THE
OF THORNS

ELLE BEAUMONT

Midnight Tide
PUBLISHING

ELLE BEAUMONT

THE CASTLE OF THORNS

For my Purple Warriors,
This one is for you. I will fight by your side and lift you up
when you need a helping hand.

℘ROLOGUE

A little girl's cry tore through the air, shattering the heart of the King of Tursch. Werner, the king, stood helplessly in the corner of his daughter's room as the five-year-old girl struggled.

"I smell it. Why does it smell so bad?" Gisela wailed as her many attendants pinned her down and fed her a thick syrup, which she promptly choked on.

There was no smell. Nothing. Werner had been told by several medicine men that Gisela wasn't of sound mind, that some devil possessed her. Of course, he didn't believe it.

"Please, Papa, no more. It tastes horrible!" the girl wailed.

Her words plucked the strings of his heart, and he crossed the room. Werner crouched beside the bed, stroking the damp brow of his youngest daughter. Her turquoise gaze darted around the room, trying to focus on something. "There, there, Mousy. It'll be all right, I promise." He bent forward, pressed a kiss to her clammy forehead, and reluctantly withdrew from her side.

In the room's doorway, the attending doctor waited, clearing his throat. Werner crossed the room and exited into the hall with the man.

1

"Have you found a cure for what ails her?" He leaned his tall frame against the wall, his hazel eyes locking onto the small graying man before him.

"Contrary to what many think, it isn't a possession. It's an affliction of the brain and no amount of bleeding her, shaking blessed water at her, or casting spells will cure her." The doctor sighed, frowning as he rubbed at the crease between his brows. "I've been told of how frequent her fits are. If what you say is true, then the next episode is likely to get worse, and each one after that." He paused, fiddling with the leather bag in front of him, as if he were nervous.

"It tires her brain, you know. I'm not sure how much it can endure before she doesn't wake, Your Majesty," the doctor said reluctantly, sadly. He looked away from Werner, then rummaged through the bag in his grasp. "There is one thing that could help, but it isn't easy to obtain." He pulled out a satchel and offered it to the king. "These herbs may or may not help, and if they do, they'll take some doing to retrieve."

Greedily, Werner snatched the small satchel and peered down at the bag in his grasp. "If they help, the cost won't matter to me."

The doctor sighed, shaking his head tiredly. "You will discover how grave a cost it will be."

Narrowing his gaze, Werner cocked his head. "What do you mean?"

Why did the doctor look so uneasy? Did it truly matter to Werner? What sort of father would he be to so easily discard the herbs without even trying? No matter the cost, if it meant an easier life for Gisela . . . he'd do it.

"Very well," drawled the doctor, nodding. "Ylga the

witch resides on the beaches of Burlitz. There you'll find her hut, and she'll know the remedy you speak of when you mention the fits. You know the ways to get there, and now you know the cost."

If he'd known the cost up front, it wouldn't have changed his mind. Not then, not ten or fifteen years later, either. There were consequences to every choice.

Werner swallowed roughly, covering his mouth with his hand. "Dear Wurdiz . . ." Would their patron god even listen to their prayers? Or had he become willingly ignorant and covered his ears? No matter how many prayers Werner uttered, they didn't seem to make a difference, and it certainly didn't save his wife's life. He only hoped that they'd be enough to save his precious daughter.

The shortest way to the beaches of Burlitz was straight through Todesfall Forest, the same place Knorren the demon lurked. He'd claimed the forest centuries ago, slaughtering any who trespassed, and over time he claimed more and more land as his own.

Other than passing through the forest, the only way to the beach was to sail from the port in the city, which meant at least two weeks of travel, when it should have only taken perhaps a week to get there.

"If you time the trips right, there should never be a shortage of the herbs, and there will never be reason to feel guilty, Your Majesty."

The doctor's words cut through Werner's thoughts. "Of course. You're right."

A few weeks later, when the herbal remedy ran low, Werner had no choice but to send a handful of men to retrieve a fresh supply for Gisela. His sweet girl's health improved with the consumption of the remedy, and perhaps he'd grown too comfortable with the fact. Someone, whoever it was, had slipped. The herbs were running low, too low for the long trip. It couldn't happen again. Werner would monitor the herbs himself, but with the limited supply, there wasn't a choice. And he wouldn't see his daughter suffer through another fit if he could help it.

There was a chance Knorren would be occupied elsewhere. So, King Werner sent two parties, just in case the first party fell victim to the beast. One would venture through the forest and another would make the long trip around the coast to the beach where Ylga dwelled.

She was known throughout Tursch and the surrounding lands as a medicine woman, but she made no attempt to hide the fact that she was also a practicing witch. Tales of her ability to heal and even curse had wound their way through the kingdom over time.

In a week, the Todesfall party returned—or what was left of it.

Werner lifted a handkerchief to his mouth, hoping to staunch the inevitable flow of vomit threatening to spew forth. A half-eaten corpse lay on a cot, flies buzzed around the exposed inner tissues, and maggots writhed around.

The sight was far too much, and the king lost his battle with his stomach. He remained bent over until he was quite emptied.

"He was alive when we found him," one man said, his voice wavering.

How in Wurdiz's name was he alive? Werner mused, noticing the man's legs had been ripped from his body, bones jutting out and vital tissues displayed. On his side, a vicious claw mark exposed his rib cage. Yet, he had been alive?

Dabbing at his mouth, Werner composed himself and let his tired brown eyes fall to the victim once more. "I will compensate his family. This is a tragedy." Turning away from his men, he walked away from them and out of the infirmary.

Another attempt to travel through Todesfall Forest would have to be made, for it would still be faster than waiting on the sea-faring party to return. Gisela needed the herbs and soon, because when she ran out, who could say how much more her mind could endure? It was not something Werner wanted to think of—no—it was something he wouldn't think of.

If he had to travel through the depths of that hellish forest himself, then he would do it.

PART I

"Treachery and violence are spears pointed at both ends; they wound those who resort to them worse than their enemies."

— *EMILY BRONTË, WUTHERING HEIGHTS*

ONE

15 years later

The scent of apple blossoms hung heavily in the hallways of Tursch Castle, but the fragrance wasn't one Gisela minded. It meant spring had finally arrived, and that the bees would down the nectar greedily. In the fall, the red apples would make for exquisite desserts, apple tarts, and strudels. For now, she'd take pleasure in the sun's growing strength, and how wonderful it felt against her skin.

She flopped onto the cushion in front of the massive window, sprawling her legs out as she basked in the sun's glorious warmth. The library was a safe place for her to hide away when the servants bustled and her sisters busied themselves with gossip. They did not welcome her among them, and that was just as well with her, because she didn't enjoy gossiping like her older sisters did.

Gisela felt much like a cat lazing about in the late afternoon. As she stretched forward, she pushed the windows open all the way.

"Ha! I knew I'd find you here. Tilda will arrive this evening, I thought I'd let you know."

Jana's voice cut through the silence, startling Gisela, but she recovered quickly and turned to her older sister. Dark ringlets sat against Jana's head. Some pieces broke free from their pins and tickled at her temple, teasing her dark skin.

"Tonight? I thought she wasn't arriving until two weeks from now."

Jana shrugged, twisting her full lips into a puckered expression. "You know how Tilda is. No plan ever remains the same." She crossed the floor and leaned against the cushions in the window. A smattering of freckles on Jana's nose stood out more prominently as the sun highlighted her brown skin. "Between you and me, I think she does it on purpose."

"What?" Gisela wrinkled her nose. "Why would you say that?"

"To remind Papa that she exists." Jana laughed. She lifted her hand and toyed with Gisela's soft brown curls. "Wurdiz help you," she murmured. "Tilda will surely team up with the others against you."

Gisela fought the urge to roll her eyes. Even after all these years, her older sisters took pleasure in tearing her down. Out of her four older sisters, Jana was the only one who took up the mantle of championing her. Not that she needed it now, but when she was little and spent most of her days tucked in bed, she needed it.

Once, Gisela dreamed of bonding with Tilda. She was ten years older than her, and could have easily filled the hole their mother's death created, but no. Tilda wanted nothing to do with her sickly little sister, and her indifference grew into contempt. What it came down to was that Tilda blamed her for their mother's death, and in some ways it was her fault.

Gisela's birth was hard, which was a prelude to her new life. Only a few days after her birth did the fits begin, and the attendants declared her possessed by some spirit and that she'd been sent to kill the queen. For it was when Gisela's convulsions began, and she started to turn blue, that the queen passed away.

The murmurs continued for a few years after that, but eventually they subsided. Whether Gisela's disposition proved that she wasn't, in fact, possessed, or that the castle servants simply grew tired of the same gossip, wasn't known.

However, as Gisela grew so did her ailment. Her sisters grew jealous as their father's free time was spent fretting over Gisela and not the others. He tried, she supposed, as much as he could, to divide his time among them evenly. But there were so many times when he'd fall asleep next to Gisela's bedside, praying to Wurdiz when he thought no one was listening that his youngest would survive the night.

Gisela huffed. "Let them. Their antics are childish, and rather unbecoming. Imagine being heavy with a child and still taking the time to belittle your youngest sister. Oh, to have the time in a day to conjure up scathing insults." She lifted a hand to her forehead, then fell against the wall dramatically. "I'm far too busy being a decent person for that nonsense."

Jana squeaked, then promptly laughed. "What was that? Where did that little mouse go, and since when did a lion stand in its place?"

This time, Gisela rolled her eyes, then hopped down from her comfortable perch. *Mousy* was her childhood nickname, one their father still called her.

"Does it surprise you? It shouldn't. Try to pick up a field

11

mouse when he feels threatened and you'll find his teeth in your flesh several times over." Gisela shrugged, pulling the fabric of her skirt up.

Jana smiled, looping her arm through Gisela's. "But what of the cat who corners the mouse? Won't the mouse become the cat's dinner?"

"Sometimes, but if the mouse is clever enough, it can outsmart the devilish cat." She winked as they walked through the library. "I could never let myself become the cat's dinner, so don't worry about me."

"Ugh!"

The sound of disgust broke through their playful banter. Gisela's eyes flicked toward the doorway, and she had to keep from giggling. There, with her hands upon her hips, stood a cross-looking Pia. Her mouth pinched together in a typical sour expression that wholly belonged to her. Pia was born two years before Gisela, but acted as though she had been born a decade prior. She also hated Gisela, partly because Tilda did, then also because she'd grown jealous of the extra time their father spent with her. Nevertheless, she didn't bother to disguise her derision, even in front of their father.

"Why are you bothering to talk of filthy mice and cats? The only purpose for a cat is to kill the vermin, otherwise, cats can wander into Todesfall Forest for all I care."

Gisela bit her tongue as Pia ranted. Todesfall Forest was a death sentence for any human, but animals wove through the woods without a care. Knorren, the demon, roamed his wooded land, searching for victims to devour. Everyone knew the tale of the giant fox that gobbled up trespassers, then spat out their bones. Parents warned their children to behave, or else Knorren would come to take them away. The terrifying part was, they did not make it up, and there truly was a fox as tall as an oak tree lurking inside the forest.

"Be kind, Pia. No one deserves Knorren's teeth." Jana shook her head. Pia's foul expression didn't seem to faze her.

Pia sniffed. Annoyance trickled into her expression, pinching her brows and thinning her full lips. "I wouldn't say that." Her dark eyes homed in on Gisela, but no scathing remark followed. "Anyway, since Tilda is arriving tonight, I thought we'd give her the presents for the baby."

Gisela's brows lifted in surprise, but she quickly lowered them so as not to offend Pia. It was a kind thought, which didn't happen often. "Of course. I think that's a lovely idea."

"Of course it is," Pia snapped. She turned on her heels, head held high, braids swinging from their twisted bun, and she strode off without another word.

Gisela erupted with laughter. Jana joined in with her, but they were careful to cover their mouths and quiet their laughing until Pia was too far down the hall to hear.

"She is so wicked." Jana sighed. "The worst of them. No wonder no suitor wants to take their chances—let alone take her to the marital bed."

Everyone possessed redeeming qualities in Gisela's mind —well, almost everyone. Some were rotten to the core, and Pia was one of them. The single redeeming quality that she had was that she didn't bother to hide her venomous traits.

"Jana!" Gisela choked on her name, trying her best to sound chastising.

"Please. We know her lips drip venom and her mouth harbors fangs, but can you imagine what her nether region bears?" Jana held her wrists together, opening and closing her hands as if they were a massive, razor-toothed mouth.

Gisela dissolved into a fit of laughter with her sister. She appreciated it, because come dinnertime, she'd need to focus on things that brought a smile to her face. No doubt the other sisters would make it a difficult dinner.

When Tilda arrived, so did their sister Mina, which spurred the servants into a frenzy as they rushed to prepare an extra room.

Tilda greeted each sister, kissing their cheeks, then stopped in front of Gisela. "My, haven't you come into your own." Her eyes, which were as dark as night, looked Gisela up and down. Tilda didn't smile as she met Gisela's gaze. Her eyes held little warmth as she approached her, and although she leaned in to offer a kiss of greeting, her actions appeared withdrawn and cold.

Was that almost a compliment? Gisela mused, but the question faded as Tilda seemed to wait for a compliment in return. "You look wonderful, Tilda. You must be ready for the baby to come."

"It cannot come soon enough. A full night's sleep would be wonderful." She frowned, rubbing at her swollen stomach. There was no hiding her pregnancy because gone was the rail-thin figure Tilda once boasted.

Gisela sighed with relief as Pia stepped in, stealing Tilda's attention. With all of the princesses reunited, it was sure to be an interesting supper.

Once the initial excitement faded, they entered the dining hall and sat down. Candles cast a warm glow on the banquet table and the scent of food wafted into the room, but the plates were empty.

Gisela twisted in her chair, idly wondering where their father was. She hadn't seen him all day, and as far as she knew, there was no pressing meeting. He'd missed the arrival of Tilda and Mina, which didn't bode well for the evening's tone.

The servants came around, placing filled plates before everyone. Finally, the warm, smiling face of their father made an appearance as he entered the dining hall. "Well, look at this. All my beautiful daughters together again." He walked to Tilda, kissed her cheek, then turned to Mina and did the same. "You're both glowing." He chuckled. The smile on his face thinned as Mina pouted. "What's this for?" He motioned to the lip jutting outward.

"You've ruined my surprise." Mina sighed. "I was going to announce my pregnancy over dinner, but seeing as how you did it for me . . ."

Werner's eyes narrowed a fraction. "I only said you were glowing, my dear."

"And everyone knows that means one is with a child, Papa!" Mina's eyes glittered with unshed tears.

Gisela shook her head. She twisted the napkin on her lap as, unsurprisingly, Mina's dramatics unfolded. "Congratulations, Mina."

She growled in frustration. "It's pointless now."

Werner sat down at the head of the table. His hazel eyes closed as he touched his brow, as if centering himself. "A child is never a pointless thing. Forgive me for my tardiness, but there were a few things to address. I've missed my two eldest daughters, so tell me how you've been."

As with any event, Tilda and Mina took control of the room, hardly letting anyone else speak. Pia forced her way in, only to be chastised by their father. However, when the conversation slowed and a quiet settled over the table, Jana spoke up.

"As you know, the Duke of Grimau's son has been courting me. He proposed, after asking Papa, of course." She paused for dramatic effect, grinning. Jana's dimples grew more apparent. "I accepted."

Gisela had spent nearly an hour with her sister and the sneak hadn't even mentioned the proposal! "What?" she squeaked. "That is wonderful news! Congratulations, Jana."

Pia, who had far too much wine with her dinner, nearly shouted her words. "It's a pity. Everyone is marrying and getting pregnant, but who will ever want a broken thing like you, Gisela?"

The fork in Gisela's hand clattered to her plate. A pit formed in her stomach, as if she'd been punched. It wasn't the worst thing Pia had ever said to her, but somehow she'd known just when to say it, as if she could sense Gisela dreaming of such a day for herself. The cold remark was like icy water running down her back and whatever appetite she'd had was now gone.

Werner's smile disappeared. The sleepy quality his eyes had taken on faded the moment Pia's words fell from her lips. "Apologize."

"Absolutely not," Pia whined.

"While you sit at my table, you will do as I say, and you will apologize right now."

Hatred swirled in her dark eyes. "I'm so sorry, Gisela."

She wasn't. Not in the least. Gisela wasn't foolish

enough to believe her words. While the words stung, they didn't take her by surprise, and she was beginning to believe them, too. Who would want a wife that could pass on whatever affliction she had to their children? In Pia's apology, she heard what her sister didn't say. She was so sorry that she was born defected, and that she'd likely live a short, lonely life.

"It's all right." Gisela swallowed.

The rest of supper was quiet after that. When everyone left for their rooms, Gisela remained seated. She could feel her father's gaze on her, and when she chanced a look in his direction, he stared back at her.

"Are you all right?" he inquired.

"Of course. Pia's remarks aren't anything new." She shrugged. "Where were you before dinner? It isn't like you to be late."

Werner took a deep drink from his goblet. "In a meeting. Knorren, it seems, has been causing unrest near Burlitz. He's trying to claim more land as his own."

Gisela's brows furrowed in confusion. "What? He already has an entire forest."

"It doesn't matter. Every so often this is what he does. He grows bored and angry, then he claims more territory."

Fear crept inside of Gisela's chest. There was nothing anyone could do to stop the beast from claiming more territory. He never left his forest but would wait for armies inside the darkness, watching them, and when they least expected it, he'd slaughter them all.

"Is there truly nothing we can do?" Gisela whispered. "Can no one bargain with Knorren?"

Werner laughed, humorlessly. "Bargain with a demon?

How does one go about that and not sentence themselves to hell while doing it? No. I will not bargain with that beast. His day is coming, Gisela, and when I discover what will bring him down, Wurdiz hold me to it, I will end him."

She shivered at her father's cold words. Gisela had never heard him speak so menacingly before, and she believed him. She only hoped that Wurdiz would keep her father safe, instead of damning him, too.

TWO

The next morning, a chill filled the air, courtesy of the gray sky. Pink blossoms drooped sadly on their wooden limbs, and Gisela could relate. The overall mood in the castle steadily declined, especially as the council swooped in after breakfast. Papa didn't say what his meeting was about, but something in the pit of Gisela's stomach said it wasn't good.

With all of her sisters occupied with preening or gossip, Gisela stalked down the hallway and stood outside the meeting room. Her father's voice resonated in the room, making it easy for her to hear what they spoke of.

" . . . I'll be sending men out to sea, but the reports of the tumultuous seas aren't promising for a successful trip. In which case, Todesfall Forest is the only way."

"But, Majesty, the men will surely die." It was one of the councilmen. Gisela didn't recognize the deep tone of his voice, but that wasn't saying much. She was never allowed to partake in the meetings.

A long pause followed, then her father spoke. "There is no other choice. Gisela's herbs are running low, and we need to replenish them. She has been well for so long, I don't want to see her suffer again. No, this is how it will be."

"And what of the unrest with the villagers? Knorren wants more territory, and the surrounding towns are growing angry with the lack of action. The farmers will lose some of their land, and houses will be destroyed if he takes what he wants. More people will die, too. What of that, Your Majesty?" It was another man's voice. He didn't hide his discontent with the current plan of action, or rather the absence of one.

Gisela's heart pounded furiously. Memories from her childhood were difficult to recall. The fits she had erased, or in the very least, muddled, making it hard to decipher what was a dream and what was real. She tried to remember the day the new doctor arrived, the small man with white hair and crystal eyes. What had he said? She couldn't recall, but she knew after he arrived her fits had lessened. The herbal mixture was the only thing to tame the spells, and to know it came at such a price sickened her.

A chair groaned as someone shifted, then a fist pounded on the table.

"Do any of you have an idea as to how to overpower the demon fox? Are any of you brave enough to step into the dark woods to take him on? When we can agree on how to kill him without condemning ourselves, then you can bark at me."

Someone scoffed. "You play a dangerous game, Your Majesty. Every time you send a party in for medicine, you risk more than just the men's lives. When bloodshed isn't enough anymore, he will come for the kingdom itself. I pray to Wurdiz that we are ready for that, and if we aren't, that our deaths are swift."

Gisela couldn't listen anymore. She covered her mouth

as she choked on a sob and ran to her room. Flopping onto her bed, she pressed her damp cheek to her pillow and wondered how many had died trying to retrieve her medicine over the years. Guilt clawed at her conscience. If Gisela had known the price, she would have refused them.

Early in the afternoon, Jana barged into the room. "I don't know why you're moping, but you can tell me on our way to the city market," she announced.

"What?"

"I didn't stutter. You're dressed already, just grab a coat—the drizzle is cold."

In the city, fog rolled along the cobblestone streets, lending it an eerie quality. Smoke billowed from chimneys as bakers prepared their goods and inns prepped their meals. Despite spring arriving, the city looked as cold and gray as it did in the winter, and the citizens wore scowls instead of smiles. Although, Gisela didn't feel like smiling either, and the weather wasn't offering any warmth.

"You've been silent the entire trip. What is the matter with you?" Jana fussed with the gloves on her hands.

"I'm thinking, that's all," Gisela replied. "I'm sorry. Tell me more about the duke's son, since you sneakily withheld that information from me."

Jana bit her bottom lip, at least having the decency to look a little ashamed. "I didn't mean to. I wanted to tell you, but things needed to be finalized, and like it or not, things took a political detour." She rolled her eyes. "Politics aside, I do truly care for him."

Gisela smiled. She wanted Jana to be happy, because out of all of them, she deserved it. Not only because she was the *only* sister to show kindness to her, but because Jana was honestly a genuinely kind individual. "But do you love him?"

Jana's pert nose twitched as she glanced in Gisela's direction. "Not yet, but I could see myself easily falling for him. Kellan is a good man, and he makes me laugh." Reaching across the cab, Jana squeezed Gisela's hand. "He truly is, I promise."

"He better be," Gisela warned.

"Or what? You'll flash your big blue eyes at him?" Jana winked.

Gisela wrinkled her nose. Everyone said she was far too soft, too kind, and quiet, but when her sisters were loud, brazen, and often cruel, someone had to be. She pulled her hand away, waving it. "I'd yell at him—or something."

"I expect no less. Perhaps you can bare your fangs, too." Jana's expression softened, and once again she grabbed Gisela's hand in hers. "You have someone for you, too. I think Wurdiz knows how special you are, and is taking a little longer ensuring that your match is as perfect as you are."

Gisela shook her head. Did she doubt her sister's words? Perhaps. She had reason to since those who discovered her affliction promptly sniffed and turned the other way. She was also the youngest daughter, with little claim to the throne.

"If not, I'll manage." Even Gisela didn't believe the words that slipped from her mouth. She was broken, and because of that, she'd inadvertently killed people. The smile fell from her face, then in a blink, she broke down into tears.

"Dear heavens, Gisela, I didn't mean . . ." Jana slid from the cushioned seat and moved next to Gisela, embracing her. "I swear it. There is someone out there for you! If I have to hunt him down myself, I'll tear him from whatever—"

"No, it's not that." Gisela interrupted. "I overheard Papa . . . Jana, I've killed people. Not with my own hands, but I might as well have! The herbs that keep me healthy— people have died trying to get them. Not just one, but dozens!"

Jana's face softened, but surprise didn't filter into her gaze. "Don't be silly, my love, it isn't your fault. Come here." Her arms encircled Gisela, pulling her against her side as she soothed her with a soft hum. "Your hands are clean of their deaths, Gisela. You've never asked for them to go."

Suspicion grew inside of Gisela. If her sister knew, why wouldn't Jana tell her something as important as this? Too lost amid her emotions, she wasn't certain whether to be angry or sad with her sister.

Gisela forced her voice out, which sounded as broken as she felt. "Did they have a choice? Or did Papa force them?" She swiped at her tears, trying her best to staunch their flow. Fifteen years, that was how long she'd been taking the herbal mixture. In that time, how many had died because of her? The urge to vomit came in a violent wave, but it passed quickly.

Jana squeezed her tightly. "I can't speak for them, or even for Papa, Gisela. But you are no murderer. Come now, I'll tell you more of Kellan, if you'd like?"

When Gisela nodded, Jana took the cue. For the rest of

the carriage ride Jana chattered about Kellan, distracting Gisela, and she found she'd like to meet him sooner rather than later.

It always surprised Gisela how loud the city was. The castle sat on a hill among the mountains and trees, so the only noise that rang out was the sounds of the wildlife or the soldiers' training. Here, in the city, people shouted what they were selling, or in passing they'd call to someone they knew. *Bustling*—that was the word she'd used to describe it. Everyone moved with a purpose, having somewhere to go or something to do, but when they saw the royal carriage rolling down the street, they turned to watch, and some shouted.

Thankfully, Jana had successfully soothed Gisela, and the prospect of browsing the city's elaborate shops tickled her. There was one in particular she wanted to visit, the first of its kind, a two-story building with several rooms of clothing.

She stood in front of the building, watching the wooden sign sway in the wind. *Seamlessly Perfect* was scrawled in tidy gold letters, contrasting with the navy background. The store had been an inn once, a rather large one, too, but now it housed clothing instead of people. She'd heard the noble women discuss the top floor, which was dedicated to ladies only. Tea was typically served during a fitting, and several appetizers, even desserts, were laid out for them to nibble on.

"Well, are you just going to stare at it?" Jana teased.

"Come on, let's go see what all the fuss is about." She slid her arm through Gisela's, then pulled her along.

They were not without their shadows. Guards followed closely as they entered the shop. A tinkling bell announced their arrival, but there was no shopkeeper in sight. Gisela tugged her sister toward a spiral staircase, where a tall vase stood on either side. Fragrant blooms nestled in the vases, greeting them.

"I wonder what they're predicting the latest trend to be," Gisela mused.

Jana hummed, then squeaked as she picked up her skirt and ran up the flight of stairs. "I'll find out before you!"

Not wanting to be left behind, Gisela ran after her sister. At the top of the stairs, both of them halted as they absorbed their surroundings. Dresses hung on display around the room reminding Gisela of an armory, not a dress shop. Some were adorned in jewels, others had necklines that plunged so low they brought a blush to Gisela's cheeks. It was a unique way of displaying them.

"Oh, these are lovely shades. Gisela, you'd look beautiful in this butter-yellow dress." Jana stood in front of it, peering down at a pair of cream-and-gold shoes.

It was a lovely dress. Although, looking around the room, Gisela didn't see one unsightly piece in the mix.

"You should get one for the summer festival. You'll need one for the ceremony." Jana walked the length of the room and turned on her heels.

Now that Gisela thought of it, she needed a gown for Heligersee, the festival of the lake. For hundreds of years it'd been a tradition in Tursch, stemming all the way back to the Gilded Prince, who fell prey to Knorren's wrath. It was said that the prince turned his back to the plight of his people, and that as he grew richer, the people grew poorer. When the rumor of a revolution rose, the Gilded Prince allegedly summoned help in the form of a demon. Knorren. The fox turned on his summoner, devouring him whole, and fled into the forest, where he remained.

"*Guten morgen,* I'll be right with you." A stout woman walked into the room and stood behind a desk, scribbling away on a piece of paper. Wire-framed glasses precariously balanced on her nose, looking as if they'd fall at any moment.

"Can I help you?" The woman approached them, her eyes nervously pinned to Galfrid, the guard who milled around behind Gisela and Jana. A moment ticked by, then recognition flashed across her features and she gasped. "Oh, Your Highnesses, Princess Jana, Princess Gisela!" She curtsied and fussed with her gray hair, which was in wiry braids. "It's an honor to have you in my shop. I'm Freya Strauss. What can I do for you?"

Smiling, Gisela motioned to the dresses. "I was admiring your work. I'm looking for a gown, something for an upcoming event." For a moment, Gisela's eyes flicked away from the woman to an ivory-colored dress. "Would you be willing to work with my seamstress? You'd be compensated for it." She ran her hand along the silken fabric, which was nice, but it wasn't the quality she was looking for. If Freya had access to finer materials, Gisela was certain she could create a sensational piece.

"Oh! Your Highness, that would be an honor. Thank you. There are other pieces I'm working on in the back, too, if you'd like to see?" Freya cocked her head and a hopeful glimmer entered her gaze.

"Of course." Gisela followed her and Jana moved with them.

The front of the shop was tidy and put together, but the back of it was chaos. Gisela wondered how Freya could remember where anything was.

"If you liked that gown against the wall, then this one may tickle your fancy." Freya pulled a dressform out from a corner. It wore a gown similar to the other, but this one had pearls strewn across the chest, and instead of gold thread woven in an array of patterns, the gold thread formed shells fanning outward.

It sparked something in Gisela; she sucked in her bottom lip and knew she'd regret asking, but had to. "I have an idea—do you have something I can draw with?"

"Certainly." Freya fetched a piece of paper and a fountain pen.

Gisela narrowed her eyes at the pen, letting her fingers slip around the cool cylinder. Once, she could draw quite well, but now? After the fits wreaked havoc on her mind, it was difficult to maintain control of the pen. She sighed, tossing those thoughts aside, and with a shaky hand drew her ideal dress. Each stroke was rough, less than straight, but the silhouette was there and so was the idea.

The gown Gisela drew was similar to the one Freya had brought out, but it was more elaborate. She sketched a small train that pooled around the feet, and on the body she drew a surcoat. It wasn't the most eloquent depiction, but it would do well enough to convey what she wanted.

"I apologize for the lack of talent." Gisela flexed her fingers. Heat rushed into her cheeks.

"Oh, no. This is lovely. I know just what to do with this,

too." Freya beamed. "I have a splendid idea! Let me show you." She broke into a flurry of movement, explaining her thoughts, the fabrics she'd use for it, and when all was said and done, Freya's face was quite red.

Freya's enthusiastic musings held Gisela and Jana prisoner. They spoke for long enough that the woman made a cup of tea for each of them and also treated them to sweet bread.

As much as Gisela enjoyed watching the seamstress fly around the tight quarters of the back room, she felt trapped. She'd drank all of her tea and the honey bread was reduced to crumbs. It was time to go, but how did they go about it without finding themselves dragged into another lengthy conversation? She shot Jana a look, who nodded in return.

"We really must be on our way. It isn't often we venture into the shops," Jana offered.

"Oh, right, right." Freya clucked her tongue and wiped her hands on her apron. "I don't want to keep you, but know this, Your Highness," she said, turning to Gisela with her head slightly bowed. "I am honored and I cannot wait to work with your seamstress to bring this design to life."

"Good. I'm gl—" An explosion outside cut off the rest of Gisela's words. Her turquoise eyes widened in shock and she looked to Galfrid, who was running to the window.

"A building is on fire up the street." He ducked to get a better view. "It looks like a riot is starting." Galfrid pulled away from the sight, motioning to the two princesses. "We have to leave before things get out of hand."

Fear sliced through Gisela. She felt faint, but her heart galloped in her chest wildly. "Is . . . do they think . . ." She couldn't finish her words. What if Knorren killed another innocent villager? "Freya, I must leave. I'll be in touch, thank you." She tried her best not to sound short, but fear tightened her throat, making it hard to speak.

Galfrid motioned toward the girls again. "No time to waste. We need to go before the entire street is blocked."

Gisela and her entourage exited the seamstress's shop in a flurry, leaving Freya flustered in their wake. It all happened in a blur, the loading into the carriage, the prompts from her guard, and Jana fretting. The sound of the horses' hooves pounding on the ground and the jangling of their harness only added to Gisela's anxiety. *Please don't let it be another death. Please!* she thought and clasped her hands together, praying to Wurdiz, to anyone who would listen to her.

THREE

The carriage sped through the city streets. Shouts rose above the crowd, making their contempt for the king known, and Gisela feared for them. To speak ill against the crown was treason, and while she didn't blame the citizens, especially when one of their own died, it wasn't wise.

"Another one. Another family dies because of Knorren, and what does the king do!" A man's voice pierced the air, but his following words faded as the carriage pulled away.

"Dear Wurdiz," Gisela breathed. She pressed her fingers against her lips and shook her head. The dread in her belly unfurled. She was right: more people had died.

"That despicable creature," Jana spat. "He cannot have all the land, and he won't kill all of us."

But won't he? Gisela mused. For centuries the tale of the fox circulated. He'd slain the Gilded Prince who once ruled Tursch, and over the decades he'd claimed more land for himself, forcing those who neighbored the village to uproot, or killing them if they stayed. Knorren had displayed no mercy, either. His victims, if left alive, weren't so for very long. They'd die from the wounds he'd inflicted, and it was never a kind death.

Gisela shuddered just thinking about it. She didn't want to imagine the absolute terror they'd experienced during the attack, and then as their life faded away.

"When will he stop?" Gisela whispered.

Jana let her head fall against the cushioned seat. "I fear he will never stop, not until we slay him—however that is, I don't know." She tipped her head forward, eyes softening. "We are safe, Gisela, don't worry about that."

But she worried. Gisela worried Knorren would step from the forest and claim the castle as his, fracturing her family as he tore into them. Jana may have thought her worries were unfounded, but their father sent men in Todesfall Forest, repeatedly, and if he continued, who could say how furious the fox would become.

"If you say so," Gisela said, then fell silent.

Upon returning to the castle, a team of individuals met them, and at the forefront was their father.

"Jana! Gisela!" Werner cried, rushing forward to embrace them as they slid from the carriage. "I didn't know you planned to go to the city. If I'd known, I would have forbidden it. The citizens are not happy with circumstances, and I feared there would be a riot today." Dark shadows clouded his hazel eyes. His normally warm smile faded into a thin, grim line. "I'm glad you're all right." He leaned down and brushed a kiss to Gisela's head. "Both of you."

"Papa, don't you think that is something important to share with all of us?" Jana asked carefully. "If we'd known then we wouldn't have ever been in danger."

Werner sighed, then motioned for them to follow. "You're right, and for that I'm sorry. I've been in and out of meetings for the last few days. Things have been a little scattered around here. There will be no shortage of riots, I'm afraid. It seems Knorren is adamant in his advances on new grounds, and whoever remains unwilling to leave their property is slaughtered. That much you girls know, but there is more . . . Because of this and the lack of action I've taken, the residents are upset. We've been told to go to war with him, but we're not sure how."

Inside the castle, Werner rubbed his face tiredly. "The forest is his domain, and to send troops in there will be certain death. Not just one party, but several hundred individuals will no doubt die. On one hand, we could successfully infiltrate, and that one party could slay him, but on the chance they don't, can we spare all those lives?"

Gisela grimaced as she listened to her father. He didn't want to spare those lives for a probable victory, but he didn't think twice about sending them to retrieve an herbal remedy? "How?" Gisela blurted.

"How what?" Her father's brows knit together.

Gisela shifted her jaw, willing her voice not to shake as she spoke. "How would you slay him? If it hasn't been done in five hundred years, please tell me how you'll slay Knorren." Did her father not see the madness in this?

Werner sighed, tiredly. "We will find a way."

"But you don't *know* the way." It seemed like a futile argument, one that was draining the both of them. But Gisela had to try, because her father was always nearsighted when it came to her.

"I'll not discuss this with you. Even if I knew, it's not something you need to worry about."

"It is when you're sending parties through the forest to retrieve my herbs," Gisela blurted, instantly regretting it.

Werner turned his head, narrowing his eyes as if trying to decipher if he'd heard her correctly. "What did you say?"

"They're only angering Knorren further. Maybe he'd stop if we'd stop!" She found the courage to raise her voice, and although it wavered, she didn't back down. Jana's hand wrapped around Gisela's, and she squeezed it.

"That is not an option, Gisela. We are done here." Werner waved his hand, dismissing the topic.

"It is an option. It's my life, and I think I have a say whether my life is worth thousands of others."

Werner laughed; it was a dark, humorless sound. "No, you don't have a say, because you don't see your worth, but I do." He walked away, the staccato of his heels keeping time with the pounding of Gisela's heart.

Jana tugged on Gisela's hand. "He is right about one thing."

"What?" Gisela frowned.

"You don't see your worth."

Two weeks passed by since the incident and Gisela felt increasingly off. The flickering of sunlight caused her head to ache, and her stomach fluttered with anxiety. Not only that, but exhaustion plagued her. It wasn't until her father approached that she understood why she felt so poorly.

"You're almost out of herbs, Gisela. We've tried rationing them out," Werner spoke softly and frowned. Deep lines creased his forehead, showcasing how worried he truly was. "The men who tried to sail around came back due to rough conditions. I fear our only option is to attempt Todesfall Forest."

Panic cut through Gisela. Of course, it made sense why she'd felt off. But the panic wasn't for herself; it was for the men who'd travel through the forest. She didn't want men to trespass into the woods, even if it meant getting the herbs. "No," she blurted. "I won't have anyone else dying because of me."

"Gisela." Her father's voice changed, hardening a fraction. "I will not have you bed ridden and close to death."

"One life isn't worth thousands. One life isn't worth riots in the street, or an uprising. I'm not a child, Papa, and I may choose."

He bristled at her words. "And I won't have you near death, Mousy. You may be a young woman now, but you are and forever will be my daughter. Besides, this time I will go, and maybe then I can barter with the fox."

Gisela choked on a sob. "But if you go, you'll surely die."

"No, my sweet girl, no. Have some faith in me—in Wurdiz. I will return to all of you." Werner closed the distance between them and embraced her. He brushed his lips against her curls and sighed. "This won't be goodbye, so please don't think you'll be rid of me that soon."

Her shoulders slumped forward as his arms encircled her. With the decision cemented in his mind, there would be no changing it. "When do you leave?" Gisela murmured against his chest.

"Tomorrow morning." He stepped back, tilting Gisela's head so he could brush a kiss to her forehead. "I'll return. I swear it, my Mousy."

Swallowing roughly, Gisela fought to believe his words.

There was no promise he'd return, and if history was any indication, Knorren would devour him as quickly as any other man, king or not.

His fate was in the hands of Wurdiz now.

The morning came far too swiftly for Gisela's liking. She watched as, piece by piece, the king's armor settled onto his person. The sound of leather stretching cut through the relative silence. Werner shifted, testing how it felt and if it needed adjusting.

She loathed that all of her sisters were in the castle during this time, although it didn't matter that they were here or not, she supposed. Either way, they'd bear down on her, shouting at her, belittling her, and ultimately accusing her of sentencing their father to death. She couldn't blame them, because wasn't it the truth? Their mother's death had been her fault. Wasn't it just as fitting that their father would also die because of her?

It made it easy for contempt to grow between the girls.

Someone knocked on the door, and a familiar voice rang out moments later. "Your Majesty, the men are ready in the courtyard, and your horse is saddled." Anselm, her father's valet, bowed at the waist. His ash-blond curls scarcely moved as he righted himself. He was a man in his midthirties, and not unsightly, but he had the personality of a wet blanket, in Gisela's opinion. "Is there anything else I can do for you, my lord?"

Werner drew in a deep breath and exhaled. "I suppose not, Anselm. Thank you." The king's dark gaze shifted to his daughter.

"Whatever the outcome, my lord, it has been a great honor." Anselm bowed his head once more.

"You don't have to do this," Gisela whispered.

Anselm left the room without another word, leaving the duo in solitude again. Gisela wasn't sure how long it would be until her sisters flooded the room.

"Please reconsider," she begged. Gisela stormed across the distance between them and placed her hands on his armored chest. Not even the armor would stop the fox's fangs, and she shuddered. "If you could just—"

"Just what? Let you go? Let you suffer? Watch you suffer? No, I've had my fill of that, my Mousy. I will return. I promise you." His arms encircled her, giving her a gentle squeeze.

Gisela wished it was that easy, that a promise would ensure his safety and that he'd return without so much as a scratch, but she wasn't naive.

The sound of her sisters' chattering in the hallway broke the moment, and she reluctantly pulled away from her father so that her sisters could wish him well.

Outside the castle, a horde of riders waited for her father's command. Gisela assumed only one party would venture into the woods, but she'd overheard a few of the mounted officers discussing their plans, and there were, in fact, three parties venturing into the forest. Hope blossomed in her chest, because perhaps her father would survive the trip.

"If our father dies, it will be on your head. It's your head that should pay. It's broken anyway." Pia ground her words out beside her. Like their father, her skin was a dark shade of ebony, but unlike their father, it held little warmth. She lacked the distinct amiability in his hazel gaze and his agreeable disposition.

Tilda sidled up to them, narrowing her ebony gaze on the two of them. "That is enough, Pia. You know Gisela can't help it. She was born that way." The words dripping from her tongue might as well have been a knife digging into Gisela's chest. "Father will return, I have no doubt."

Pia sneered. "You don't even live here anymore, neither of you." She motioned to Tilda and Mina. "So why don't you return to your lofty lives in your own castles with your husbands?" Pia cocked her head, and her lips pulled back into a saccharine smile. "Or have they all expired?"

"Enough," Gisela broke into the middle of the argument. "We are all upset about Papa, but cutting each other down won't bring him home safely. Let us send him off with a positive mind and heart."

Pia rounded on Gisela, lifting her hand as if to smack her, but Jana abruptly appeared out of nowhere and situated herself between them. "How dare you get in the way!" Pia hissed, moving her head so she could glare at Gisela. "Mark my words, if Papa dies because of you, you'll spend the rest of your days confined to a room!"

The sisters said no more to one another.

Jana motioned for Gisela to take her arm. "Pay no mind to them, love. They don't understand, and they're scared."

That was always their excuse. Papa used it, Suli the handmaid used it, and other servants used it—they always had an excuse. When did her sisters' words just become mean and unacceptable? As much as Gisela wanted to believe the best of anyone, some individuals lacked goodness. All of her sisters would blame her if their father died, and Gisela would blame herself, too.

"I'm so tired of hearing that. Wild beasts lash out when

they're cornered and scared, but they are beasts. Our sisters are grown and should know better." Gisela frowned.

"Not all beasts have fangs or claws, Gisela. Some wear pretty smiles and their words drip with venom." Jana squeezed her arm as they watched their father ride away with the horde of mounted riders.

It wasn't the fanged beasts Gisela worried about as their father rode off, but the one with a vibrant pelt who was far deadlier than any viper, be it human or creature.

FOUR

a gentle breeze tickled the tiny hairs on Knorren's black-tipped ears; they twitched periodically when the hairs caught on one another. The fox lazed on the ground, soaking up the warmth from the sun. He stretched his front paws before him and had every intention of lying back down to sunbathe, except a voice snagged his attention.

"Be quiet, or you'll alert him to our presence," the voice hissed.

"We're almost through the woods. I doubt he's noticed us and is likely feasting on the others."

Knorren's ears flattened against his skull. The fools hadn't realized they'd already declared themselves, and also divulged there were more of them, too. As large as he was, Knorren stood quietly and hid in the tangles of overgrown brush and trees. Sure enough, a fairly decent-sized party of soldiers walked by on the path. Their horses spooked as his scent wafted their way, but the riders were clueless.

He followed them at a distance, only emerging from the woods when the riders focused on crossing a large stream. Knorren took it as an opportunity to attack. He bolted forward, snatching a man from the horse, and carried him into the woods. Cries erupted from the victim, but the struggling didn't last, not as sword-like teeth cut into him.

A spray of blood rushed into the back of his throat the moment his canines pierced the human's flesh. Bones crunched beneath the pressure of Knorren's jaw and metallic liquid coated his tongue and trickled from his jowls as he chewed on the lifeless corpse.

Too quickly Knorren devoured the human, but there were more waiting for him. However, before he shifted his weight, a thorn pricked his paw. Rather than yelp, he moved, and from the ground sprung a new rose bush.

Annoyed, he bared his teeth at it. Such was his existence in Todesfall. For every drop of blood and every bone left to decay, a rosebush grew or a burdock sprouted.

"Did you see it? Was it him?" a panicked voice cried.

"Dear heavens! We're all going to die," another one wailed.

"We will not die!" one finally growled.

A deep, melodic laugh rose from the woodline. "No, I think he had it right. You *will* die, and you should begin praying for your souls, immediately." Knorren leaped from the cover of overgrowth and landed on an unsuspecting rider. One by one, he tore into them. Bones crunched beneath his teeth and muscles squelched. Knorren didn't cease until they were dead or close to it.

Knorren hummed to himself, flicking his long-plumed tail. "More toy soldiers sent my way?" A grin tugged at his lips, and he bared his sharp teeth. "It must be my lucky day." He bounded off into the woods, racing toward the nearest road. There *were* only three paths, and they all led to the one major road he was running toward.

Branches full of green leaves whipped against his limbs as he galloped. His nose drank in the surrounding scents while his ears swiveled, hoping to pick up neighboring sounds. The pads of his feet fell lightly. He couldn't chance giving away his location to a foe.

Knorren heard the party long before they caught sight of him. He lowered himself to the ground, listening as they chatted.

"My good men, we do this for my beloved Gisela. We will tread quietly, and should that beastly Knorren show himself, you must not provoke him. You mustn't flee, for he will kill you."

The leader spoke. Knorren could see him from where he lay. He watched as the man turned in his saddle to regard the men behind him.

"And if he corners us?" another asked.

"Pray he doesn't, for he will kill you then, too. Knorren is as clever as he is merciless, and he will use your bones to pick his teeth if it so pleases him." Bringing a hand toward his mouth, he kissed his fingers and looked toward the heavens, muttering a prayer to the gods.

Knorren's body shuddered as he strained to not laugh. He'd never thought to use a human's *bones* to pick his teeth. He assumed they'd splinter at once if he tried. Delicate little bones—like those of a bird.

As quiet as their leader wished for them to be, it was impossible. Beneath their mounts, leaves crunched and branches snapped, echoing around them. Every noise seemed amplified.

Around a bend, the stallion belonging to the man Knorren assumed was the captain balked, hooves slipping on the slick leaves, and he refused to move forward, but the man pushed him on. The horse squealed in protest, stomping his front leg as if to strike at an invisible foe. *Thud, thud, thump, thud.* The man's heels banged into the horse's sides, but the stallion bent around his rider's leg, trying to avoid the path. Eventually, he gave in and moved forward, but not without bucking.

Light from the late spring sun cast a golden glow on the sandy forest floor, but for as beautiful as the forest was, it was eerily quiet. None of the birds chirped, no squirrels chattered, nothing.

Not until a rabbit screamed in the distance. It was a shrill, bloodcurdling noise, and one that annoyed Knorren. He used the moment of distraction to his advantage and slid from the briar patch with ease.

The men, still occupied by their spooking horses, were oblivious to him. "Well, well, well," Knorren crooned behind the party, startling everyone anew. "What have we here? I wasn't expecting another meal so soon." Gleaming yellow eyes locked onto the men. A bloody smile pulled back the fox's lips, exposing his canines. No story could do Knorren justice. He wasn't a cuddly woodland fox that one admired from afar. His eyes were too intelligent to be *animal*, and yet they weren't human either. Monstrous, that was what he was.

Knorren's eyes flicked to the guards but didn't linger for long and instead settled on the armor of the leader. Something akin to recognition flickered in his gaze. "The highways have blessed me as of late." Lifting a paw, he chuckled and licked the blood away. "You will not be passing," he continued. "You are all dead, so choose who dies first." Mid-lick, he paused and surveyed the party. "Unless you'd like to play a game with me. Would you?" His shrewd gaze narrowed on them.

"No one dies today. We won't be playing any of your games, either, Knorren," the leader said roughly.

Knorren placed his paw down, stilling as the man spoke his name. He could certainly draw out their deaths, allow them to believe they were free of the woods . . . "Aren't you bold? And wrong. Your sigil looks familiar . . . are you a king?" He knew now, by looking at the man's armor and the art drawn onto the shoulder plates, that this man was a king. In the past decade or more, Knorren had seen the sigil more times than he could count.

Amusement laced his tone, causing him to sound almost giddy. "A king has stumbled into my *den of death*. How enchanting."

"I am King Werner of Tursch." Werner shifted in his saddle. "We don't mean to trespass. I must retrieve medicinal herbs for—"

"I don't care." Knorren stood to his fours, looming over the stunned party. "Your excuses are lacking, *Your Majesty*. Besides, you know the natural law of the forest. You trespass, you die." He snarled. "I'll pick who dies first." Knorren's mouth opened, showing the rows of jagged teeth. His ears laid flat against his skull as he snapped his mouth shut inches from Werner. It was enough to spook his horse, and its legs buckled. There was nowhere for him to run, sandwiched between the group of horses and the looming fox, the horse was stuck.

Desperation was an ugly trait, but the king apparently had no qualms regarding displaying it. Perhaps Knorren would make his death a quick one.

"Wait!" Werner cried. "Wait! This is for my daughter! She is very ill! Let one of us pass so she may have the herbs she needs. Please, I beg you. She will die without them."

Knorren's tufted ears swiveled, his movements halting at the king's words. He continued to hover over Werner, his fiery breath washing over him. "Is that so?" The king was willing to die for his daughter? The thought intrigued Knorren. What made her so special, that Werner would willingly venture into Todesfall? His shrewd eyes lit up. Greed flared to life within him and found himself wanting what would break the king to lose. "I have a proposition for you, dear king. Bring me your precious daughter that you're willing to die for, and you and your men shall continue on your merry way. Two dozen lives for the price of one. But should you trick me, I warn you, I will not be pleased. Think about it for a moment." Knorren's thick tail wrapped around his front legs as he sat, watching the men like a cat transfixed by a mouse. What was so special about the girl that he was willing to die for her? Father or not, everyone was selfish in the end.

Boredom plagued Knorren as much as the roses and burdocks. It was time to change that.

"What could you possibly want with my daughter?" the king stammered.

"Whatever I wish. But shall I go into gruesome details?" Knorren averted his gaze, then glanced at his bloodstained paws. "Even demons enjoy pets, Your Majesty."

The king's fear dissipated, at least outwardly, for anger

made him bolder, stupider, and mouthier. "You'll only eat her. I will not send my daughter to her death."

"And if you cannot pass, she dies anyway. It seems we are at an impasse." Knorren bared his bloodied teeth. Bits of sinew rattled as he chuckled. "Death or possible death. What a tricky decision." He reveled in the king's visible discomfort. He shifted, swore none too quietly, and glared at Knorren.

Silence fell on the forest once more as the king visibly considered his options. "I'll do it." Werner garnered the surprise of his men.

"Your Majesty! You cannot—"

The king shot a venomous look toward the captain as he spoke. "Bite your tongue. I am the *king* and I can do as I wish."

Knorren leaned forward, his snout mere inches from Werner's face. Blood-tinged saliva dripped from his jowls. "I've had enough with your bickering. Since you've agreed to hand over your *beloved* daughter, I expect no tricks from you. None." If a fox could look gleeful, Knorren did, and a deep chuckle resonated in his chest. "You have a month to deliver your daughter to me. If she still hasn't been delivered by the Heligersee Festival, I will come for you, and not just you. I will take payment by way of *other* lives, too."

"Is that mercy?" one man asked.

"Are you not alive?" Honey-colored eyes scanned the faces gaping at him. "I call that mercy, toy soldier." Knorren laughed as he turned away. "One month, Your Majesty." His voice carried on the wind, even as his bright red figure faded into the green foliage.

Knorren weaved through the trees, bowing his head when a low limb stuck out. A small, white-headed man crossed his path, and the fox's ears pinned against his head. As the small man turned around, his bulbous eyes focused on Knorren. His buck teeth flashed as he smiled.

"Greetings, *beast*," the dwarf crooned.

Knorren snarled at the insult, snapping at the offender. "You won't call me such a thing, Egon."

"I call you as I see you, a beast." Egon flicked a bug from his shoulder and walked toward the fox, unafraid of nearing him. "Ylga requests your presence."

Shaking his head, Knorren stepped over the tiny man, snorting when Egon tugged at his tail. If he had half the mind, he could have launched the pest into the darkest part of the forest. "Ylga will receive the king and his men soon. Surely she can wait."

The dwarf quickened his stride and clung to Knorren's fur. "What? What did you say? You let someone pass?" He clucked his tongue and stroked his chin. "Interesting."

Knorren snarled in response to the singular word. "It's only interesting if you dwell on it longer than you should. Be gone before I lose my patience. I've spent the rest of my good nature for the day."

"Ylga demanded you see her. You know what happens when she's angry."

Knorren knew all too well what happened when the old witch was angry. She held grudges longer than anyone he'd ever known, and when someone tested her patience, and used all of their chances, she acted without mercy. Ylga's wrath made Knorren look like a petulant child, and while he wasn't afraid of her, he wasn't keen on testing her either.

"Tomorrow. Not any sooner than that, and that will have to be enough for her."

Egon bowed. "Very well. I will pass on the message."

As the dwarf turned to scurry off, Knorren couldn't help but flick his tail and send the annoying man tumbling to the ground. "Oh, dear, didn't see you there." Knorren chuckled darkly, leaping away before the little one could curse at him.

FIVE

wo days after her father departed, Gisela's herbs ran out entirely. All it took was a day without them for one fit to occur. Exhaustion tugged at her mind, weakening her limbs and muddling her thoughts. Even the sunlight flickering into the library was enough to bring on a wave of dizziness. Perhaps she could avoid another bout of convulsions and vomiting, at least until her father returned, because he *would* return. He had to.

Walking through the castle gardens, Gisela teased the petals of a freshly bloomed rose. With care, she snipped the stem and placed it inside a basket. Suli, her handmaid, sat primly on a bench. She wore her chestnut hair braided into a crown, pinned tightly against her head.

All was quiet in the garden until it wasn't. Voices rang out above the chattering birds, sounding alarm to all in the vicinity.

A guard dodged into the garden, bowing to Gisela. "Pardon the intrusion, Your Highness." His gaze turned to his fellow guardsmen, and his voice lowered, but not enough that Gisela couldn't hear him. "A body, too badly mangled to determine who it is."

At once, Gisela's heart cantered away in her chest. She

needed to know if it was *him*. As much as her heart told her it wasn't, she wanted to see for herself that her father hadn't succumbed to Knorren's snapping jaws.

"Your Highness, no—" Suli bolted from her seat, her hand outstretched to halt Gisela, but she was much too late.

Gisela dropped the pruning shears, clutched her skirt in a death grip, then sprinted from the garden, leaving a panicked Suli in her wake. Gisela was certain her heart would pound free from her ribcage. Dread unfurled within, poisoning her mind with bloody images of her father torn asunder. His beautiful hazel eyes milky in death instead of vibrant.

No no no, he isn't dead, Gisela. Stop this! she reprimanded herself as she darted through the castle, shoving aside the dizziness she experienced.

Time stilled. It felt much like she was in a dream where her limbs refused to obey and speed ahead. Her feet didn't pound against the marble flooring as quickly as she'd like; if only she possessed wings instead of arms!

Gisela choked on a sob as she ran through the halls, darted through a large oak door, and rushed outside toward the barracks.

She was almost to the infirmary when she collided with a familiar face. Galfrid. His lips pursed as he regarded her with a curt bow. "Your Highness, you shouldn't be here."

"Is it him?" she blurted, leaning in toward him. "Please tell me." Gisela told herself she could take the bad news, but that wasn't true.

"Thanks be to Wurdiz, it wasn't. It was an unfortunate merchant. We found his cart just outside of the forest. I wish we knew *why* he went inside." It was another man behind Galfrid who spoke.

Gisela's bones turned to jelly as relief flooded her. She covered her mouth, muting a sob of relief. But it was also mixed with sorrow for the man whose life Knorren had cut short. "May I see the man?"

Galfrid turned to Gisela, his brows furrowing. "Your Highness, that is not wise—or proper."

Suli gasped behind her, panting heavily. "It isn't."

Someone should pay their respects to the slain man, and why couldn't it be Gisela? Besides, guilt tore away at her core. She had wished this on someone else when she pleaded with the gods that it wasn't Papa.

Gisela bristled. These men didn't hold authority over her; she was their princess. "A man has died. We don't know who he is or who his family is. Someone should pray for him. Have you called the priest? Alerted the townsfolk, so that they may inquire about the man?" Gisela pinched the bridge of her nose, wondering why it was she who had the most sense out of them all. Where were her sisters? Likely sipping tea. Did Tilda care? Or was she mourning the loss of the kingdom's throne that was nearly in her grasp?

"Very well, Your Highness." Galfrid bowed his head then turned to the other men.

Suli wound her fingers around Gisela's subtly. Lowering her voice, she whispered, "I don't think this is the wisest decision. He's dead and nothing you can do will change that."

"I don't mean to change it. I mean to apologize, and I mean to pray for his soul and his family, Suli." She slid her hand from the handmaid's and followed Galfrid inside the infirmary.

It was stuffy, smelling of sweat and steel. When the small group rounded the corner, Gisela caught a whiff of something. She recognized the smell from when Suli tended to the few bumps Gisela gained during a fit. Then it struck her nose: the horrible smell of death.

Schooling her face, Gisela moved toward the occupied cot. The man's figure lay wrapped in heavy cloth, but blood had seeped through the fabric, staining it. His mouth hung open in a silent cry of fear—or maybe pain warped his expression. His dark features were like her father's and she could see why one would confuse them. The broad nose, strong forehead, and wide-set jaw. Gisela thought he may have been handsome, had his face not been distorted from death.

Bile crept up Gisela's throat as she peered down at the lifeless form. "Was he alive when you . . ." She couldn't finish the words, and her tongue felt thick. If she forced them out, she was certain she'd expel her stomach's contents.

"No, my lady. He was dead when we found him. Most of his blood had been drained, too." The guard rubbed the back of his neck, shifting foot to foot. "We didn't dare venture inside the forest. We didn't even want to linger outside it much longer." Shame painted his cheeks, and he averted his gaze.

"You poor man," Gisela said softly and crouched beside the cot. "I will pray for you, and I will pray for your family. I vow to put a stop to these senseless killings, too." But *how* was the question. Gisela needed to devise a plan, one that her father wouldn't agree with, and one that her sisters *would*.

No one, not in Gisela's lifetime, or her father's, had appealed to the demon of the forest. Many begged and pleaded with him to change his ways, to spare the lost ones in the forest. But Knorren never did, and each year he grew crueler and crueler. His killings increased, as did his territory, making it more difficult for people to travel through the kingdom. It became necessary to clear new roads, and Gisela wondered why no one had ever hunted him.

Was Knorren truly a demon of the woods? Was he guarded by darkness that would only leach into those who hunted him? It would explain why he still plagued the land. What was she to do? What *could* Gisela do?

Pray, she supposed, that Wurdiz would grant her the knowledge to know what to do next. For her father's safe return. And that Knorren would, for once, show mercy on those who stumbled into his woods.

SIX

On the third night of her father's absence, Gisela woke to the sensation of the bed humming, except it wasn't the mattress. It was her muscles. Tiny, pinprick-like sensations covered her body and it was a feeling she knew far too well. The room tilted in the dark, signaling that Gisela only had a few moments before she'd be in a full-blown state of convulsions. *Where is Suli?* she wondered. Her maid was never too far away; because of Gisela's health complications, Suli slept in Gisela's room. The last thing Gisela wanted was to be alone.

"Suli?" Gisela croaked, trying to keep the panic from her voice. "Suli, are you there?" No response. Wherever Suli was, Gisela had to signal for help.

Precious moments ticked by, building the panic within. Gisela threw back the covers, unsteadily placing her feet on the floor. It was a chore crossing the room in the dark as her world shifted, but as soon as her hand met the doorknob, she yanked it open.

"I need . . . I need help." She slurred her words, which was only the beginning. A guard caught her as her muscles jerked and sent her toppling over. Gisela wanted to sob, but all that came out were shaky moans as her body moved of its own accord. A few moments more—that was all they had before she fell into a violent fit.

"Fetch the physician, now!" The guard barked his orders and carefully brought Gisela to the bed.

She could hear everything, including the guard attempting to soothe her. But Gisela's jaw clamped shut as all of her muscles grew rigid, and she couldn't reassure *him*. In the next few moments, everything faded away.

It felt like only a minute had passed by when she opened her eyes, but the first light of the sun was peeking through her window, which meant it'd been at least an hour. Sweat coated Gisela's skin. She felt as though she were floating amid the room, but it wasn't a giddy feeling—it was alarming. It wasn't right, and every inch of her body tingled with dread. No, no, not again. Panic crept up her neck and as much as she wanted to yell, she couldn't. Gisela's muscles stiffened, signaling another fit was about to occur. All she could manage was a moan, which was enough to alert Suli.

The handmaid turned Gisela onto her side and removed the pillows from the bed. Quickly, she retrieved a bowl and waited for the inevitable.

When the fit was through, Gisela felt arms carefully lifting her from the soiled bed and into a refreshing bath. Out of habit, she lifted her arms and gingerly moved to the side as hands cleansed her. She thought, not for the first time, *Why did Wurdiz inflict such an illness on me?*

Moments when she'd lose control of her body and convulsions ravaged her mind. After each one, she felt useless—unable to walk steadily, or even talk.

Once, a visiting doctor attempted to explain her condition to her father. A *defect*, he'd said. Nothing contagious, but something that would plague Gisela for the rest of her life, and potentially be hereditary.

A defect.

Those words haunted her when she was a little girl, but it was something she had grown used to in her older years. Gisela *wasn't* normal, especially not if placed beside her older sisters. They cared so little about the trivial things she noticed. Small things like birds nesting in the trees outside, or how the leaves danced in the wind. If paying heed to the beauty of the world around them meant she wasn't *normal*, then so be it.

A servant gently brushed now-clean hair away from Gisela's face. In her current state, she couldn't make out who it was. "You're all right, my lady, we are with you."

All she wished to do was sleep off the dreadful feeling weighing her down. The sluggishness, the foggy memory. As she settled into the freshly changed bed, she listened to the quiet murmurs in the room.

"They're going to become worse and His Majesty isn't back yet," Adrienne, another attending handmaid, murmured. "What if she—"

"No," Suli interjected. "We won't talk like that."

Eventually the voices grew distant. The weight of her body pulled her down into the mattress and as she drifted off, she wondered what Adrienne was about to say. Was she afraid of Gisela dying?

Gisela woke to limbs that wouldn't cooperate. They were slow to respond, but eventually they did. Suli sat up in the chair beside her and leaned forward.

"You're awake, my lady." Suli brushed her fingers against Gisela's cool brow. "Just in time, too. Your father is about to arrive. One guard saw His Majesty's party on the patrols." Suli's lips spread into a wide smile. "He did it. He's alive."

Elation spread through Gisela's tired mind. She smiled crookedly and waved at her maid. "Help me dress so I can greet him." Unsteadily, Gisela stood then took a moment to balance herself. He'd done it. Her father had survived Todesfall and somehow escaped Knorren's wrath. But how?

Suli fetched the day's gown, which was a deep purple verging on black. Normally, a bone corset would hug a woman's torso, but considering Gisela's health, no one wanted to hamper her ability to breathe. Suli aided Gisela, tugging the cotton fabric over her head. Once in place, her fingers pulled the stays, securing them.

Luckily, the braid from her bath was mostly still intact. One less thing to fuss over. When she slid her feet into her slippers, the pair headed out the door.

Suli's arm looped around hers in case she lost her balance. Down the hall they traversed, to the stairs by the hoist which was crafted for her special chair for when there were hard days.

Hushed voices carried down the hall, and Gisela knew her sisters were already waiting for their father to burst through the doors. She could hear Tilda's nasally voice and Pia's bitter laugh.

Annoyance wound its way through her at the sight of almost all of her sisters. She lifted an eyebrow, lips pressing together in a firm line as she watched their act. Because that was all it was to them, excluding Jana. Perhaps deep down, Gisela's sisters truly did care for their father, but they were so self involved, it was difficult for her to picture them caring for anyone outside of themselves.

Jana noticed Gisela first, her head canting to the side, indicating for her to join them. Steeling herself, Gisela approached, anticipating the bitter remarks from the others.

Gisela realized she'd been wrong to assume they'd hurl bitter words her way, for instead, they turned their back to her in an obvious display of aversion. Her shoulders slumped forward in defeat. It would seem even when her sisters shared the same sentiment, they still set Gisela apart from them.

"Nevermind them, my heart. They're as frigid as Altergipfel." Jana scrunched her nose in distaste.

Altergipfel was the tallest mountain peak in the kingdom, known for its unforgiving terrain and deadly cold. The comparison to their sisters was a bold but accurate statement.

Gisela bit her lip to keep from laughing out loud. "Shall we go outside then?"

Jana nodded. "I think so."

They pushed past the dawdling sisters, spilling into the courtyard. The sun peeked from behind the tall pines, casting a warm, inviting glow onto the cobblestones. In the distance, voices rang out, garbled at first, then they grew closer, the shouting louder.

Gisela's heart cantered away in her chest. She lost all sense of decorum as she rushed forward, leaving Suli in her wake. It was reckless, of course, as Gisela wobbled where she halted. But the sight beyond the iron gate gave her heart flight.

Her father.

He was alive.

"The king is alive. He's alive! He has returned!" a guard she didn't know the name of shouted. His youthful face split into a broad grin.

The sentries at the gate opened it hurriedly, ushering in King Werner. The king's eyes searched the gathering crowd in the courtyard, and when Gisela found his hazel pair locked onto hers, she couldn't simply remain rooted in place.

"Papa! You made it! You're alive!" she shouted across the way, moving slower than usual. When she got to his mount, she clung to her father's armored leg like a small child would. With eyes rapidly filling with tears, she peered up at him and smiled. No one knew the amount of relief she felt, for no one knew how heavily guilt weighed on her. If she'd caused her father's death, she'd never forgive herself.

"Of course, my Mousy." Werner dismounted and embraced his youngest daughter. His smile faded, replaced with storm clouds in his gaze. "I'm afraid my return didn't come without a price." Werner's lips thinned. His words were quiet, for Gisela's ears only.

She looked up at him, brow furrowing in question. "What do you mean?"

"A steep price and one I will not pay, for you are my beloved daughter." Without another word, his arms encircled Gisela, squeezing her tight against his armored chest.

The armored plate bit into her cheek, hurting, but Gisela didn't complain. There was time to unravel the riddle of his words. For now, she simply reveled in the fact that he was alive.

"I thought you died. They reported a man *dead*, and I assumed it was you," Gisela blurted out. "It wasn't, but then I saw him . . . the blood, his bones, and . . ." She sucked in a breath, choking on the words as a whimper threatened to crawl out.

Surprised entered Werner's gaze. His brows lifted when he peered down at her. "What? He said there would be no deaths." He paused, shaking his head ruefully. "This has to stop at once. I'm so sorry you had to go through that, Gisela, but I am fine."

"Who?" She blinked, wondering if he spoke of Knorren. Had he seen him and had the fox let him go unharmed?

"He's here, he's alive!" Tilda cried.

The king's other girls forced him to relinquish his grip on Gisela. Much to her dismay, they didn't take care of where their feet stepped or where their arms flew.

"Easy, girls. Easy. I am well, I assure you. I have some dreadful news." He turned to the captain, who still flanked him. "Send a message to all the councilmen. We need a meeting and right away."

All the girls paled. "What?" they inquired in unison.

"Let's get inside." Werner motioned for his men to take the horse, and he strode inside the castle. Servants swarmed him, removing pieces of his armor quickly.

Apprehension snaked around Gisela's heart and mind— not for the first time this week, and she was certain it wouldn't be the last. Whatever news her father held couldn't bode well for any of them.

SEVEN

*G*isela followed her father, along with her sisters, into a sitting room. Their father paced the width of the room, his hand dragging down his face as he prepared to speak. But every time his lips parted, he shook his head and continued to wear a path in the carpet.

"Knorren met us halfway," he finally said. "We bargained with him, because it was the only way to get the herbs."

Gisela felt the prick of apprehension along her skin, dotting it in goosebumps. Something dreadful was about to happen. She could feel it in the tension exuding from her father. What had he done?

"What? Impossible. No one has." Tilda eyed him as if he'd lost it. "It's purely a trick of his, Papa. Why have you bargained with him? He's never tried to bargain with anyone before!"

"Yesterday, he did. I can't fathom why he'd change his mind *now*, but he has. For Gisela." A moment ticked by, and the king's pacing didn't ease—it only grew more frantic. "Knorren wants Gisela, as a gift. As a . . . token of peace."

Gisela gasped, stiffening as her father's words dangled in

the air. "What?" she cried. Panic curled around her heart, squeezing it as it thundered away in her chest. Hadn't this always been an option? Peace in trade for her? It would end the killings, wouldn't it? Still, dread ensnared her, chilling her to the core.

Tilda's eyes narrowed, her lips puckering. "For centuries Knorren has haunted the woods and slain Tursch's people, and he stops the killings for *Gisela?*" she asked, shrilly. "Why *her?*"

Werner frowned. "I don't know, but we won't be sending Gisela away. We will send someone else."

"Send her away, Papa! We could achieve peace with her gone!" Tilda whined.

"Absolutely *not*, Tilda," Werner snapped. His lips twisted into an unforgiving scowl. "That will never be an option, do I make myself clear?" He clenched a fist, then pointed a finger at her, shaking it. "One more word from you . . ."

Why Gisela felt the sting of hurt was beyond her. It shouldn't have surprised her and yet . . . Tilda's contempt for her was so strong that she would send her to Knorren, without a thought? Frowning, Gisela bowed her head and covered her face. Horror washed over her, causing her exhausted limbs to tremble. "Just send me," she murmured. No one heard her, judging by the continuation of conversation.

"I saw the man and what Knorren did. No one else here did. If there is any chance that I could put a stop to—"

"No. That's the end of this discussion. I have to prepare for a meeting. No more." Werner sliced his hand through the air, pointing a finger at Gisela. "I'll hear none of it. Do you understand? I will send no daughter of mine off to Knorren to become his plaything or meal, not while I'm still breathing."

Which was exactly what Gisela feared most. That Knorren would come for her father, that he'd come and slaughter them all.

Just as her father abruptly left the room, a servant walked in with Gisela's prepared tea. Reluctantly, she took it, and she thought it tasted far more bitter than usual.

It had been a week since her father had returned. And in that time, Gisela had scarcely seen him. Perhaps he feared she would drag him into another discussion of why she should venture to Knorren. Whatever it was, he hid himself away well.

Gisela milled around the garden, drinking tea and picking roses to fill the vases in her room. Today was a good day. She felt her equilibrium return; her grasp strengthened and her head didn't swim nearly as much. It was on days like this that Gisela felt *normal* and carefree. On particularly bad days, she required a wheeled chair, but when she was invigorated as this she didn't need it, could use the stairs, and she felt well enough to venture into the gardens.

"My lady," Suli chided. "Careful of thorns, they'll prick your skin."

Gisela eyed her, smiling to herself as she carefully ran a finger along a thorn. "What is a little bite, Suli?" With care, she manipulated the stem and broke off the rose, lifting the soft pink blossom to sniff at it. The sweet aroma flooded her senses, and the pink petals brushed against her skin.

Sitting down, Gisela gathered the flowers she collected, removing the thorns, and started weaving them into the crown she crafted earlier. A moment later, the sound of boots scuffling along the stone pathway caught her attention. She paused her work, placing it in her lap.

Galfrid, who was typically in charge of guarding Gisela, bowed. "Your Highness, the king requests your presence in the Great Hall." As he righted himself, his dark gaze settled on the roses in Gisela's grasp.

The guard possessed a handsomeness that was uncommon. Instead of the typical broad build of Tursch, he was slender with sharp-angled features. The severity of his stare matched the rigid way he held himself. Gisela often wondered what it would look like if he smiled. He bowed again, then turned on his heels and left without another word.

Suli nodded, abandoning her stitching as she reached for Gisela's hand to help her up. "What do you think it could be?"

Gisela watched the retreating figure, hesitant to follow him. Although he was only following orders, she narrowed her eyes at his back. Did the vague request have something to do with Knorren?

"I don't know. There is only one way to find out." She looked to Suli. Bless her maid, she looked as ill as Gisela felt at the unknown. "Come on." Gisela fisted her skirt in each hand, leading the way inside the castle, forgetting, for the moment, the peaceful time with the flower crowns.

Much to Gisela's surprise, the Great Hall bustled with activity. The scent of wine filled the air, sweet and overpowering as the councilmen filled their goblets to the brim.

"You'll need more than that to soothe your nerves," one man said with a chuckle.

Councilman Orloff barked in laughter. "You're right. Perhaps the entire cellar's worth."

What on earth were they on about? Gisela narrowed her eyes, then heard a woman's voice raise in the hall behind her.

"No, please." The woman stumbled in behind Gisela with tears streaming down her dark face. Light brown curls framed her features, not so unlike Gisela's hair. But her wide, woeful eyes cut into Gisela's heart, piercing her soul. What was going on? Why was she here, and why was she looking at Gisela in such a way?

Conversation ceased as Gisela approached her father and bowed her head. "Papa, what is going on?" She looked over her shoulder toward the intrusive eyes of the councilmen. A knot formed in her belly as she turned her gaze back to her father.

The king turned to her, frowning deeply. The space between his brows wrinkled with dismay. "This is the only way, I'm afraid," he said in a lower tone. "I wish it weren't so. She will go to Knorren in your place."

Gisela pulled her gaze from her father and looked to the other girl, whose tears cascaded down her cheeks. "What? No. You . . . you can't do that!" She withdrew from her father, even as his hands sought her out. She continued backing away until she collided with Suli. "Please! Just send me." Gisela's turquoise gaze slid toward the panicking girl, whose sobbing grew louder, weighing on her already burdened heart.

Her father took her face in his hands and whispered harshly, "Never. I will *never*." His thumbs ran across her cheeks. "Now, you must teach this girl how to act like you. We will fool that cursed creature yet. Lady Anna will stay with us for a few days." Werner smiled broadly and motioned for the girl to speak up.

"Do I not have a say in this at all?" Gisela's voice sounded so pitiful, even to herself. She couldn't swat her father away like she wished to, not with the entire room watching her.

"No, Mousy." Werner dropped his hands and motioned toward the crying girl.

Through her sniffling, Anna spoke. "Your Highness, it's a pleasure." Except her face said it was anything but. The way her eyes narrowed, the tightness of her lips. She was being forced.

Truly, is it a pleasure? Guilt ate the last part of Gisela's thrumming heart. Why wasn't she part of these discussions, the decisions? A week was all it had taken for her father to make a monumental decision on her behalf. He stole not only her choice, but Anna's too.

One councilman cleared his throat, reminding Gisela she'd yet to respond.

"Anna, you are brave. Thank you for your help in this matter." Gisela offered her hand to Anna, smiling despite the circumstance. A lump formed in her throat and she squeezed Anna's hand. "Let's enjoy the sunny afternoon and learn more about one another." Let the others in the room dare to speak against it.

Anna wiped the tears from beneath her eyes. "Thank you."

Outside the Great Hall, Gisela lowered her voice, turning to Anna. "Was this your choice, Lady Anna?" The hallway was silent in contrast to the room, which had resumed the chaotic hum.

Anna nodded. "It was. I want the slaughtering to end, too. My brother is on the list of Knorren's victims."

Freezing in her stride, Gisela gaped at her as if she'd lost her mind. "And you still wish to go?"

"If it stops him, yes, my lady."

"Oh, Anna, you are quite brave. I am glad I get to know you better."

Even if their acquaintance was brief.

Over the course of a week, Gisela spent most of her time with Anna, teaching her everything she could think of in case Knorren thought to question her. This seemed like an impossible task, one that Knorren would see through, but Gisela's father wouldn't listen to her, no matter how much she begged him to. He meant well; Gisela saw that in his gaze and in the way he clung to her desperately when he spoke.

Unfortunately, as much as she despised the plan to send Anna away, there was nothing she could do to convince her father it was a terrible idea. "Anna, I'll be leaving you in the company of my sister Jana." The look on the other woman's face said it all. Wide-eyed and brows furrowed. Her panic was almost tangible. "Don't worry, it's Jana, the nice one." She laughed as Anna visibly relaxed.

"Good. The last time I was alone with Tilda, it was uncomfortable."

Gisela blinked. "Why is that?"

"She kept making remarks of how unfortunate my impending death was." Anna fidgeted with the skirt of her dress. "And that it was tragic that I bore such a likeness to you." She flushed as the words left her.

Gisela bit her bottom lip and stamped down the sting. "You are beautiful, Anna. Don't let Tilda convince you otherwise. And you will live." But could she promise that? She wished she could. "I have a fitting appointment for a gown, but when it's over, I'll come find you again." She reluctantly left the room.

In the few days she'd spent with Anna, a mutual fondness developed between them. And had Anna not been leaving, Gisela could have easily allowed a genuine friendship to blossom.

Suli accompanied Gisela down the hall to a room next to her bedchamber. Inside, Delia the seamstress awaited, but she wasn't alone. Freya paced in the back of the room, her braided gray hair swinging behind her like a pendulum.

"Good afternoon," Gisela greeted them. The click of the door ensured it was safe to undress. Suli tugged at the back stays and made quick work of them, pulling them loose. In a blink, Gisela's slender frame was free of the dress and stood only in her underthings.

"Good afternoon, my lady. We look forward to working with you today." Delia inclined her head, lowering herself into a small curtsy. Freya was quick to do the same.

It seemed silly to follow through with the fitting for the Heligersee Festival. Gisela couldn't wrap her head around the idea of continuing with it. The times were uncertain rather than happy, but if this was what the people of Tursch needed, so be it. If she could bring a small amount of joy to their lives for an evening, it was worth it. Still, there was a bitter taste on her tongue.

"What was it you were hoping for, my lady?" Delia inquired.

Freya moved away from Delia, then rummaged around in the bag she brought with her. "Oh, she left this with me." She pulled free a sketch and handed it to Delia.

"I see," Delia mused out loud and motioned for Gisela to step onto the pedestal. "This is good. I think we can make this work."

Gisela stood atop the platform, thankful the afternoon sun still warmed the castle. "Freya is talented. I think you'd enjoy her workmanship, Delia."

Delia peered down at the paper. "It looks like she took your measurements at the shop." She paused and laughed. "What do you want me to do then?"

"A collaboration. Freya needs higher quality fabric, and I know you *both* will do wonders on the gown."

Seeming to grasp the hint, Delia nodded and set to grabbing a few bolts of fabric she brought with her. "I was thinking this red, but what did you have in mind, Freya?"

"I thought ivory, with gold threading."

"I think both would look exquisite," Gisela chimed in, lifting her brows.

"Oh! You are quite right." Delia clucked her tongue and

for the next two hours she and Freya cut fabric, discussed stitching, and teased one another.

By the time they were through, Gisela longed to sit. Suli helped her into the discarded dress when someone knocked on the door.

EIGHT

"Come in," Gisela called, spinning to face the door.

"I hope you decided on your gown's design." Her father's words trailed toward the end, as if he wasn't sure how to collect his words. "I'm leaving tomorrow to deliver Lady Anna to Knorren." He lifted a hand to silence Gisela's growing protest. "When I return, we must begin our final plans for the festival. There are only two months left until the celebration." He chuckled, the corners of his eyes crinkling with mirth.

How could he be so at ease? How could he *laugh?* Knorren was not to be trifled with, and more than that, Lady Anna's life was on the line. Panic pierced her to the core. Gisela feared for her father because when Knorren discovered the truth he would spare no one, of that she was certain.

"I don't know if Anna is ready to go," Gisela blurted, suddenly desperate to prolong her departure. "Knorren is clever, and you know that. What if he questions her, tricks her, and then she cannot answer properly?"

"Lady Anna doesn't have a choice. I know you've bonded with her, but Knorren gave us a deadline. I don't want to ruin the festival planning. The sooner we leave, the sooner we can return. Knorren will have his trinket and we can be done with his antics."

"And *celebrate*?" She couldn't help how her voice went up an octave. Gisela's fingers slid up her face, then stroked her forehead. The fact that her father stood there and spoke of Anna leaving with such ease chilled Gisela's blood. "There will be nothing to celebrate."

"Nothing?" Werner scoffed. "There will be every reason to celebrate. We will celebrate your health and the agreement Knorren will have no choice but to accept." He stepped forward and cupped Gisela's chin. "Don't mistake my words for being cold. I don't want to do this either, yet it's our only option."

"No, it isn't," she whispered.

"Gisela." He released her chin. "You're being difficult."

Sucking her bottom lip in, she quieted. A thousand words tumbled around in her mind. But what difference would they make to her father when he was so bent on sending someone else? He may have thought that he was saving his daughter, but he was dooming his people.

"If you wish to say your goodbyes to Lady Anna, do so today. I'll not have any more arguing from you, understand?"

Gisela's eyes widened, her cheeks burning from the reprimand. Embarrassment wound its way through her, curbing her tongue from lashing out. To retort now would be disrespectful in front of the seamstresses, but there was nothing more she wanted.

Instead, Gisela's head canted to the side, her eyes lowered and her lips pressed tightly together. "As you wish, Papa."

"Good. I'll leave you to your dealings." He motioned toward the papers, measuring tape, and quiet seamstresses.

As soon as the door shut behind him, Suli rushed up to Gisela, gathering Gisela's hand between hers. "It will be all right, my lady, I know it will be."

"No. I don't think it will." Gisela flopped down on the pedestal, taking a moment to clear her thoughts. Her father possessed the uncanny ability to make her feel as though she were naught more than a child, floundering in life without a voice.

Maybe she was.

In the morning, Anna fussed over what little belongings she could pack—it wasn't as if she had a lot in her possession—while Gisela pensively watched. A flicker of hope danced in the princess's heart, for if Anna could convince Knorren that she was truly the youngest princess, she'd be saving many lives. Yet, if she failed, if she didn't convince the fox, Gisela shuddered to think of what would happen.

"I've committed everything I can to memory," Anna breathed. "I will do my best, for my brother and for the country." She spoke earnestly as she walked up to Gisela. Anna's fingers swept a strand of Gisela's hair from her brow. "Believe in me. I need that more than anything." With a sigh, she sat down, gripping Gisela's hand. "I've come to cherish you and our budding friendship. I can see why His Majesty refused to send you, but know this: I hold no grudge toward you. Only, I wish Knorren would meet a gruesome end."

Will he ever meet his end? The idea tumbled around in Gisela's head as she stroked the top of Anna's hand. Tears pricked her eyes the more she dwelled on what would become of her new friend. Just another ounce of guilt to lay on the heaviness of her heart. "Oh Anna. I wish things were different, but I'm afraid wishes accomplish very little." And Gisela might as well have been born mute because her father didn't listen.

A knock sounded on the door, startling both girls. "Come in," Lady Anna called.

The king stood in the doorway, looking far more composed than Gisela thought he should have. "Excuse me, girls." Werner's hazel eyes flicked between Gisela and Anna, finally settling on Anna. "Lady Anna, it is time. The carriage is ready for us."

Anna sucked in a breath. Moving her hand toward her stomach, she clutched the loose fabric of her dress and stiffly stepped forward. "Yes, Your Majesty." She curtsied to Gisela, allowing her eyes to linger.

Time seemed to slow. Gisela wanted to lunge toward Anna, to hold her back and cause a fuss in front of her father, but instead of doing so, she turned her gaze on him and simply stared. Heavy tension writhed between them, like a living creature.

"I will pray for you, Anna," was all she could say.

Werner opened his mouth to speak but promptly closed it. He shook his head and exited the room, leaving Gisela alone in the empty guest room. One last chance was all she had, one more to change his mind and save Anna from a dismal fate.

Hurrying after her father, she sped down the hallway,

toward the stairs, and called to him. "Papa, please. Reconsider, please, I beg of you." She didn't shout, didn't cry. She just reached out and held his arm. Desperation clawed at her, leaving ugly marks on her soul. This was her last chance.

"Gisela, please don't make this more difficult than it has to be. Lady Anna knows this is for the best. As you should, too. We must go at once. Knorren will lose his patience."

A scream grew inside of Gisela. But would it change anything if she unleashed it? If she stomped her feet, howled in dismay, or pounded her father's chest, would it convince him to try another way? No. All it would do was cause a scene, and she'd potentially find herself escorted to her room and told to calm herself before a bout of convulsions came on.

Instead of the thousands of ways she wanted to lash out, Gisela moved to embrace her father. "Be safe, Papa." Gisela glanced up at him, not bothering to disguise the disappointment etched on her face. Pleased with him or not, she still loved him and wished him a safe journey.

When she turned away and walked down the hall, she could hear the clattering of hooves on the courtyard echoing off the castle walls, and the creaking of the carriage pierced the air as it rolled forward.

With her forefinger and middle finger pressed to her brow, Gisela whispered a prayer to Wurdiz, asking for protection for her father and the rest of the party.

NINE

Ylga cackled, watching as Knorren shifted uncomfortably on his paws in her presence. He'd put off visiting the witch, conveniently forgetting the tiresome dwarf's demands. Unfortunately, the woman found Knorren deep in the Todesfall, patrolling the area for trespassers. Tiny flowers and pieces of bramble clung to his bushy tail.

"You let a king pass through the forest unharmed, which surprises me, old friend."

Although he didn't visibly flinch, Knorren's insides jolted in awareness at the grating quality the familiar voice had. "We are not *friends*," Knorren barked at her.

Ylga emitted a nasally sound, then continued, unfazed by his dramatics, "But you bargained for his precious daughter." Faded gray eyes studied the fox closely, watching for any tic that would give him away. "Interesting. What will you do with her?"

"Eat her, for all I care. What does it matter to you, and why did you request me?" Knorren's patience wore thin. He wanted nothing to do with Ylga. As far as he was concerned, it was she who summoned him from the depths of hell to plague the forest. Knorren recalled nothing of his origins, including the underworld and the summoning.

Anger swirled in Ylga's gaze, tightening the skin beneath her eyes. She rolled her loose sleeves up, revealing aged, freckled flesh. Words that meant nothing to Knorren passed her lips, which seemed to move too fast or too slow for the flow of speech.

As soon as she finished speaking, Knorren's entire body flattened to the ground, pinned and immobile. A rumbling growl rolled through the clearing as he fought against her binding magic. He should have known Ylga would flex her ability to show she was still in control.

"I will not eat her! Bloody hell, let me up, you abominable cantankerous wretch!" The pressure increased on his body, squeezing him so tightly his breath fled from his lungs. Knorren's obstinance vanished, rendering him limp on the ground. "Mercy," Knorren wheezed, refusing to submit further by whimpering.

At once the pressure eased, and Knorren stood unsteadily.

"I've known you for centuries, Knorren, and not once in the years past have you ever allowed someone to pass through your woods alive—or shall I say without life-threatening injuries." She steepled her fingers, staring at him. "Why now?"

Knorren didn't know why. It was some unspoken emotion in the king's gaze that struck him. Whether it was curiosity, pity, or mercy was unknown to Knorren. Or maybe it was because the king was so willing to endanger himself, a man of his station, for the life of his daughter that intrigued him so much. "I don't know." The reply held a hint of annoyance, which was because of the unknown and not Ylga's tactics.

The old woman pursed her lips, swiping silver strands from her eyes as she considered his reply. "Does Knorren the Merciless suddenly have a conscience?"

It was a question Knorren knew better than to answer. Instead, he watched as she bent over a low-growing bush and plucked a plethora of small black berries.

"Ylga, if all you wanted was to gloat . . ." He twisted on his haunches, itching to leap into the cover of the summer's foliage and patrol the border of Todesfall Forest.

The witch emptied handfuls of the berries into a small woven basket. She tsked at the fox as if he were a mere child. "No. The girl in question is truly ill and requires the remedy only I make. I find it interesting that your paths should cross in such a way."

"Do you?" Knorren asked blandly. "You find it strange when the fastest way is through my forest and toward your hut?" he snapped. Considering all he knew about the woman, this could have been her plan from the start. This could be a plot of hers, to end his miserable, lengthy existence.

"No. I find it strange that for well over two hundred years you've slaughtered countless men and even women who step foot onto the forest floor. But the king pleads for his daughter's life, a daughter whose health relies on my knowledge of herbal remedies and magic. I find the notion of your fate linked to mine *yet again* fascinating, demon."

At the slur, Knorren's ears pinned to his head. But was it truly a slur? He was a wicked one, up from the depths of the underworld to wreak havoc and lay waste to humankind as if they were naught more than fodder for the plants.

"We are done here," Knorren rumbled. Without another word, he leaped over the crone, dashing into the undergrowth with his lips pulled into a snarl. In the distance, close to the clearing he was in, someone milled around.

Not for long.

Blood dripped from Knorren's chin as he carried the corpse of a young man in his mouth. The weight of the limp body shifted, causing him to bite down and crunch into a bone. Why the human considered trespassing was beyond him. It had only been a month since slaughtering another bold nobleman's son. *Noble indeed,* Knorren thought. What made him different from a beggar? The same metallic tang filled his mouth, give or take a little perfume. He'd cried the same as Knorren's teeth tore the flesh from his bones.

Still crunching on the body, Knorren wove his way through the oak and birch trees until he came across the sound of a feminine voice. Cloaked by the overgrowth, and still a ways away, Knorren froze in his tracks, wondering if the king returned already with the princess.

Sniffling accompanied the soft voice, then a masculine tone cut through the woman's apparent upset. "Fear not, little one, you won't perish. You have my word." The male voice wavered ever so slightly.

Curiosity got the better of him and Knorren slunk forward, crouching as low as he could without rustling the forest floor. Although their voices were audible, the confines of a carriage shrouded the pair. But Knorren recognized the king's voice, even from inside.

Black horses with gold-plated buckles and crimson trappings jigged in place, scenting death in the air. They were a part of the king's entourage. Knorren faced them, although they couldn't see him yet, and he saw the whites of their eyes as their gaze darted back and forth.

Quietly, the fox dropped the body in his mouth with a *plop*. Knorren's honey gaze narrowed as he crooned, "*Throughout the dreaded winter, thorns and bones splinter, the desperate hands of the Old One's child.*" His voice slithered through the bramble. "*Nary a traveler lived, though the lands were once blessed. The gods turned their backs, and they lay the children to rest.*"

Silence.

In the next moment, Knorren snatched the discarded body at his paws, darted through the cover of the woods in a circle, then leaped out at the guards flanking the carriage. He dropped the dead body on top of the roof. Fresh blood rained down from above and onto the ground. Roses sprung from the earth, tangling in the carriage wheels and jabbing at the horses. Whatever sinews kept the human's head intact snapped, allowing for it to roll off the carriage and onto the ground. There was no way the king and his daughter would mistake the contents for anything but what they were.

The team of horses spooked, lurching forward to run away from the fox, from death and the trap they knew the forest to be. However, the driver and a nearby guard coaxed them into staying and enduring the suffocating tension.

"King Werner," Knorren called from behind them. "You

return so soon." Knorren's calculating gaze darted to the men on horseback. Fear froze their expressions in place. They sat trembling and had every right to fear him. He pressed forward, cocked his head, then peered into the carriage. "I hope you said your goodbyes, *Princess*." His eyes narrowed as the girl's shock dissolved into tears.

"Knorren, we are to make a deal," Werner began. "Before I hand my daughter over—"

"Oh no, *Your Majesty*." Knorren bared his teeth as he slunk forward. "There will be no more bargains. I spared you once. Shall you test my patience?" He snapped his jaw at the king, vexed by the notion King Werner would even contemplate another deal. "Give the girl to me." He drew out each word with a growl.

Werner held his hand up, waving off the men that lifted their weapons. Wiping a fleck of the fox's bloody spit from his face, Werner locked his gaze with the fox. "Be that as it may, if I am to give you my daughter, I expect peace. Allow the citizens to travel to Hurletz to trade and to pass into Burlitz. Through this very road."

Red invaded Knorren's vision. This insignificant man thought to barter with him once more? A thunderous rumble echoed in the forest, not from the sky, but from the depths of Knorren's chest. "There is nothing of import in Hurletz or Burlitz. Nothing that you should need now that I have your daughter." His ears swiveled, lips pulling back to reveal a wicked, blood-tinged grin. "Isn't that right, *Your Majesty*?"

The king's face remained impassive. "Not for my daughter, but for those in Burlitz and Hurletz. Shutting them off from the city isn't a kindness."

"Who do you think you are speaking to?" Knorren's

tufted brows furrowed as his lip curled in derision. "As if I care what is kind or not for the wretched people?" He'd sooner eat them than care what befell them.

Werner sliced his hand through the air as he spoke. "You have what you want, don't you? You've taken much from me," he shouted. "What more do you want?"

Knorren yawned, stretching in an obvious display of boredom. "Very well. Your people may pass to and from Hurletz and Burlitz, but if I find you have tricked me . . ." His eyes followed to where the headless corpse lay. "I'm afraid you'll find yourself in quite the predicament." Standing to his paws, Knorren eyed the girl. "What is your name?"

Werner nodded to the girl, encouraging her to speak.

"G-Gisela," she stammered and cast her gaze to the ground.

"Gisela," the fox echoed her name. He almost pitied the girl, for she trembled in her slippers, and her breath came in quick spurts. "Come now, Gisela. We shall see if you truly are the princess. For your sake—let's hope you are. Climb onto my back and hold on. We wouldn't want you to take a spill now."

Knorren lowered himself for the girl, allowing her to situate herself on top of him, clinging to his fur as if her life depended on it. When she was as settled as she could be, he leaped off, leaving the king and his men much as they were when he'd stumbled on them.

TEN

*R*ain pelted against the castle's windows, dulling the sound of twittering birds. Gisela glanced outside the library window and watched as a few sparrows fluttered in puddles, while others sat on branches and spread their wings, fully enjoying the luxury of a midday bath.

A hint of a smile touched Gisela's lips as she crossed the room and sat on the leather couch. She curled herself into the nook in the corner, then scooped up the book she'd been reading. Since it was raining, she couldn't venture outside in the gardens, much to her dismay. The warm droplets would have felt good against her skin.

The sound of rustling skirts pulled Gisela from the world beyond the ink and pages. She blinked, focusing on reality. Regrettably, she glanced up from the fascinating read of a goddess tossed from the heavens, forced to live among a house of girls, and how she had to fight against all odds to save not only the surrounding kingdoms, but the heavens as well.

Across the room, Tilda perused a bookshelf. Gisela assumed her sister had memorized the books on that shelf, because it was the same one she always visited.

If Gisela didn't move, would Tilda simply leave the library? She sat frozen, not wanting to garner her sister's attention, but it was as if Tilda heard the very thought.

Tilda spun around, clutching a book in her grasp. The gown she wore was a touch too tight, considering her swollen belly.

"Why are you hiding in here like some hermit?" Tilda's mouth twisted in a scowl, her dark eyes pinning Gisela where she sat.

"I'm reading, the same as you, I suspect." She lifted the book from her lap, peering up through curls that had sprung loose from their braid.

"Always thinking you're above everyone else." Tilda strode forward, into a spot where the window cast shadows against her face, veiling her almost. "If Papa should pass away during one of his ridiculous travels because of you, I want you to know, little sister, you won't be spoiled any longer. I'll be named queen, as the rightful heir to Tursch, and my family will hold the throne. Not you, not any of the others. Do you understand?" Tilda spoke through her teeth now, her upper body lowering as much as it could as she spat her words.

Gisela's muscles tensed as her sister drew near. Of course, it wasn't a new act for Tilda when it came to spitting venom. But she'd never boasted of the eventual status as queen. Anger built inside of Gisela. She tired of her sister's ruthless demeanor. Tilda was too sharp, even for their father's liking. However, he ignored the daggers she often tossed, and missed many arrows she let fly when he wasn't looking.

"I don't understand you." Gisela's gaze never wavered. "Nor will I ever."

"That isn't saying much." Tilda sniffed, straightening her posture. "Pray to Wurdiz that Papa returns, because your days will consist of your room, and the life of one plagued with madness."

Gisela dropped the book to the side, then bolted to her feet. "Tilda! I am not mad. How can you say such things?" She curled her fingers into her palms, squeezing to keep herself in check. What good would it do to lash out? Hate was a strong word, but in that moment, she despised her sister.

"One day, you'll kill him, too, Gisela—" Tilda's mouth remained open as a squealing echoed in the halls. Abruptly, a little freckle-faced boy appeared in the room, racing across the distance separating himself and his mother. His dark curly hair bounced with every leaping step he took.

"Mama! Ma—" he interrupted himself, wide hazel eyes focusing on Gisela. "Tante!" This time he bellowed, twisting to hurl himself at Gisela's lap. "I missed you!"

"Byron, my sweetest and most favorite nephew." She laughed, bending over to scoop him up.

"I'm your *only* nephew."

Gisela tapped the tip of his nose and beamed. "That may be so, but it makes you even more special."

Tilda held her hand out as she spoke. "Byron, let's let Tante have her peace."

"But, I want Tante," Byron whined, clinging to Gisela even tighter than before.

Tilda's eyes narrowed at her son's disobedience. She

reached for him, awkwardly trying to peel him from her sister.

"Go with your mama, Byron. I'll see you at supper, and you can sit next to me." With one more hug, Gisela released the boy and helped him down from the couch. She watched as they left the library and lifted her hand to rub at the invisible arrow in her chest.

Once, long ago, she wanted to believe Tilda and Pia loved her, but as time passed Tilda gave her no reason to believe that was how she felt. Time and time again, Tilda relentlessly teased her little sister for being useless and for stealing their father's attention. At first, Gisela could understand it, but then as Tilda grew more aggressive and sour, it was difficult to see the good in her.

Pia was, in some ways, far worse than Tilda ever could be. Jealousy didn't taint her, it was just a cruel disposition.

That evening, supper was fairly quiet, if one discounted Byron's enthusiasm when it came to his stories, or the way his father—Lord Geralt—laughed and it echoed in the room. Tilda stared icily at her husband, but even Geralt's warmth did nothing to break the frigid tension exuding from his wife in the hall. His amiable smiles, rumbling laugh, and playful nature only seemed to annoy Tilda all the more.

Gisela secretly delighted in it.

Byron, as promised, sat next to her. He rambled on about his most recent mishap in his estate's pond.

"I fell while trying to catch a toad. He was right there! I almost had him, but he leaped away from the water, and then I fell off the rock. Splat!" He smacked his hands together to emphasize his point, laughing hysterically as he reenacted it.

Gisela couldn't help but join him in laughter. "My goodness. I'm glad you're all right, because I would have missed you had you needed to stay behind instead of surprising me with a visit!"

"Never!" He lifted his fork in the air, rising from his chair in protest. "I would never miss a visit with you."

Tilda scowled at Gisela, as if she'd been encouraging Byron's antics.

Laughing, Gisela eased her nephew into his seat once again. "I'm glad, because I'd miss your freckled face." She tapped his nose lightly.

Throughout dinner, Byron kept Gisela entertained with his endless stories. There was the mishap with the vase in the hallway at his home, the time his pony dumped him into a pile of manure, and most recently, his refusal to bathe for the rest of his life. Byron was more like his father than his mother. *Thanks be to Wurdiz*, Gisela thought. He was full of happiness, but more than that, a contagious energy that threatened to swallow Gisela whole. Not that she'd mind.

The aroma of spiced cake wafted through the air as servants brought the dishes out. More candles were lit to add light to the dimming hall, but the constant shift of air in the room made them all flicker.

Gisela bowed her head, covering her eyes as she tried to block out the swiftly moving light. A knot of apprehension formed in her belly. Maybe she wouldn't have a fit. She had the herbs in her system, but the telltale tingling ran up her spine.

No one noticed her silent turmoil.

She stood from her chair, clutching the edge as her voice

THE CASTLE OF THORNS

died on her tongue. In the next moment, her father appeared in the room, and a choked cry escaped her. "Papa!" Her face paled as nausea bubbled within, then her legs twitched subtly against her will.

"Good news!" Werner's voice boomed in the hall, his arms spread wide as he strode in. "Knorren has agreed to cease the killings! And the highway is open!" He pumped his fist in the air, but as his eyes zeroed in on Gisela, he frowned and darted into motion.

Uneasily, she swayed on her feet, then crashed to the floor. As much as she wanted to think of anything else, of how the candles were the trigger, or of Byron's protesting to bathe, her thoughts ceased all at once.

Gisela's body grew rigid on the floor, then convulsed violently. She was a prisoner, trapped inside a body that couldn't break free of its torture, nor could she speak. The contents of her stomach disagreed with her, twisting and sloshing in her belly like a turbulent sea. At once, she spewed.

"Tante?" Byron asked, alarmed, but Tilda drew him away from the sight.

Werner crossed the room as soon as she fell to the floor. Too many times he'd seen her collapse, or writhe in bed. He knew what came next. All the chairs scraped against the floor as everyone moved to ensure Gisela wouldn't hurt herself, or perhaps vomit on them. With a care, Werner turned Gisela as she spewed, pulling her braid away from her mouth.

"You're all right. I promise, my girl," he encouraged her softly.

Just a few moments. That was all this episode was, and it left Gisela feeling boneless. She could scarcely lift her head to acknowledge her father.

"I have you, Mousy-girl." Werner brushed wet strands of hair from her face. "Let's get you to your room."

"But the news—" Gisela mumbled, cutting her own words off as they failed to form in her head. As much as she wanted to cling to consciousness, darkness pulled her under.

While she slept, she dreamed of Crown Prince Jannik from centuries ago. The Gilded Prince, they called him. His story was one they all knew well. A recent successor to the throne after his father passed away from fever, Prince Jannik was a generous ruler, albeit a frivolous one. He spent the kingdom's coin freely, but when he nearly spent them into debt, he became cruel and calculating.

She dreamed of Knorren, who commanded the prince to do his bidding. The bite of the late autumn air nipped at Gisela's neck as she watched the prince submit to the fox. Immediately, Knorren tore into the castle, shredding the walls, slaughtering the servants.

Prince Jannik demanded the fox to cease, his hands held up in protest. Anguish warped his pale, beautiful face. But the fox only slanted him an impish look, then leaped at him, mouth open wide. In one bite, the prince was dead.

Knorren turned his bloody grin to where Gisela stood, watching in horror. He laughed, then fled, retreating into the cover of one of the castle's estates in the Todesfall Forest, and he claimed it for his own.

The dream shifted. Years trickled by, the Todesfall Forest grew each year, and with it, Knorren's claim to the land.

Gisela couldn't understand why this history lesson plagued her now, but as she dreamed, she saw a flash of red hair. As she investigated the underbrush of the forest, she heard a rumble of laughter, then hot breath washed over her, and she felt fangs clamp around her neck.

Jolting herself awake, she thrashed for a moment, settling only when she saw her father sitting beside her. That wasn't a dream, at least.

Her father leaned forward, grasping Gisela's clammy hand. "It was just a dream. Rest easy, and know that Knorren will no longer bother us. I'm sure your anxieties over the situation aren't helping your health."

Maybe, but it was the perfect storm in the dining hall. Gisela was tired. The candles flickered. And yes, she was eager for her father to stay, but it wasn't as dire as he made it sound.

She frowned, squeezing his hand. "Won't he though?" she croaked, sounding every bit as parched as she felt. Her father retrieved a glass of water, then lifted it to her lips. She drank greedily, closing her eyes as the refreshing liquid washed down her throat.

"Why should he? He thinks he has what he wants. Knorren has no reason to haunt us any longer." Leaning back in the chair, Werner set the glass down on the nightstand. He tapped his fingers on his knee, visibly pondering his next words. "You know, this talk can wait. Byron has been worried about you—he's been pawing at the door for hours."

"Let him in, I think it would do us both some good."

So he did.

Byron leaped onto the bed. A million questions spilled from his mouth about his aunt's health, and why her fit happened, how long it had been occurring, or if he'd ever have it happen to him.

Gisela prayed not, but if it did, at least he wouldn't be alone.

&LEVEN

Deep in the heart of Todesfall, a castle stood encased in thorny vines that suffocated the stone beneath them. Blossoms of crimson contrasted with the greenery, offering not only a lethal beauty, but a sweet fragrance, too.

Amid the sweetness, death wafted, for it was a graveyard as much as it was a monument of times gone by. Bones littered the forest floor, and from the decomposing bodies grew burdocks. They stretched toward the hidden sky, even daring to bloom in such a vile garden, flaunting their purple petals for their demon lord to see, and to curse.

Ever since Knorren had devoured the Gilded Prince, the castle in the forest had been buried in a mass of thorns and burdocks. Each time Knorren extinguished a life, another rose bush and another burdock bush grew in its place. They were the bane of his existence, reminding him of each wicked deed.

Once, the castle sat as proudly as the castle on the hill and, from what Knorren remembered, served as the prince's secondary estate. But when he was slain, it was the first piece of land the fox stole.

Evergreen trees grew in thick clusters, ensuring no sun

poked through, which made the blooming flowers an anomaly, but they were nothing more than an annoyance to Knorren. A constant reminder that he was a blight on this realm, summoned by some hate-filled witch to wreak havoc on the kingdom. Long ago, when Ylga had first called to him, Knorren had been filled with melancholy. Each time he killed someone it tore away a piece of him, but the sorrow bled into rage and disgust. Why, he hadn't known then, and he certainly didn't know now. Despair turned into contempt over centuries, until he nearly forgot what started it all.

Gisela, the princess, wept the entire journey to the hidden castle. Several times she nearly tumbled to the ground, and each time Knorren paused, allowing her to regain her balance and wits.

By the time they arrived, Knorren wanted to throw her to the ground. He swung his head to the side and bared his teeth.

"Get off." He sunk to the ground, rolling to the side so the bumbling girl could dismount. "Now go inside the castle." Knorren jumped to his paws, shaking out his fur to smooth it once again.

The princess looked pitiful standing in the dirt-covered pathway. In her hands she held the only possessions she could bring—a small bag with a few changes of clothes, Knorren assumed. Tears streamed down her cheeks, but it was the horror in her gaze that spoke volumes.

"Did I not make myself clear?"

"Yes, b-but the door—where is it?" She half turned to the castle, eyeing the wall of thorns dubiously.

Knorren's eyes narrowed. He strode forward, jabbing his nose at a camouflaged wooden door. It groaned loudly as it swung inward, blowing dust and wilted petals across the floor.

He sighed, then sat on his haunches and dug at the wall, stripping away the overgrowth and blooming flowers. When he finished, the door's archway became clear. "Here."

The princess whimpered in response, crossing the threshold into the darkness of the Great Hall.

None save for Egon and Ylga had stepped inside, let alone cleaned the stone structure in decades. Neither Egon nor Ylga would deign to lift a finger to dust a shelf or shovel the bones from the floor. Not that Knorren cared. Guests weren't likely to knock on his door, and if they were brazen enough to traipse into his forest, they soon met an ugly fate.

More bones for the forest floor, more burdocks to sprout from flesh and roses to flourish in droplets of blood.

The princess gasped as she stumbled over the graveyard inside, then promptly doubled over to vomit, as if she could expel the evil that threatened to sink into her marrow.

Knorren rolled his eyes. He ducked his head and entered the castle.

He lifted a paw, swiping at the wall, which sent a broom swathed in cobwebs clattering to the floor. "If it bothers you so, grab the broom and clean it. While you're at it, discard the contents of your stomach you so carelessly deposited on the floor." He curled his lip, showing a gleaming pair of fangs. "Do it now. Don't make me lose my patience."

The girl scurried toward the broom, dropping her bag so she could clutch the handle. She quivered violently, gagging amid her terror.

A delicate one, Knorren mused, wondering if all royals were so weak. A thought occurred to him that perhaps he should test the girl's resilience. Yes, test her resilience, and in the process see if she was truly the king's daughter.

For why would King Werner give his beloved daughter over to him so easily? If he was willing to die in the forest, wouldn't he be willing to trick his foe?

The girl was as delicate as a rose's silken petal. No doubt as liable to bruise as one too. She'd need someone to look after her if Knorren intended to keep her alive. There were farm houses not far from the edge of Todesfall. He could nab a villager and force them to care for her. "Princess, I must go and summon aid for you, but while I'm gone, you will clean all of this hall." Knorren spun on his haunches and exited the castle, bounding into the greenery of the forest.

Over the course of three weeks, the princess said little and refused dinners, but she accomplished all the tasks he set her without so much as a peep. She had, as far as Knorren knew, befriended the mousy woman known as Violet from the neighboring village. Much to his dismay, the venomous shrew did everything in her power to shield the princess from him.

Try as Knorren may, whether he spoke softly or bellowed at her, Gisela refused to speak to him. Before his eyes, she withered away. Knorren wondered if this was her illness at work, but one thing bothered him. She didn't drink or consume the life-sustaining herbs Ylga and Werner claimed she needed.

Early in the morning, after a hunt, Knorren returned to

the castle with his prize hanging from his mouth. The deer flopped to the ground with a sickening thud, blood oozing from the puncture wounds anew.

The sound of madness echoing in the castle gave Knorren pause. He listened carefully. Pushing open the door to his home, he crept forward.

"I can't, I can't. No longer, I can't. I thought I could, but I can't. Not for the king, not for my brother, and not for Gisela." The girl's tantric words fled from her quivering lips. When she finally took notice, she gawped at him, relief flooding her eyes, then fear mangled her features. Tears spilled onto her cheeks as she balled her hands up. "I can't anymore. I am Anna, I am not your princess."

Anger bloomed heatedly in his chest. Instinct gnawed at him, urging him to lay waste to her at once. *So, King Werner has decided to trick me, has he?* A deep growl resonated in Knorren's chest, but he didn't lash out at the girl. Not yet. While patience wasn't a virtue he possessed, it served him well to wait for the entire story. All of it. As *Anna* babbled on about Werner's ploy, Knorren's vision reddened.

"I've failed." A simple statement, but it was true. The weakened girl sank to the floor, eyes focused on the dull tile beneath her. "All I ask is that you have mer—"

Knorren moved as quick as lightning, his paw swatting Anna with enough force to shove her into the stairwell. She fell limply, her head twisted at an odd angle. As he loomed over her lifeless body, his snout pressed against her chest. No movement came. No weak thump of her heart either.

Anna was dead.

"Mercy? What comes from showing mercy but trickery?

I showed your sovereign mercy, and I won't do it again." He snarled, dipping his head down to pluck up the lifeless body.

Bones cracked under the pressure of his teeth, shifting and jabbing the human's flesh as he trotted down the castle's pathway, into the brush and toward the neighboring village.

It was still early enough that no humans were milling around close to the forest. Besides, darkness still claimed the edge of the farmlands, disguising Knorren's hulking figure as he slunk toward the main road.

With a toss of his head, he disposed of Anna's body. It collided with the ground, contorted like a child's doll, with her limbs pointing in grotesque directions. Her left leg twisted in the joint at her hip, angling so that her foot pointed toward the opposing one. One of her arms had loosened from its socket, barely hanging on. She looked much like a rumpled marionette where she lay.

"Mercy," Knorren growled. "The last strand of my mercy is this: I gave the king one month, and I'll make good on that, but the death toll will rise in the meantime. For you, Your Majesty, didn't uphold your end of the bargain. Trickery begets trickery, and I'll be paid what is owed to me, King Werner!" He spun toward the woods, letting out a shrieking cry. "And I'll go to the castle myself."

TWELVE

*N*early a month after Lady Anna's departure, spring started relinquishing her grip on the land. Blossoms powdered the ground, giving way to full green leaves, and the browned, withered brush grew lively once more. Birds flew in from the corners of the world, scattering themselves across Tursch in a loud display that one season would soon fall into another.

Despite the warming days and greenery, the sun remained curtained behind a veil of gray. Too dreary to spend time in the city, or among her beloved gardens, Gisela perched on the window seat in her room, reading a new novel.

Suli poked her head around the corner in the room, moving toward the lazing princess with her afternoon tea.

"Thank you." Gisela folded the book, placing it beside her, then took up the tea and drank. "Suli, do you think Knorren is truly done with his antics?"

"May I speak freely, my lady?" Suli's gaze lifted, locking with Gisela's in a hopeful manner.

"Always. I hope you know that." She patted the cushion next to her, longing for some form of companionship. It wasn't as if she'd find it among her sisters, and the one sister she could count on was busy with her betrothed. She watched her handmaid carefully, noting the reluctance before she spoke.

Suli sat, turning at the waist to glance outside. "I believe demons will always return to the grounds they choose to haunt. Boredom may distract them for a while, but they'll always return to annihilate what they intended to." She grimaced as she spoke. But instead of shifting her gaze to look at Gisela, she studied the floor in the room.

"I appreciate your candor, Suli." Gisela took hold of one of her hands, squeezing it gently. "I agree with your sentiment, but it seems you and I are alone in that. How could anyone believe Knorren has simply given up?"

"Denial, my lady, I think that is what it is."

Unfortunately, the belief that Knorren had ceased his games was as imprudent as it was perilous. Dread unfurled within Gisela, as if she could sense a storm brewing within the forest. Although she couldn't possibly know, there was a knife dragging along her nerves, pricking each one as it danced along.

"My lady, are you—"

A shrill scream tore through the air, cutting off whatever Suli was about to say.

Startled, Gisela bumped into the saucer with her teacup, causing both to tumble from the cushion and onto the floor, shattering. The remaining liquid stained the light marble floor. Gisela craned her neck to glance out the window, but from the current vantage point she couldn't see a thing.

Without a second thought, she dashed out of her room, into the hall, and ran toward a massive window that overlooked the courtyard. From this vantage point she could see a woman screaming at the gates, bellowing for the king to show his face.

"Murderer!" Lady Catherine howled. "You promised my daughter would be safe! Show yourself, you coward! Was my son not enough? You had to take my Anna!" The woman twisted away from the guard approaching her, and as he calmly attempted to usher her away, the woman lashed out. She slapped at him, screaming at the top of her lungs. "King Werner, you wretched man, there is blood on your hands, and blood on your soul. You will pay for this."

Anna. No. Not Anna. Gisela fought to remain upright, and she clutched the windowsill, steadying herself. Tears burned her eyes, blurring her vision. "Wurdiz, may you keep her." She choked on the words. Anna's brother had been a victim, now she was also dead. All because of Knorren.

Backing away from the window, Gisela covered her mouth then looked to Suli. Bile worked its way up her throat, but she swallowed back the acid. "He found out. Knorren knows. He knows, and he won't stop until he has what he wants." She choked on the words. Anna was dead, and it was because of her father's deception.

Knorren wanted Gisela. That was the price for her father crossing the forest safely, and one Gisela didn't think was too steep. Her life in exchange for thousands, and for the ability to live peacefully beside the forest without fear gnawing at the inhabitants, body and soul? Knorren had been fair, and her father was a fool.

"Get away from the window!" Suli hissed, reaching for Gisela's arm so she could pull her away.

There wasn't any genuine threat. Lady Catherine held no weapons, at least not that Gisela could discern. And if she did, the guards would have hurled the woman to the ground like a sack of potatoes. Instead, they attempted to placate her.

"I need to speak with my father at once," Gisela said, tugging her arm away from Suli. She shrugged off Suli's second attempt to grab her, then ran. Down the hall, beyond the stairs, and around the corner. She could hear her father's raised voice—he was angry. As quietly as her nickname, she crept closer toward where he was. When Suli slid to a halt behind her, Gisela lifted a finger to silence her.

"What would you have me do then, Tilda, send your sister to the demon? Knorren cares little of life! He is death's vassal, bound to serve his wicked master. You would send your sister to the depths of hell?" His voice shook with anger.

"If it would cease the endless killing, yes I would," Tilda replied in a glacial tone.

"You are even colder than I thought. After the festival, I think it would be wise to leave." Werner growled his words.

Tilda gasped. "Papa, you cannot mean—"

"If you think for one moment I'll tolerate your blatant contempt for your sister, you're wrong." It grew quiet for a moment. "I am done here." He dashed around the corner of the hall, stopping short as he nearly collided with his daughter. "Gisela," he rasped.

"I will go, for the love of Wurdiz, just send me!" She watched the emotions play across her father's face. First surprise, then anger, which was quickly replaced by feigned indifference.

"No. I can't. Gisela, don't ask me to do this." Even with his features schooled, his emotions bubbled up in the inflection of his voice. It wavered ever so slightly.

Gisela shook her head. "I am not asking. Let me go, please."

"I can't!" he shouted, startling the nearby servants who eavesdropped.

Her jaw clenched as she stared at him. "But you must."

"Gisela . . ."

From behind them, the wailing woman cursed the king's name. Gisela wrapped her arms even tighter around her father and then released him. She gazed up into his eyes, trying her best to read what he wouldn't say.

You're my beloved. You're my mouse, and I cannot let you go.

"But you must." She willed herself to say.

His lips parted, as if he were about to speak, but he tore himself away from Gisela and stormed outside, leaving her with Tilda. Tilda, who wore a smug look on her face and not an ounce of affection.

"One day, Wurdiz will peer inside your soul and rain down on you what you've put out in this world. Hate and greed fill your heart, sister, and that is what you'll receive." Gisela balled her hands into fists, shooting one last look in Tilda's direction.

The words startled Tilda. Her mouth was agape and her eyes were wide, but her expression quickly turned to fury.

If only Gisela could take in the moment a little longer, but she couldn't. She rushed after her father and outside into the courtyard. The sound of her father's voice booming over the pouring rain struck her ears.

"We all offer our deepest condolences—" Much to Werner's credit, his tone was genuine, but his words were cut short as the woman snapped.

"Condolences? My daughter is dead because of your ludicrous plan! Both of my children—gone! I don't want your pity, or your gold. I want you to do what is right for once!" She reached through the iron gate, nearly swiping at him, but the guards batted her hands away.

Gisela had heard enough. She walked into the courtyard, rain pelting down onto her, drenching her almost instantly. If her father couldn't bring himself to do it, or in the very least, say it, she would.

"Enough of this! I won't have any more deaths on my hands." Gisela's bottom lip quivered from fear and anguish. She met Lady Catherine's gaze, which looked so much like Anna's. With a frown, Gisela spoke. "I am truly sorry for the loss of your children. Anna was . . . such a lovely girl." Gisela pushed through the guards and grabbed the woman's outstretched hand. "I will right the wrongs," she whispered.

Werner swore beneath his breath, then louder for everyone to hear. "Get back in the castle."

"I will not. In fact, I vow before everyone standing here that I will give myself to Knorren, because I will not watch everyone suffer around me." Rain cascaded down Gisela's face, making it difficult for her to focus. She spun, facing her father, who glared down at her. "I will go to Knorren alone."

Short of locking her away in a tower, he couldn't stop Gisela from venturing to the forest. She didn't believe he could lock her away, even if it was for her safety.

"I want to hear it from your mouth, Your Majesty." The woman retracted her hand, gripped the bars, and watched him like a hawk.

Werner's gaze flicked from Gisela to the woman. An argument formed on his lips, then withered away. "I . . .

promise to send Gisela to Knorren, should he come looking for her."

It was good enough, Gisela supposed. He'd sworn it in front of an audience, and it was enough for the woman to relax and withdraw.

"May Wurdiz be with you, Your Highness." The noblewoman sobbed, shakily moving toward the carriage a few yards away.

Werner hissed, "We aren't finished here."

"I am not a child, and I think you forget that. I'm far more capable than you give me credit for." Gisela paused as she walked around him. "I love you dearly, but it is time the killings stop. If my . . . If I can stop them, let me help."

Her father stood rigidly, helplessly, and silently. There was nothing left to say between them. How many times could they hash out this argument?

Nodding to herself, she turned away from him and walked back into the castle. Gisela's slippers squelched on the marble floor and Suli rushed up to her, clucking her tongue.

"You'll catch a cold in no time if you remain in sopping wet clothes." Suli looked Gisela up and down, shaking her head. "I'll draw a warm bath for you. Come now, my lady."

Numbly, she followed her handmaid, but all the while, Gisela kept thinking of that poor woman's face and the emptiness in her gaze. Nothing would ever bring her children back or replace them, but something could stop it from happening again.

At least, she hoped.

Vanishing into her bedchamber, Gisela allowed Suli to fuss over her and scrub the feeling and blood back into her bones after standing in the chilly rain. If luck was on her side, she could remain in her room, uninterrupted for the rest of the day.

Guilt consumed her as she dwelled on Anna's demise. If it hadn't been for her, she'd still be alive. Gisela blamed herself first and her father second. It was her ailment that drove her father to foolishness and desperation, and had she not needed the herbal remedy, Lady Catherine would still have her beautiful daughter.

After bathing, Gisela slid beneath the covers of her bed and willed herself into a deep sleep. She could at least escape reality there, if only temporarily.

THIRTEEN

*H*eligersee Festival swept into the kingdom, and everyone decorated their homes and shops with gold and crimson. Banners flew from Tursch Castle, and even the lowliest of patrons hung a drape or rug in the colors to celebrate the annual celebration.

Gisela grimaced as Suli tugged the last few strands of hair into place, securing her crown braid tightly. Despite the maid's attempt, wild curls sprang loose, spiraling against Gisela's temples. She'd given up years ago trying to tame them entirely, and instead said they were part of her personality.

"Do you think the gown is a little . . . much?" The final product was astounding. Ivory skirts pooled at Gisela's feet, behind her, and around her. It was a sea of ivory fluff, and had it not been for the silken material of rich crimson, she would've looked like dandelion fuzz gliding across the room. But the work on the bodice of the dress, the golden threading of roses on vines, was stunning.

The cut was far different from what Gisela was used to. This wasn't a modest-fitting dress; the cut exposed her skin until midway down her back. The sleeves clung to her biceps instead of resting on her shoulders, and the front cut downward into a heart shape. This was more skin than she'd ever exposed before, and while the idea of it felt thrilling during the designing process, Gisela's confidence waned.

"You look absolutely stunning. I think everyone will see you for the young woman you are."

She doubted they would. They'd soon recall the youngest princess was tainted—poisoned even—as far as her bloodline went.

Smoothing her hands down the silken fabric, Gisela drew in a deep breath. "Thank you, Suli."

Gisela didn't feel as though they should be celebrating. In her marrow, she knew Knorren's threat wasn't over, and yet her father seemed to think he'd forgotten—or grown bored with—waiting for Gisela, and that he'd let it go. But when did Knorren ever let anything go? Did the demon forget the trespassers or land people attempted to fight back for? No, he never did.

Suli stared into the looking glass in front of them. "What's wrong?" She frowned.

Gisela cleared her throat, toying with a loose curl. "Nothing. Just a little anxious, I suppose. The speech I have to make . . ." It wasn't a lie, per se. She'd worked on the speech for weeks, but it was that nauseating knowledge that Knorren's terms weren't met and that today was his deadline that set her stomach into a fluttering frenzy.

A knock disrupted their conversation.

Suli went to the door, cracking it enough to speak. She half turned toward Gisela. "The carriage awaits. Everyone is getting ready to depart for the lake."

Gisela walked to the window in her dressing room, pushing the curtains open. Outside, dusk settled over the kingdom, painting the sky a blood red, and the sun looked like nothing more than an orange eye, gleaming amid the ominous blanket of crimson.

Disbelief wrinkled her brow. She couldn't fathom why her father thought Knorren would let the bargain fall through, but Gisela knew what had to be done if the fox came to collect his end of the bargain.

"Are you ready?" Suli prompted.

"As ready as I will be." Gisela stepped away from the window and walked out of the room.

In the carriage, the lanterns only added to the eerie quality of the roads. The ground looked as though apparitions writhed along it, which didn't bode well for any of them. Luckily, Jana accompanied her, and not the others, on the ride to the lake.

Jana laughed, taking up a swath of the tulle skirt. "Is this what you wanted? It's gorgeous, but not your typical style." Her fingers rubbed the fabric between her gloved hands.

Gisela flushed, biting her bottom lip. "Somewhat. It's a little more than I wanted, but at the time it seemed a good idea. Mostly, it was to show Papa that I'm not a little girl anymore."

"Oh, I think he'll grasp that fairly well when he sees you."

Pressing her lips together, Gisela flicked her gaze out the carriage window. "Will your other half be accompanying you tonight at some point?"

Jana's dark eyes lit up. She reached forward, grabbing her sister's hand and squeezing it. "Yes! He will be there, and I want you to stay with us for most of the night. We'll shield you from the wicked ones. Although I'm not sure how to keep little Byron away from us." She tapped a finger to her lips, then smiled. "Not that I want to. How he came out so kind and generous is beyond me, because his mother certainly isn't." Jana bent, placing a kiss against Gisela's bare knuckles.

"Thankfully, Wurdiz ensured Byron took after his papa." Gisela shrugged. The boy had a big heart. A bigger heart than his mother ever possessed, that was for certain.

During the ride, apprehension bloomed within Gisela's chest. No doubt Tilda would be in rare form, especially since their father excused her from the castle promptly after the festival. Gisela could only imagine what atrocities she and Pia may have planned, and she could only hope the prying eyes of their citizens would be enough to keep them in line. But Byron's affection would always be something Gisela looked forward to. His cheerfulness, bright eyes, and broad smile warmed her heart.

The carriage jostled the two sisters, and had it not been for the overabundant skirt surrounding Gisela, she might have collided with the door of the carriage. The fabric caught her, bouncing her back into place. She grunted, placing her hands on either side of her to catch her balance.

Outside, the lanterns grew bright as the sky darkened further, giving it an even more nightmarish appearance. Inky patterns scrawled on the road, crawling as they traveled. It looked as if the shadows were, in fact, alive and following them. It was a foolish thought, but one that unsettled Gisela just the same.

Several hundred lit lanterns offered their golden brilliance, chasing away whatever specters yearned to bask in the shadows. As the carriage turned onto the road by the lake, Gisela gasped softly as the body of water came into view. The luminaries reflected in the water lent it a star-like appearance, glittering brightly on the mirror-like surface.

Jana pressed her fingers against the glass window, staring at the view. "Wurdiz above. How beautiful is this? Every year those designers seem to outdo themselves."

Across the lake from where they were, staging loomed over the body of water as if it were floating. Gold banners waved in the gentle summer breeze, surrounded by dark crimson drapery.

"Oh, I can see Tilda's scowl from here." Jana twisted her head, winking at Gisela.

Waving her sister off, Gisela shook her head. "She can be put off about Papa's decision to let me speak, but it wasn't my choice." Gisela had tried to dissuade her father, but he was firm in his decision to let Gisela speak. It was a bold move in her eyes, knowing the threat that loomed in the distance.

"Stop that." Jana swatted at her hands.

"What?"

"You're going to ruin your dress if you keep twisting it like that."

Gisela's hands stilled. She'd twisted the tulle without even realizing it. "I'm just . . . What if Knorren comes for me tonight?"

Jana sighed. "We have a small army prepared to attack. I think we can ward off Knorren."

If that was all it took, wouldn't that have been enough to conquer him in the first place? Gisela sucked her bottom lip into her mouth and said no more. Which was just as well, because they soon arrived at the staging and were greeted by helping hands.

Jana left the cab first, then Gisela followed suit. In a rush of movements, guards escorted them up the stairs to where the rest of their family awaited.

A little body flung itself into Gisela's skirts, which absorbed the weight as the small frame disappeared into the several layers of fabric.

"Tante!" Byron squeaked.

With a laugh, she bent at the waist and picked her nephew up. "What in Wurdiz's name . . ." Her gaze dropped to the suit he wore. Byron looked like a perfect gentleman, with his hair slicked back and crimson doublet buttoned properly. For how long, she didn't know, but for the minute he was composed.

Tilda beckoned to her son from afar. He wiggled, warring between obedience and staying with his aunt. But Tilda's growl won over the warmth of Gisela's arms. "Be good," Gisela whispered.

Servants ushered trays of finger foods up the stairs and placed them on a small wooden table that held the appetizers and drinks. Later on, the main course would come, but for now, the small morsels would have to do.

"Mousy, is that you?" A warm hand settled against Gisela's bare shoulder.

She turned, facing her father, and smiled. He wore a suit similar to Byron's, except on his lapel a golden birch leaf brooch hung alongside several other medals. "Who else would it be, Papa?"

His honey gaze lit up. "You look radiant. The older you get, the more you look like your mother." He cupped her chin tenderly. "But I'm not sure if I'm ready to accept you as a grown woman," he groused.

"Ready or not, I am." Gisela grabbed his wrist, cupping it with both her hands and placing a kiss to it.

Before Gisela knew it, the festival started. Citizens spilled onto the grounds, milling around the lake and offering their praises to the royal family.

Beneath the staging, several soldiers created a barrier, barring the path from anyone attempting to climb the staging or access the royals.

When the moment to speak arrived, Gisela trembled. Anna's face swirled in the forefront of her mind. Her shy laugh and willingness to endure Knorren's cruelty. It wasn't something Gisela could ever forgive herself for, or even forget. She took a deep breath, approached the railing, and looked down over the citizens. The thrum of her heart echoed in her ears, drowning out all other noise, and although she wanted to speak, she couldn't seem to find her voice.

"You can do this," Jana whispered from behind her.

She believed her. Although, the prying eyes of the individuals below, the whispers, the years of judgment . . . it all made her squirm.

Gisela reached out, grabbing the railing. Her fingers curled around the metal, grounding her in the moment. "Good evening, citizens of Tursch. Thank you for joining us in our celebration of the Heligersee. Tonight, we honor the Golden Prince and his untimely sacrifice to the country. Tonight, we remember a fallen ruler and honor our current times. We choose to celebrate you, our citizens, for your hard work and fealty. For this evening, we are all sisters and brothers. We are all united."

It was short and sweet, but it cut to the point: they were one for the evening.

Despite her fears, the crowd of people cheered for her. Hands clapping, voices calling out in glee, and whistles slicing above it all.

One moment they cheered, in the next, they shrieked in horror.

Across the lake, trees shuddered. The royal family stood in alarm, unsure of what was happening. Gisela remained glued to the railing, squinting toward the treeline.

"Gisela! Get back!"

As she swung her head around to look at her father, she heard the groaning of trees and then the cracking of them as they toppled over. The cry of a fox was not of this world. It was not unlike the shriek of a woman and held an otherworldly rasp. The sound was alarming, and enough to wake anyone from a dead sleep.

The guards barked their orders, prompting the royals to stay where they were. Bows drawn, swords at the ready.

Frozen in place, Gisela turned and took in the terrifying display before them. Knorren. He was here, and he had come to collect his debt.

Knorren barked. A bone-chilling noise that made Gisela's ears ring and sent her to the floor of the platform. Her hands covered her ears and tears unwillingly fell, because this was how she was going to die.

"Can't we try to fight him?" Gisela heard her father ask pitifully.

"We will try, and if we can hold him back, then you must flee," a guard said lowly.

The sound of terror swept across the lake, echoing. It only worsened as Knorren moved forward.

"Oh, King Werner, I believe you owe me something."

PART II

"*The problem of restoring to the world original and eternal beauty is solved by redemption of the soul.*"

— *RALPH WALDO EMERSON, NATURE*

FOURTEEN

*K*norren's shrill cry cut through the air, ringing out above the hysteria. A nearby horse squealed in terror as it attempted to run away. Gisela watched in horror as the frightened animal's shriek abruptly ended when the fox's mouth descended on it. A sickeningly wet crunch seemed to echo across the lake.

Through the bars of the platform, she could see the giant fox standing with his head lowered. Blood oozed from his mouth, staining the white fur crimson. The glow from the lanterns lent him an even more menacing appearance as the lights flickered along his deep red pelt. Gisela thought she was going to be sick. Her stomach lurched as the half-eaten horse dangled from his jaws. In a fluid movement, Knorren flung the horse in the air, caught it, and gulped it down. It was that which made her stomach rebel, and she vomited on the platform.

"Gisela, to me!" Her father extended his hand, wiggling his fingers. Panic coated his voice, but he still moved forward, inching toward her. "Just crawl to me, Mousy."

Urged on by his voice, Gisela ducked down, peeling her eyes from the discord below. The cries of the small army rang out as the captain shouted his orders, but a twisted laugh filled the air. She'd heard nothing quite like it. Caught between a growl and shriek, it pierced her to the core, threatening to unleash the rest of her stomach's contents.

Gisela stole a glance toward Knorren, which had been a terrible idea. His ears flattened against his skull as his yellow eyes focused on her. He must have heard her father's plea, because his head dipped low, aiming toward a cluster of individuals.

No, no, no! No more deaths because of her. No more bloodshed because of her father's foolishness. Despite her shaking limbs, she bolted to her feet at the last moment. "Don't! Please, stop." The words threatened to gag her, tightening her throat further.

The archers readied beneath the platform, letting loose the arrows on command. Knorren crouched low, brushing them off as most barely made it past his thick fur. A few struck home, but they appeared a minor annoyance.

Patrons dashed out of the way as Knorren darted forward, teeth bared.

"Stop! All of you." Gisela's voice sounded far away, and when the guards below didn't listen, she raised her voice again. "I said *stop!*"

They obeyed too late. Knorren crouched low and pounced at them, tearing into the throng of soldiers like they were nothing more than children's toys. His teeth scissored along their bodies, and the audible *crack* of bones coated Gisela's skin in goosebumps.

"Knorren!" Gisela leaned over the rail, meeting the yellow eyes of the demon. He was close. Too close. The scent of blood and rot wafted from his mouth as he lifted his head.

"I am the *something* you wished for." She swallowed roughly.

The fox grew silent, his ears pricking forward as Gisela shouted at him. "I don't believe I ever wished for you. Demanded, yes—but wished for?" His lips pulled back to reveal sharp bloodstained teeth. Sinew jutted from between his canines and had it not been for the others in danger, Gisela would have flattened herself to the platform again.

A light flickered from below. Gisela realized it was a lantern's glow reflecting off a blade as a guard swung his sword near Knorren's leg. The fox ducked his head, crouching as he snapped his teeth around the offender's figure.

"Fall back, fall back!" the captain shouted above the madness as he ran for cover beneath the platform.

Fury bubbled up within Gisela, displacing the fear. She grabbed the pitcher of wine and flung it over the railing. It struck Knorren's head with a hollow *thunk*. Although the gesture was feeble, it reeled in his attention once more.

"You . . ." A growl rumbled low as he swung his head around. "You belong to me now. Gisela, that is your name, isn't it?"

"No!" From behind them, Werner bellowed, daring to step from the shadows the rest of the family hid in.

Knorren's cheeks puffed in annoyance, but his eyes widened in what almost appeared to be delight. "Silence. You lied to me and tricked me. I'll hear no more of your filth." He bared his teeth, shifting his gaze to Gisela once more. "Judging by how put out the king is, I daresay you're the *real* Gisela." He swept his calculating gaze over her trembling figure.

His eyes chilled Gisela to the core. Fear threatened to cut her breath off. Reaching her hand out to the beast, she could feel the warmth coming from him long before he lowered his nose to her hand. "Gisela is my true name. I didn't come to trick you, Knorren. I want this to end, and if you'll still make good on your bargain, I will go with you tonight." If it was the only way . . . if it bought Tursch more time . . .

"A trait you no doubt inherited from your mother." He cut a look at her father and lowered his head so he was at eye level with Gisela. "Climb onto my neck, Your Highness. You are coming with me."

"No! She will not." From behind Gisela, her father clambered to his feet and approached.

"I wouldn't," Knorren sang. "How easy it would be for me to devour your precious daughter in one go right now."

Fascination and disgust held Gisela captive in equal parts. She'd never seen something so beautiful and horrifying at once. A myth come to life. She rubbed at her chest, willing her galloping heart to slow its unrelenting pace. "Yes, Papa," she said, twisting on her heel. "I will go." Her father's arms crushed Gisela tightly. She leaned in to his warm embrace, committing the feel and smell of him to memory. "Let me go. Papa, I will be all right. You may call me Mousy, but I am a warrior at heart." She wanted to say more, but the look in his eyes told her she was just his little mouse, that he didn't know how hard she fought on the daily. To not succumb to melancholy. To keep practicing her fine needling so she didn't lose the ability to correctly enunciate the words her brain longed to muddle. Everything was a battle for her, and this would be yet another she faced.

"You don't understand. She needs . . . aid," Werner tried to plead again, resting his head against Gisela's.

"Perhaps you shouldn't have struck a bargain with your daughter's life on the line." Knorren swished his tail, moving his neck closer to the rail. "Now, *Your Highness*. I suggest climbing on my neck. Otherwise, you'll end up riding my tail."

Across the way, Byron wailed, thrashing in Tilda's grasp.

Gisela took a moment to squeeze her father's arm, then pulled away. "This isn't goodbye." Turning to face the rail, she clumsily climbed over, maneuvering around the folds of her dress. Could one's heart beat its way free from their chest? Gisela's chest ached from the breakneck rhythm. Knorren's fur was warm and thick, allowing her to use it as handholds to climb onto his neck.

She gripped the fur tightly. Numbness spread throughout her, fear tearing through her like a cannonball.

"Do not follow us," he said. "For if you do, I will kill you all." His voice rumbled low with the threat, then Knorren turned on his haunches and walked away.

Much to Gisela's surprise, he didn't lope as swiftly as he could have; he took his time sauntering home, which made riding on his back much easier. Try as she may, she couldn't seem to subdue the mounting questions in her mind. Would he kill her? Was she to be a toy? What gratification did he receive from this?

The soft fibers of his fur tickled her nose as the breeze created by his movement tussled them. Away from the lanterns, darkness consumed them, and, unable to see, Gisela clung closer to Knorren's neck.

It felt as though hours passed by, but it'd likely been at

most an hour. Unable to endure the silence any longer, Gisela blurted, "Will you harm me?"

A soft chuckle came from him. "Kill you, I think you mean? Don't run away and we won't have to find out, Princess."

Had Anna tried to run? If she had, what prompted it outside of fear? Gisela couldn't promise she wouldn't do the same. As much as she longed to save her people, could they fault her for running from Knorren? "I won't run away." The fox's ears swiveled backward as she spoke, but he said nothing.

The trees grew thicker the deeper Knorren walked into the forest. Even with a full moon in the sky, it was still far too dark for her to make anything out. Above them, the canopy of trees looked more like tendrils reaching down from the sky, waiting to snatch up a victim. And the thick trunks appeared as black masses. If she were to live among the woods, could she truly fall asleep out here? "Where will I sleep?"

An owl hooted in laughter after the question. Gisela didn't appreciate its input.

"In bramble amid the forest, and you'll be forced to dine on field mice instead of koel ruben or sauerbraten." Knorren sneered. "You'll grow used to it." He paused, as if waiting for a reaction, but when Gisela didn't make so much as a peep, he continued, "I live in a castle. I am not some *wild thing*, fair Princess."

"You are a fox—"

"I am a fox," he stated coldly. "A giant fox who talks as eloquently as a human and the fact I live in a castle is what you find strange?" He picked up his pace, treading lightly on the ground as he trotted down a path not as beaten as the others.

Instead of dirt, the path Knorren took was lined with burdocks and roses. A trail of beauty and pain. *Prickly things*, Gisela thought. The burdocks weren't unlike a rose bush, for in the warmer months they grew beautiful purple blossoms. In the winter they looked ugly and would become stuck to one's clothes or hair. She had seen Father's hounds covered in them before. If the plant's older limbs died off, the dried-up flower remained, waiting for someone or something to cling to.

At the end of the path was the *castle* Knorren spoke of, and it made Gisela gasp. Even under the cover of darkness, she could see the outline of the structure. She'd expected a small manor, but this was nearly the size of her home. Instead of being constructed strictly of stone, this one had additions crafted of wood. Several spires jutted from the top, creating the appearance that they were tines of a crown.

No gate barred their path to the entrance, and no guards stood at attention. Gisela supposed that it would have been senseless, for who would dare trespass into his home?

"Off now," Knorren ordered, coming to a halt at the entrance.

Idly, she wondered how he'd fit inside the establishment as she slid from his shoulder. Surely he couldn't?

The double doors leaned inward, clearly for his benefit. Knorren's nose nudged them open further, then he hunkered down and squeezed through the opening.

Oh, that was how.

Gisela passed over the threshold, scooting around Knorren's backside. The vaulted ceilings allowed for him to stand tall without curling into a ball. Aside from what was right in front of her, thanks to the moonlight, she couldn't see much else.

To say the air inside was musty was an understatement. It smelled of mold and something acrid. She didn't want to consider what it might have been.

"Violet," Knorren bellowed.

Gisela grasped the skirt of her dress. Who was Violet, and why on earth was she here? She swept her gaze from side to side, hoping to catch a moving figure.

"Violet!" Knorren snarled. This time, a lantern appeared from the hallway. It seemed to float of its own accord, until, as it drew closer, Gisela saw a pale face. A woman's face. Judging by her features, she was only a little older than Gisela. No deep wrinkles on her face, no lines of worry, but her thin lips pressed together as if she fought to restrain a shout of her own.

Movement in the corner of Gisela's eye caught her attention. Against the cobweb-covered wallpaper, shadows leaped and jostled as Violet approached. But it wasn't the eerie figures writhing against the wall that caught her attention. It was the cobwebs, so thick Gisela wondered if they couldn't be used to weave. On the floor, by her feet, small and large bones lay in haphazard piles. She wanted to scream, to bolt out the door, but as her heart thundered in her chest, she found herself rooted in place. Again, she wondered how and why this Violet was here, and why hadn't she fled?

How was this not living like some wild thing?

She frowned as Violet gawked at her. The other woman's irritated expression swiftly changed into one of dread. Gisela sucked her bottom lip into her mouth and chewed on it.

"What is it?" Violet inquired, but her eyes didn't leave Gisela.

She leaped back as Knorren swung his head too close to hers. His acrid breath washed over her in hot waves, wreaking of death. She wanted to vomit.

"Show the little princess her room." His teeth gleamed in the flickering lamplight. "Tomorrow your work begins."

Violet glanced in Knorren's direction, then back to Gisela. She didn't have to say it, for it was as clear as day in her eyes. *I'm sorry that you're here.*

"Pardon?" Gisela stammered. Work? She paled, wondering what on earth he would have her do. But when she looked to Violet and then back to Knorren, he was gone. If she were braver, she would've ventured into the shadows to see if he lingered, but she was neither courageous nor a fool.

"Come with me, Your Highness." Violet led the way toward the stairs.

Exhaustion seeped into Gisela's bones. With each step she made up the stairs, her shoulders slumped forward a little more and the muscles in her legs quaked. Gone was the boost from her adrenaline. Violet remained quiet as they ascended, but Gisela couldn't take the silence any longer. "Why are you here?" She hoped she didn't regret the question.

On the second floor, Violet paused and rested a hand against the banister. "I am here for you." She chewed her lip then cast a glance over the rail, as if half expecting Knorren to appear again.

Gisela hadn't expected a roof over her head, let alone

someone to help her. *But why?* she wondered. *Why bother at all?*

"My name, as you heard, is Violet. Should you need me, ring the bell in your room." She said no more, then continued down the hall and stopped in front of the first door on the left. The scent of cinnamon and vanilla tickled Gisela's senses.

Violet walked to the farside wall, using her lantern to light the sconces to illuminate the room. Much to Gisela's surprise, the room was nearly pristine. Had Anna cleaned it so thoroughly, or had Violet? The thought tightened her chest instantly. Anna. She'd died here, or close to it. When Gisela thought she could handle it, she'd press Violet for information about what actually happened.

She shifted her thoughts to the room, taking it all into account. The drapes were a deep red, with silver edelweiss embroidered on them, matching the oversized down blanket on the bed.

Gisela twisted, turning to glance at a looking glass. Her dress was torn, tulle hanging limply from branches snagging it on the journey through the trees. She frowned, reaching behind herself to undo the stays in the back.

Violet placed the lamp down and helped Gisela out of the heavy dress. "There you are, my lady. I know it isn't much, but there are spare clothes in the wardrobe, and a chemise . . ." Instead of finishing her words, she silently crossed the room and withdrew a chemise from the wardrobe.

Glad to be rid of the gown, Gisela quickly changed into the cotton shift, but she felt Violet's eyes nearly burning a hole in her person. "Is . . . there something . . . Are you all right?" It sounded odd to her, asking whether Violet was all right when she was sentenced to live here, and yet . . .

"Are you truly Princess Gisela? I know the last one wasn't, but are you the princess?" She stood rigidly as she ran a critical glance over Gisela. The planes of her face remained tight as she waited for Gisela's reply.

Gisela's heart ached at the question. She nodded and plopped onto the edge of the bed. "I am. And for what it's worth, I wish it had been me instead of Anna. She didn't deserve that." None of them did.

FIFTEEN

hree days passed. Three days of Gisela hiding in her room, refusing to come out. Despite Knorren's threats and clawing outside her window, she refused to answer him. *Brazen little thing*, Knorren mused.

If Violet hadn't reported to him she was, in fact, alive, he would have assumed she'd expired in her sleep, but the details on her well-being—though brief—were positive ones.

Not that he cared. In fact, he still wasn't certain what he wanted from her. Would she be another one of his meals? He didn't know. But one thing was for certain: The look on the king's face when Knorren whisked his daughter away was enough to elicit glee from him for the full three days. He chuckled to himself, recalling the shock, the horror, and the defeat plastered on his face.

Still, it irritated Knorren that the princess hid away in her room. If he could fit through the halls and barge into her room, he would have yanked her outside.

Frustration snaked through him and he rumbled his discontent. In no mood to deal with anyone, he snarled as Ylga appeared before him, smoke pluming from behind her. He despised when she teleported in front of him.

Ylga ran a long fingernail beneath her chin as she

watched him with clear curiosity. She tugged at the thread-bare cloak that hardly shrouded her spindly figure. Wisps of silver hair slid from the cover of her hood, waving in the gentle breeze. Ylga's gnarled fingers pushed her sleeves up, revealing pale, age spot–riddled skin. She pursed her thin, chapped lips and pointed a crooked finger at him. "Mark my words, Knorren, every ill deed has a consequence."

His lips curled over his fangs as he leaped toward her. "Your cryptic threats grow tiresome, old woman."

Ylga pushed her sleeves back, shoulders stiffening as she stared up at the fox. "You're not invincible, Knorren. There is nothing binding you to this earth for eternity, which means a well-aimed arrow, or sword, could easily pierce your heart." She motioned to his under belly, shaking her head. "Of course, your size and penchant for lurking in the shadows has saved your pretty hide for centuries. But don't be so foolish as to think you can't die. You've stolen away the king's daughter—his *beloved* daughter. You will face consequences."

Of course he wasn't invulnerable. He knew that. The wounds inflicted by the arrows stung, but they'd heal. None had pierced vital areas, thankfully.

"She was owed to me."

Ylga hissed. "You're a fool if you think that." She paused. "Why? Why do you think the king owed you the price of his daughter?"

Knorren ground his teeth as the witch questioned him further. If he could snap his mouth around her before she hurled him to the ground, he would have done so. "You know why."

The witch's lip curled, and without another word she strode by him.

Offended, Knorren spun on his paws and leaped in front of her, barring her path. He narrowed his eyes. "You know as well as I do, if I didn't the king would storm into the woods looking to flay me."

"If you didn't what? Assert yourself, kill hundreds, if not thousands of innocents? As I said, there are consequences to every ill action you take. You have quite the tally against you."

Anger melded with frustration. Knorren growled in annoyance, his teeth gleaming in the early morning sun. What was the point of her chatter?

"What would you have me do? Lie down and die?" Knorren sneered. "I know you would."

Ylga glared up at the fox's face. "Do you now? I would have you learn, you fool. Learn that death equals death, and that somehow you must break the cycle. But you won't. So you must wait for one who will aid you."

He blinked several times. This was news to him, but was it true, or was she tricking him? Knorren's ears flattened as he crouched low to the ground, peering into the witch's faded blue eyes. "What do you mean?"

"I told you, foolish one. You're fated to die as the demon you are. A noble's blood shall remove your taint, should they perform a selfless act." Ylga swept strands of silver from her eyes, then clucked her tongue. "Maybe then you can return to where you came from."

Knorren snarled, exasperated by the wretched hag's vague terms. "I have shed countless drops of blood from nobles. I have tried bringing them to you, and you laugh, or shun me. You lie and I tire of it." Knorren had done every-thing she requested of him. Except for that last human . . . they had outright lied to him. Lying wasn't a noble act. Surely she'd not been the vital key . . . *Dammit*, he cursed inwardly.

He lunged at the witch one moment, and the next he found himself thrown to the ground, unable to move. Much to his dismay, he whimpered as Ylga forced him into a submissive position. Knorren saw the glint of a charm in the sunlight.

"Get out of my sight, Knorren." The witch waved her hand, pocketing the medallion. "Come to me when you have something of use and take care of that child. Her death will be your undoing."

Scrambling to his paws, Knorren gave her a withering glare before skulking away.

Knorren didn't know what the witch wanted from him when it was her fault he walked the earth. She had summoned him all those years ago. What had been her plan once he roamed the earthly plains? Often, he wondered if it was her plan to have him destroy the surrounding villages one by one and chastise him. All the while, she cackled in her hut.

But something didn't settle right with him. Ylga expected change from him, and more than what he was, like she was waiting for a monumental moment. Knorren had shown mercy once, and if the witch was right, it would be his undoing.

With a bark, he bounded through the forest, snagging burdocks along the way. They were flowering, which meant they were harder to pluck free, but some still embedded themselves into his red fur, tangling themselves thoroughly.

Today, Gisela had no option. She would emerge from her bedchamber and entertain him. Even if he had to tear the castle apart to ensure it.

SIXTEEN

A shriek cut through Gisela's slumber, startling her awake. Sitting up, she glanced around to recount where she was. Had the scream been in her dreams, or was that Knorren hunting? She lifted her hands, stroking errant curls from her face. Her heart pounded wildly in her chest. Over the past few days, Knorren had yowled at her window, clawed at the sides of the castle, and hurled rotting corpses into the room. To say he'd induced her into a panic was an understatement.

Frightened, she'd taken to sleeping on the floor in case he could look into her window. She'd wept herself to sleep and every morning Violet would reassure her the best she could.

When it was clear he'd ended his violent tactics, Gisela grew braver and peered out the window. He was lounging in the sun, tail flicking and flies buzzing around his blood-covered paws. But her toe caught against the drape, shifting it along the iron pole, and it was enough to stir the beast.

Through slitted eyes, he glanced up at her window and smiled, if one could call it that. All teeth and squinted eyes. "Come to me. You cannot hide in your hole forever," his silken voice rumbled.

Gisela wanted no part of whatever he classified as work.

When she continuously refused, he'd grown more agitated, clawing and barking at her window again.

She hid again, until he grew quiet once more. Then, she crawled along the floor to investigate. She stood, shivering as her bare foot hit the chilled floor. Already slivers of sunlight dappled the floor in her room, which meant it was morning. How long could this beast keep this up for? And would he ever relent?

Pressing the heels of her palms to her eyes, she continued forward.

Another bloodcurdling howl tore through the air. She stiffened. The noise pierced her ears, but more than that it grated on every nerve in her body, freezing her where she stood.

Moments later, she heard something scratching or screeching against stones outside; it threatened to chase her back under the covers. Terror seized her. Gisela's skin grew cold, and she stumbled backward. Had Knorren decided he'd grown tired of her already?

Dizziness melded with fear. An uneasiness spread through her as a familiar nausea fluttered in her belly. *No,* she thought. *Not now.* She drew in a deep breath, willing herself to calm, willing the aura away. But she knew it was only a matter of time before one of her fits came . . . four days without her herbs. Gisela knew what awaited her.

"Gisela!" came Knorren's bellow. "Come at once."

On my terms, she thought. *Mine.* His howling, huffing, and scraping outside did nothing to quell any fear. Each time he barked or bellowed, she clamped her hands over her ears, dulling the shrillness. Could she stay trapped in her room?

How long would it take for him to tear the castle down to get to her?

"Now, Gisela!"

The ornately carved door mocked her. She stared at it, wondering if she should open it, but a fresh wave of guilt washed over her. Anna. This was for Anna, for her brother, and for all those who came before them. Gisela steadied her trembling bottom lip and angrily swiped at the fresh tears spilling onto her cheeks, then crossed the room and opened the door.

Gisela screamed so loud she thought her throat would bleed. As if her heart hadn't been hammering away already, the sight threatened to bring her to her knees. Before her, a bloodied muzzle crammed itself into the hallway.

Knorren's teeth gleamed in the morning light. Bits of whatever he'd eaten last still hung from between his fangs. When she gathered her wits, she realized he couldn't shove himself any farther into the hall and was, if not wholly, then nearly stuck. As she pressed forward, it became clear why he was so ornery. Burrs clung to the stop of his snout and the tufts of hair above and at the corners of his eyes. One of them was so tightly bound in burrs, it caused his eye to swell shut.

"Have you stuffed wool in your ears?" he snarled. One unaffected eye shifted, but he likely could not see out of the closest to her. Tears oozed down his cheek from the irritation of the burr's spikes. "You need to pluck the burrs from my pelt." Knorren's head swung in the other direction as he shifted in the hall, not fully capable of moving through it.

Prisoner or plaything, it didn't matter. He would not speak to her that way—especially if he wanted to be preened by her! Despite the fear numbing every inch of her, she finally spoke to him after three days of silence.

"I don't think you're in any position to make demands, Knorren. Those burrs will scratch your eye and you'll get an infection, possibly rendering you blind. Ask me kindly." Her voice wavered, belying her confidence. She shifted from foot to foot, weighing her options. Gisela knew eye injuries were terrible. All the healers and physicians that visited from afar told her stories while tending to her. They were stories of health, recovery, and infectious diseases. Among them, she'd heard of a young man who had lost his eye to an infection from a tiny splinter.

Knorren growled deeply. The sound echoed off the castle walls, which lent it an unearthly quality. Flexing his claws, he ground them into the floor, but then his body grew lax. "*Please*, can you help me?" If a voice could have venom in it, Knorren's surely did. His *please* was anything but genuine. All the same, Gisela delighted in the fact she could even pull the word from him.

Despite Knorren's growling and the flash of fangs and claws, which were precariously close to her, Gisela smiled. Laughed even. The wicked beast of the forest lay prone in the hallway, unable to see well, and was so bound in unsightly burrs that he looked more akin to a porcupine than a fox.

Without saying a word, she turned away from the door and went to the room's vanity. Rummaging around, she looked for a pair of grooming scissors and a long-toothed comb.

"What are you doing?" he snapped at her, using his paw to pull himself farther down the hall.

Was he mad? If he continued inching down the hall, he truly would be stuck! Gisela's lips parted as she gawked at him. "I will help you! But you need to stop crawling, or you'll never be able to pull yourself free." Tentatively, she moved forward, but the very idea of being so close to his mouth sent warning bells off.

Violet's voice called from down the opposite end of the hall. Her eyes widened as she registered Knorren wedged between the walls. Gisela couldn't be sure, but it almost looked as if Violet were angry. Red crept into her cheeks, and her jaw tightened.

"What does it look like?" Knorren bit out.

Gisela sighed. "I'm all right. Burrs are stuck in Knorren's fur and I'm trying to help him." *Why should I help him?* she wondered. *If he only ever leaves a trail of death in his wake?* But in his current state, he was rather pathetic. Trapped within the hallway, covered in burrs that blinded him. If she was careful, he wouldn't be able to snap at her. "Hold still."

Violet's shoulders visibly relaxed. "Oh." She gathered up a bit of her skirt and rolled it between her fingers. "There is some leftover lard in the kitchen from boiling down deer bones. I think it'll help with the removal—"

"You'll do no such thing." Knorren stiffened as he snapped at her.

Gisela hadn't considered that. Violet was right. She tilted her head as she glanced up at Knorren's good eye. "And if we can't remove them with a brush, fingers, or scissors . . ."

Knorren quieted, but his countenance burned with indignation.

Violet turned on her heel and disappeared down the end of the hallway. Gisela hadn't a chance to explore yet, but she assumed there was another way down to the kitchens from there.

It occurred to Gisela in that moment that she could have stabbed the comb into Knorren's unaffected eye, rendering him blind. She could have run away, deep into the woods, and hoped she found her way out. But to what end? She'd been days without her herbs, which meant a spell was on its way. If she fell into a fit out there, she may as well consider herself dead. Instead, she resigned herself to the menial task, and Gisela plucked what she could with her fingers.

Disgust twisted her lips as she pulled clumps of hair and dried pieces of burrs out. With each new burr she yanked free, Knorren settled, which in turn soothed her anxieties. But her hands ached from the tedious work and she wished she could be done already.

Little by little she made headway, and when the stubborn bits of burr refused to come out she used the brush. When that didn't work, she used the lard that Violet brought up.

Knorren snarled, but every so often he'd whimper. Once, his head swung toward her, shoving Gisela onto her backside. Thankfully, she didn't hit her head on the floor as she crashed to it, but it took coaxing from Knorren to pull her out again. Still, her heart hammered in her chest and she felt much like a rabbit, cornered and on the verge of being eaten.

After completely combing Knorren's face, no burrs remained. She surveyed his body, which was covered in the blasted burrs. "What did you do?"

"I thought it was clear that I ran into a patch of burdocks." His tone was low, just above a growl.

"I meant *why*? You're lucky no fur had to be cut." The

long-haired hounds that usually caught burrs in their hair always needed them cut out, for their hair matted around the burrs almost instantly. Knorren's coat appeared no worse for the wear and actually looked better than it had before. Aside from a few spots where the lard greased his coat, it seemed to have a new luster to it.

"That is none of your business." Knorren twisted his neck, watching as Gisela backed away from him. "Mayhap you'll need to cut them from *your* hair, *Klette*."

Stilling, Gisela turned her head and looked down at the braid on her shoulder. He had called her a *burr*! The insult filled Gisela with indignation. Whether it came from the mouth of a demon or not. She lifted the braid and the clusters of burrs that clung to it, and tears of frustration burned her eyes. Gisela didn't want to give in to them and allow the beast to see how his remark bothered her, because it didn't hurt. Not when she'd heard so much worse. It was the frustration that steadily built up inside of her. "Maybe, but the hair will grow back." She forced the words out, and to her surprise, her voice didn't waver. *Who would see her now to call her ugly?*

Still, if the lard removed the burrs from Knorren's fur, it would remove them from her coarse curls.

Knorren's eyes narrowed on her as she stood in the middle of the hallway. "Continue. I didn't say stop." He spoke in a clipped tone as he watched her, as if he could see into her soul.

For you, Anna, for you. What had this devil demanded from her while she lived? Did he insist she pluck burrs from his pelt, or worse?

Gisela stepped forward, closing the distance between

them once again, and ran her fingers through his coat to find more burrs. But instead of finding more burrs, she found several newly scabbed-over wounds. Some of which even oozed a bloody liquid from them. Common sense said it was only from the thorns or a tree if he'd been running so carelessly through the forest, but the location was too high for thorns. At the lake, the soldiers had unleashed arrows on him, and Gisela recalled a few arrows jutting from his side.

"Do these hurt?" Concern laced her tone, but she didn't give it much thought. It wasn't as if Knorren thought about whether something hurt one of his victims, but Gisela wasn't him.

"No, leave it be." His tone left no room for argument.

Gisela noted each wound, then went back to the task at hand.

As soon as the last burr came free, the fox scrambled backward and fled down the stairway without so much as a thank you. His tail flagged high over his back, knocking into a hidden mirror, which tumbled to the marble stairs and shattered.

She flinched as the glass rained down the stairwell. At that moment, she related to the broken shards. Her life felt much like the splintered pieces.

Gisela's mouth opened as if to call Violet, but she'd already returned to the kitchen to prepare breakfast. Gisela glanced around for a broom and dustpan to clean up the mess. It would do no good to cut herself or slip on the stairs. Finding the broomstick, she sighed as she scooped up the dustpan, wondering why she'd thought for a moment Knorren might have thanked her.

It wasn't as if Gisela expected thanks from him. Or that

he was even capable of it. But there had been the briefest of moments where she thought she'd seen something other than wickedness in his gaze. Perhaps something akin to gratitude. It wasn't chilling, and it didn't frighten her. Could there be more to Knorren than simply death?

After she cleaned the glass up, Gisela returned to her room with the lard in hand. Plopping down in front of the vanity, she examined the tangled state of her braid. "No wonder he called me Klette." Annoyed, she started plucking the loose pieces of burrs away, and what didn't pull free, she slathered in lard and combed out.

A wave of dizziness overcame her. She gripped the vanity, closing her eyes. How much longer did she have before the convulsions would wrack her body? Tonight, tomorrow? Her lips tipped downward as worry filled her.

Choking on a sob, she cradled her face in her palms. Never had she missed home so much before. She missed the knowledge of the staff and would take their condescending glances any day over this—being alone with someone she didn't know to help her.

Most of all, she missed Suli's companionship.

Crying would do nothing but blur her vision, stuff her nose, and leave her tired. Sniffling, she wiped the tears away and went to find Violet.

SEVENTEEN

With Knorren gone, Gisela braved the stairwell again, and this time ventured deeper into the first floor. Cobwebs clung to the wall so thickly it almost appeared as if they had been purposely spun that way. She dreaded thinking of how many creatures actually lurked inside—dead or alive. The chandeliers above were also swathed in the thick cotton-like webbing, but the candles had long since burned down to stubs and some iron sections had rotted off.

The early morning heat only intensified the aroma of mold, and with it the perfumed fragrance of roses. Luckily, the castle itself was cool, but the air wafting in wasn't, and it rustled the stale air inside. Gisela brought a hand to her nose; if only the roses covered the dreadful smell.

She swept her gaze along the maze of a hallway and caught the soft melody drifting toward her. Aside from Gisela, there was only Violet in the castle. So who was singing down the hall? The thought caused her heart to thump faster. Curiously, she followed the woman's voice, careful not to touch the walls or trip on a discarded bone. *Is it human or animal?* Gisela mused, but did she truly want to know? No. But it nagged at her as to why the bones remained scattered throughout. Frowning, she continued down the dimly lit hall until she reached another stairwell. The stairs were slick from moisture, so she took extra care as she descended into the dark.

Surprisingly, in the depths, light streamed in through windows and onto what must have been the kitchens. The smell of bread filled her senses. Her belly rumbled in protest, reminding her she'd not yet eaten breakfast.

Just as she rounded the corner, Violet popped up from behind the island counter.

Gisela yelped in surprise, clutching her chest. She bent over, laughing nervously. "You nearly scared the life out of me."

Violet had the good grace to look apologetic. "I'm sorry, my lady. I was making you something to eat." She glanced to the side, eyeing the cast iron stove. "Not that it's a particularly healthy breakfast . . . but I thought, considering everything, it may be the best one." Wisps of her ash-blond hair sprung around her face, lending her a frenzied appearance.

Gisela's nose wrinkled in confusion. "What do you mean?"

"Ah, well, I made bienenstich kuchen." She motioned toward the counter, which still had the remains of the ingredients on it. Honey, flour, almonds . . .

Ah, so that was the smell that snaked through the halls. Not bread, but bienenstich. It happened to be one of Gisela's favorite desserts. The sweet two-layer cake with a vanilla cream filling and crunchy topping of honey-drizzled almonds was something she'd gladly indulge in.

Gisela's eyes widened in delight. "I'll never turn down kuchen for breakfast." She crossed the floor and plucked an almond from its bowl. Plopping it into her mouth, she munched on it happily. While it certainly wasn't a nutritious breakfast, it was appreciated. "Thank you, Violet."

Violet tilted her head and offered a warm smile. "You're welcome." Her lips parted and she glanced to the side, as if she was uncertain whether to speak or not. "If you don't mind me asking, my lady, why are you down here?"

Gisela's shoulders slumped forward. She leaned against the counter and scooped up a handful of almonds, then let them pass between her fingers into her awaiting hand. Violet deserved the truth, and Gisela knew it had to come out. The woman needed to know how to handle Gisela amid one of her episodes.

"I need to tell you something important." Gisela lifted her gaze from her hands to the other woman. She paused, as if startled, as if suddenly Gisela would admit she wasn't who she said she was.

The color drained from Violet's face as she whipped some cream in a bowl. "Oh? What is it, my lady?"

"I wasn't able to pack my herbs since Knorren . . ." She didn't finish, but Gisela didn't need to. Violet knew just as well as she did that Knorren had abducted her. She closed her eyes and curled her fingers over the handful of almonds. They bit into her flesh, but it brought her away from the images of Knorren tearing into the horse, the soldiers . . . "Without them, my health will decline, and I need to let you know how to handle it." So, she told her precisely that. There wasn't much one could do amid the fit, except ensure she didn't choke on vomit or crash into something that would hurt her.

By the time Gisela finished explaining, Violet had

completed the cake. She nodded as she slid a piece of the cake over. "I promise I'll do my best to take care of you."

And that meant more to Gisela than she could voice. "Thank you," she whispered and dug in to the dessert. A smile tugged at her lips as her eyes connected with Violet's. Sincerity swirled within the other woman's eyes, warming Gisela to the core. Amid the horrendous situation, if one good thing could come from it, then she'd be gladdened. A new friend was always welcomed.

After Gisela ate her fill of cake, she decided to brave it and venture outside. As soon as she stepped foot onto the court-yard, the telltale crunch of bones met her ears. She fought to keep her breakfast from revisiting her and didn't stop to consider whether the bones were human or not. For the most part, the courtyard was like any other stone. But in between the cracks, where the earth peeked through, roses and burdocks grew. She'd never seen so many in her life and wondered why, of all places, this area was overburdened with them.

Despite there being no evidence of Knorren in the area— no shrieking, twigs snapping, or taunting—Gisela's heart thundered in her ears. If he saw her outside, would he chase her back inside? Thrash her like he did with Anna?

Each stride Gisela took brought her farther from the castle until it appeared as though the trees would consume it. She hadn't recalled venturing that far, but there was a path of roses and burdocks that caught her interest. For every burdock, it looked as though there were fragments of bone near it. So if burdocks grew from bone, what of the roses? Gisela tapped a finger against a silken bloom. The fragrance wafted toward her, washing over her senses. It was sweet and lovely. With bones came blood; did that mean the roses sprouted from the crimson?

A low growl rolled into the clearing, but Gisela couldn't pinpoint where it came from. She froze in place, her eyes widened, and her self-preservation kicked in. She ran. Ran as fast as her slippered feet would take her. From behind, she could hear tree limbs creaking then snapping as the weight of whatever was behind her pursued her.

If it was Knorren, wouldn't he have yelled at her? She didn't dare look back to check, because if she saw what it was, she knew her limbs would freeze up and that she'd succumb to fear.

One moment she was running and then the next it felt as though she were tumbling into the air. The sun vanished instantly, but Gisela wasn't tumbling, she was rising. A quick look around and she saw a cage of porcelain-white teeth. Her hands sank down onto a roughened moist surface—a tongue! She was within a mouth—Knorren's mouth.

A bloodcurdling scream left her and as much as she might have wanted to cling to consciousness, she faded into the darkness.

When Gisela roused, the sound of gulls laughing confused her. Gulls lived by the sea and she was in Todesfall, wasn't she? Fear spiked in her chest, chasing her from the comfort of the foreign bed. Where was she? She glanced around hurriedly, noting the small hut with a dirt floor. Shelves lined the wall farthest from where she stood, holding dark and light liquids, drying herbs, and several bowls in various sizes.

Panic replaced fear, which brought on sharp pains of anxiety in her chest. Her vision grew black around the edges as she drew in greedy, gulping breaths. "No . . . where am I?" She twisted around in search of the hut's door. When her hands collided with the porous wood, she slammed her hand against it as she twisted the knob and shoved it open.

A hot breeze drifted toward her, carrying with it the scent of brine. Everything within Gisela told her to run, but she'd never been this close to the sea before and as she surveyed the glittering waves, she found herself positively transfixed. The sound of the waves crashing against the shoreline, the whipping of the breeze against her face . . . it was enough to lull her into a lazy state. Except the anxiety of where she was hadn't disappeared.

She remembered herself and staggered through the deep sand, awkwardly making her way down the beach.

"Where do you think you're going, young one?" a crackling voice called to her from behind.

Gisela froze, then twisted around to face a silver-haired woman. Age wrinkled her features, but there had been beauty there once. "I don't know. I don't even know where I am." She clasped her hands, steadying herself in the sand. Dizziness threatened to buckle her knees.

The old woman moved forward and grabbed Gisela by the elbow with a surprisingly sturdy grip. "You're in Burlitz." Her eyes darted toward the water. "If it wasn't obvious by the beach, and if you haven't figured it out yet . . . I'm the witch supplying you with your herbs." While her face held an honest, open expression with a hint of kindness, the woman's voice was anything but that. Clipped and hoarse, she sounded as if she were two seconds from tossing Gisela into the sea. A moment later, the woman tightened her grip on Gisela's elbow and tugged her back toward the hut.

Stumbling, Gisela pulled her arm back and shot the woman an accusatory glance. "Excuse me." Her arm coiled against her chest as her eyes flicked from the woman to the hut. "I don't know you still . . ." Nausea rolled around in her stomach and her head ached, as if a fit were just around the corner.

"Don't be foolish," the woman hissed. "You've been without herbs for days now." She jutted her chin out and looked down her nose at Gisela. "Feeling dizzy, are you? Perhaps experiencing oddness with your vision?" She jabbed her gnarled finger in Gisela's direction. "In the hut, because I'm not catching you if you collapse."

Everything in Gisela screamed at her to run, but the crone was right. Already Gisela felt a familiar tingling sensation run along her limbs, and if she didn't take her herbs soon, she'd succumb to convulsions. What other options did she have? She frowned and tentatively moved forward, staying a distance behind the woman as they entered the small hut.

"I am Ylga." The witch turned to look at Gisela. "Even though you didn't ask, I thought you may want to know." Ylga crossed the floor, unstopped a clear glass, and poured the contents onto a wooden spoon, then offered it to Gisela. "Take this. It's a concentrated form of your herbs."

Gisela eyed the amber liquid dubiously. Did the woman think she'd gladly take syrup from a stranger?

"Child, I am not in the habit of killing royalty." Ylga rolled her eyes, sighing. "Your father sends his men to me monthly. It's skullcap, just like your tea, but this is coupled with honey and elderberry to make it taste better." As if to prove a point, Ylga took the spoon for herself and devoured the contents. She discarded it, then scooped up another spoon with another helping of the syrup. "Now take it."

Frowning, Gisela took the spoon and shoved it into her mouth. The syrup was sweet. Far sweeter than tea, and less bitter. With her brows furrowing, Gisela handed the spoon back. "Where is Knorren?"

"Oh, that beast." Ylga sighed. "Sulking somewhere, I suppose."

Gisela blinked, then turned to look out the nearest open window. Was Knorren in earshot? How could the woman speak so boldly about Knorren without a care?

The image of Knorren curled up in a corner somewhere while brooding was an interesting one, but it warred with the villainous creature she'd dealt with. "Why would he sulk?" she whispered, not realizing how quietly she'd asked until Ylga tilted her head. "Why would Knorren hide and sulk?"

Ylga waved a hand in the air, then shrugged. "As if I know his motives for anything."

From the window, a low growl came and ivory teeth gleamed in the sunlight. "You witch."

EIGHTEEN

own the beach, Knorren had heard Gisela and Ylga's exchange, but couldn't be bothered to rise from the cover of the tall beach grass or the warmth of the sand. Nor did he want to endure Ylga's presence more than he had to. Why had Knorren brought Gisela to Burlitz to begin with? He wasn't certain. Outside of Ylga's nosing around and the fact that Gisela allegedly needed a remedy only the witch could provide, *why* gnawed at him.

It certainly had little to do with approval from Ylga. Knorren didn't trust her as far as he could throw her. But as Ylga tutted and teased Gisela, it prodded Knorren into venturing toward the hut.

As usual, Ylga's tongue sparked his ire. Knorren didn't sulk. While he was careful around the witch, for good reason, he wasn't one to sulk.

"What are you doing with the girl?" Knorren snapped, then shifted his head so his eye took up the window. "Don't trust the crone." A deep laugh resonated from his chest and his eyes shut as he barked with laughter. "Do you want to end up in one of her bottles, Klette?"

When he opened his eyes, Gisela had stiffened at the

nickname and pink tinted her sandalwood cheeks. "Why should I trust either of you?"

Laughter shook Knorren's body and he closed his eyes as the bite of Gisela's words tumbled around in his head. Despite finding the remark amusing, he quieted himself, deciding it would be far *more* amusing if he listened to Ylga's sage advice.

In turn, the crone hissed toward the window, then turned to Gisela. "You don't have a choice. Trust Knorren or trust me, but I've been the one caring for you for years, whether you know it or not, Princess." It was the first time Knorren had ever heard a softness to Ylga's tone, and if he wasn't mistaken an equally soft and maternal look entered her gaze as well. Ylga plucked up a towel and wiped her hands clean of the syrup. "Don't let him intimidate you. While he's vile, he isn't *entirely* so."

Out of all the things Ylga could have said or done, those words surprised him the most. She minced no words with him whenever they crossed paths and she didn't shy away from degrading him verbally. Not that he cared overly much; it was more tiresome than hurtful.

Years ago, it rankled Knorren to the core. Like little barbs, Ylga's words would prick his humor until he'd turn on Ylga. Now, she annoyed him, taunting him with those dart-like insults, and when he did rise to the occasion, she ensured Knorren couldn't retaliate.

"You have every reason to be intimidated by me." He stuck his nose in the window and blew out a breath. The whoosh of air was replaced by a guttural growl. When Knorren shifted his head, he noticed Gisela had retreated to the farthest corner in the hut.

As if that would stop me, Knorren mused.

Ylga scoffed. "I preferred it when you were sulking." She sat down not far from the window.

"I wasn't sulking." Knorren bristled at the accusation. "I was letting you deal with her after she fainted." His words came out with a growl. "She ran from me. I should have eaten her."

"I ran because you were chasing me!" Her fingers curled into her palms, only adding a more indignant air to her, including the proud set to her chin.

The girl pushed away from the wall she'd attempted to blend in with and narrowed her eyes at the window, at *him.* Such boldness wasn't lost on Knorren, but it was her shout that truly surprised him. His tufted eyebrows lifted in amusement. How he longed to shrink in size enough so he could walk up to her and commend her for her sheer idiocy— and bravery.

"Aren't you a bottle of mettle . . ." Knorren murmured, then reclined on his haunches. Above him, gulls shrieked as they dove toward the shoreline, pecking at ambling crabs.

"All right," Ylga interrupted. She turned to Gisela and motioned for her to sit. "You better think twice about leaping to your feet. That syrup is far stronger, and it has a tendency to bring on drowsiness." The crone swept her gaze toward Knorren, then shook her head. The wrinkles between her eyebrows shifted as annoyance swept over her expression. "At least someone other than myself is brave enough to stand up to you."

Gisela's shoulders shifted. She didn't hold them so close to her ears any longer and she complied with Ylga's wishes, taking a seat. Her eyelids seemed to grow heavier, and Knorren wondered if it was, in fact, the concoction that was fed to her.

"I feel peculiar." Gisela raised her hand and placed it against her forehead. Little by little, she seemed to wilt. "I'm so tired." Her tone was breathy and drawn out, as if the words took a great deal of energy to say.

Knorren leaned as close to the window as he could. At once, his eyes narrowed. "What did you do?" he snarled at Ylga. A foreign feeling sprouted within, discomforting him. His heart pounded and a new irritation developed. *Worry.* No, he refused to acknowledge it. He would not fuss over an insignificant human.

"It's just the herbs. As I said, it's compounded and brings on sleepiness." Ylga stood from her chair and crossed the room to Gisela. With care, she helped Gisela to her feet. "Come. Sleep it off. Knorren doesn't have any pressing plans." In a maternal display, the crone tucked in Gisela, who seemed half asleep already. For her head lolled to the side and her breathing grew slower.

If Knorren didn't know any better, he would have suspected she had poisoned her, but Ylga never condoned his killings. In fact, her fury was unmatched with each death. Her temper rained down on him in the form of pain, more than any cursed rose or burdock could inflict. Ylga was capable of making it feel as though his insides were ablaze, and he wasn't mad enough to *try* and rile her.

Knorren stood, then stepped around to the front of the hut as the crone exited. She lifted her silver eyebrows as if to say *I told you.* "Why does it affect her so?"

"Why do you care?" She didn't wait for an answer before continuing, "The herb does that, and when compounded it tires the body out. Gisela hasn't had her doses and she was bound to fall into a wretched cycle of fits if she didn't rest properly and take the syrup."

Whatever doubts he'd had before on whether or not the girl was the true princess vanished. The princess, as he knew, was quite ill and drove her father to Todesfall for a remedy. Knorren tossed his head back, chuckling. No wonder Werner had looked so panicked, so heartbroken on that platform.

"Why are you laughing?" Ylga snapped.

"She *is* the true princess then." His gaze slid to Ylga, who only nodded. "There is hope," he offered quietly. To return to his prior existence, to be rid of the pests of Todesfall . . . "Is she . . . the noble?"

Ylga nodded then frowned. "Not if you kill her, and you know I cannot tell you anything of the sort." Her eyes softened, but she didn't look at Knorren. Instead she focused on the sea grass dancing in the breeze. If Knorren wasn't mistaken, he could nearly see a hint of regret within her faded blue eyes. He decided then that he wasn't keen on it, and he'd much rather deal with her wrath.

"And what am I to do while she sleeps here?" He flicked his tail at a swarm of black flies. While the gulls cried above, a group of crows hidden in the trees cried out. There would be no leaving Gisela with Ylga. He didn't trust her and certainly wouldn't put it past her to return the princess to the king for a handsome reward. She'd done nothing in their long history together to prove otherwise.

Ylga ran her worn fingers over her face. She looked every year her age, which neared six hundred years, if he wasn't mistaken. "I don't care what you do. Laze on the beach. Go for a swim." Ylga flicked her hand toward him. "Just stay out of my way." Her tone brooked no further argument from Knorren.

It struck Knorren as odd, that the witch was curter than usual. She usually possessed a higher tolerance for his grumblings, but whatever was going on in that rotten head of hers surely must be eating away at any semblance of patience Ylga had left.

None of this matters, he thought, *for it'll all be for nothing.*

Gisela, whether or not she was the true princess, would fall like all the others who entered Todesfall. It was what Knorren did and he knew himself—knew that he wasn't capable of change. Which meant there was no hope, no matter what Ylga said.

With a snarl, he bounded down the shoreline, kicking up the sea water and sand behind him. While the truce with Werner and the people still lay firmly intact, Knorren was curious as to how many braved the woodlands around the beach, and who from the neighboring village thought to embark toward the city.

Knorren's eyes opened as the sound of crunching leaves disrupted his slumber. After patrolling the forest, he'd decided to nestle among the foliage and sleep while Gisela rested. It would do no good to have her flopping around uselessly atop of him or falling ill suddenly. There was also the fact he'd little desire to deal with Ylga's foulness. If she was of the mind, she could hold him captive or inflict pain on him as she'd done in the past.

He lifted his head, yawning as a little boy ran into the clearing directly in front of him. Tears streamed down the little human's sullied face and he shook in his worn leather boots. Tufts of bright red hair stuck up in wayward directions, like he'd slept with wet hair.

"All right!" His voice squeaked as he shouted. "I did it." The boy spun around to face where he'd come from. "Can I come out now?"

Fear radiated from him. Knorren could nearly taste the sweet fragrance and it beckoned to him. His teeth ached to sink into the rail-thin figure, but even as he thought such things, a briar from a rose bush pricked the pad of his paw. A twisted reminder of what the boy's remains would become.

"Who are you shouting at?" Knorren stood from where he lay and cocked his head. His voice had been enough to startle the boy, but when the boy turned around and saw who spoke, the scream that spilled from him drilled into Knorren's ears. "Stop that! At once!" He dipped his head down, his nose hovering close to the trembling child. The boy scrambled backward, fell, then promptly vomited on the forest floor. Humans were revolting.

"You—you're the demon of Todesfall." If the boy could curl into himself anymore, he might've, but as it were he shrank back toward a tree.

The sounds of other children rang out as they called to

him. From what Knorren discerned it was mostly teasing, but a feminine voice sounded more concerned.

"The one and only." Knorren lowered his front in a bizarre mockery of a bow. "Who wishes to know?"

"Please don't eat me." The child's brown eyes darted toward the treeline. "I was dared to enter the forest . . . they said you couldn't eat me."

The news had spread, clearly. Which meant while there were no trespassers currently, there soon would be. It grated on him, but it had been his terms and while Knorren possessed few admirable qualities, he did keep his word.

"And then what?" Knorren drawled. "What was the plan once you entered the woods?" He stepped around the tree the boy cowered against and rubbed against the bark, which shook the tree.

"They wanted proof!"

The reply stilled Knorren's movements. What sort of proof? A tooth? A toe? "How?"

The boy's shoulders lowered a fraction. "I don't know. They didn't say." Red crept into his cheeks. "Maybe fur."

Knorren rolled his eyes. "What is your name?"

"Luka."

Knorren lifted his head and let loose a shrieking bark. "Luka!" The boy's name thundered from him, which sent the human into another hysterical fit. "Quit your sniveling. Your friends no doubt heard that." Knorren twisted in half so his teeth could find purchase on his fur, and when he did, he plucked a tuft loose. Spitting it out near the boy, he motioned with his paw. "There is your proof."

The boy scrambled toward the hair, snatching it before

he clumsily stood and ran off. "Berto. I got it! He didn't eat me. I got it."

In a leap Knorren could have pinned the boy down and snuffed the life out of him, but he didn't. He only hoped that this display of mercy, that the irksome treaty, didn't come to bite him in the arse. For if it did, there would be hell to pay.

NINETEEN

*A*fter the little boy ran off, Knorren decided it was best to return to Ylga's hut. If Gisela wasn't awake yet, it was time she roused. The sun had dipped down, which meant darkness was already spreading within the woods. By some miracle the princess was, in fact, awake and she managed to avoid toppling from his back.

But when they returned to the castle, she was still out of sorts. It didn't worry Knorren, for he knew the concoction Ylga gave her was stronger than Gisela was used to. However, he didn't realize *how much* stronger.

Gisela tripped over her foot and barely caught herself in time. She swayed in place like a drunkard deep in his cups. Still, she gathered her skirt up with as much dignity as possible and stumbled forward.

"Violet!" Knorren bellowed. "Come deal with this girl before she plunges to her demise." His lip curled over his canines and he watched Violet reach for the satchel hanging from Gisela's shoulder as she herded her into the castle.

Ylga's herbal remedy lay inside the bag. She'd assured Knorren it'd keep Gisela's convulsions under control far better than the tea had. The only downside was, she'd grow tired shortly after consuming the tincture and thus it was best to use it in the evening.

What a troublesome little thing, he mused. Was she worth the bargain? He wasn't certain, but time would tell.

A breeze ruffled his fur. The passing wind brought the scent of deer toward him. Drawing in a deep breath, Knorren could practically taste the deer's flesh. His stomach rumbled in protest, reminding him that he hadn't eaten all day. The boy had been tempting, but Ylga's talk of hope had him considering things in a new light. Was redemption possible for a demon like him? Which prompted a deeper, more troubling question—did he want it?

With a grumble, he padded off into the woods again, this time to eat his fill of deer—or if he was lucky, a few elk.

In the evening, after a successful hunt, Knorren dozed on the bridge leading toward the castle. He'd almost wanted to drag himself inside to check on the princess. Gisela had yet to venture back outside and he wondered if she was still asleep.

Knorren found himself entangled, vexed even, by his thoughts. Why did he care whether or not she slept? Foreign emotions reared their ugly heads within him. The girl was a nuisance, her father a wretched fool, and yet when his mind raced back to Ylga's words . . . he longed for something else.

Violet's footsteps cut through his thoughts. She rushed up to him, breathing heavily. The woman was stocky, not old, but not as youthful as Gisela either. She had hair in a shade that reminded him of a field mouse, and come to think of it, her small facial features reminded him of one, too.

Violet had threatened to skewer him on the daily when he'd forced her to reside in the castle to attend the imposter.

However, when she saw how little he lurked around, she settled and resorted to spewing threats. Knorren still didn't trust her entirely. Violet was, after all, from Hurletz, and if anyone should hate him most, it was the neighboring village. All the lives he stole, land he claimed . . .

"Well?" Knorren asked lazily, licking blood from his paw.

"It's the princess." The color drained from her already pale face, leaving her with a ghostly appearance. "I found her on the floor of her bedroom . . . She hit her head. I think she's about to . . ."

"To what?" he ground out.

Violet worried on her bottom lip but wasted no time with words. "One of her fits, as she calls them."

Knorren studied the woman, looking for an indication that this was yet another trick, but in the time he'd spent with Violet, she'd never attempted to double-cross him. She was blunt and didn't think twice of cursing him out. But amid his assessment, he saw quiet panic deep in the woman's gaze and it was enough to send him to his feet. "What am I supposed to do?" He cocked his head, then swung it toward the window to Gisela's room.

You're a demon. You can scarcely fit within the walls of the castle, let alone be of assistance.

Frustration was an old friend, one Knorren was keen on thrashing, but it seemed as though it wouldn't be thwarted any time soon. He was useless at that moment.

"Go to her. Stay with her." He hissed the words, then quickly snapped, "Why did you leave Gisela's side in the first place, you nit. I'll do what I can." Knorren glanced toward Ylga's hut. Outside of Werner, the witch was the only one who knew what to do. When Violet finally dashed back into the castle, Knorren leaped away toward the seaside.

Barreling through the woods, Knorren emerged on a knoll facing the open water. Wind whipped against his face, kicking up sand and air thick with salt. A scent similar to the smell of a decomposing body tickled his nose, but it wasn't death. Beyond Ylga's cottage was a marsh, with long blades of sea grass that danced in the breeze. The aroma originated from there and he suspected the tides were low.

"Ylga!" Knorren barked, stepping up toward the cottage. His facial muscles tightened, forming a scowl on his muzzle, as he waited impatiently for the old woman to appear.

She didn't answer.

Losing his patience, Knorren swatted at her door, his nose pushing inside. A deep inhale of the hut told him she wasn't home. Damn, damn, damn.

A twig snapped behind him. Knorren whirled around, facing the small, perplexed woman.

"Why are you here . . . again? And you better not have broken my door." Shrewd eyes narrowed as she peered around the fox's body toward her house. "I should charge more for your bothersome company."

Snarling, Knorren used a paw to bar her path. "I think you charge quite enough. Sanity isn't currency, Ylga."

"Oh, to me it is." She waved him off but looked him up and down, interest gleaming in her eyes. "Let me ask again, why are you here?"

Why in the blazing depths was she wasting time? Knorren nearly growled his next words out. "The girl. She fell and hit her head. She isn't well."

Infuriatingly, Ylga considered his words, as if weighing their importance, then nodded. She stepped around him and went into her hut as if she hadn't heard his urgency, but moments later she emerged with a knapsack and said, "The tincture I made wards them off but doesn't stop them entirely. Take me to her. These fits are serious things, whether you wish to believe it or not."

Werner had stumbled into the forest in desperation and now Knorren knew why. If this was true . . . this poor, broken little bird lived a life of suffering. "She could die then?"

Ylga clucked her tongue. "As if I know. These spells she has . . . they wreak havoc on her body and mind. She could die with any one of them, but what do you care? You're no stranger to death." She pointed to the ground, motioning for Knorren to lower himself, and so he did. Ylga tugged at his fur as she climbed onto him with a little more grace than Gisela had.

"I don't care. But I'm not done with her yet."

Knorren didn't care—at least he told himself such things. He didn't know what he wanted from the human girl, or what her fate would be, but he knew that as of the moment, he certainly didn't want her dead. The game he'd drawn out for months with the girl's father would be over, and then what?

The witch let loose a wet laugh as she shook a handful of his fur to and fro. "I will help her, but certainly not for you. I will do it for the girl, because she is *good*. A goodness the world needs to balance out evil." Ylga's heels dug into his shoulders, but he was careful not to snap at her or grumble. "Take me to her then. I have no desire to spend more time with you today."

Neither did he. And so, he ran as fast as Ylga would allow him to. Through the brush, beneath low-hanging limbs, and through the wetlands of the forest.

By the time the castle of thorns came into view, Knorren panted heavily. He lowered himself to the ground, allowing his ornery passenger to clamber down. When Ylga righted herself, even in the dark of evening, Knorren could see her cheeks puff from exertion.

"Go! To the staircase and call for Violet." Knorren spoke between breaths, grimacing as his ribs ached from sucking in sharp breaths. Curiosity filled him as to what Ylga could do for the girl, so despite the pain burning in his sides, he crept toward the princess's window and stood on his hind legs.

The window was still wide open, so the hushed voices of the women carried to him. Gisela's prone body wasn't on the floor, but in bed, and her body grew rigid then her back arched as she moaned.

What the devil is this? This was no jest. An odd, unexplainable sensation ran through him and traveled along his spine. Gisela was truly ill. This was nothing in comparison to Ylga's hut. Knorren's ears flattened as he watched the two women aid her.

"How long has she been like this for?" Ylga hurried to the side of the bed, carefully rolling Gisela onto her side as she retched unproductively.

"A little more than half an hour." Violet rushed to say as she carried a bowl of water and a cloth to the nightstand by the bed. "She felt unwell and then had a small spell, which became this." She motioned to Gisela.

Ylga turned to the chair by the bed and rummaged in her bag. She took out two vials and poured them into a bowl. The substance was oily and it smelled of the earth. When it was mixed together, she painted the mixture across the girl's forehead, chest, back, stomach, and more delicate areas that had Knorren wondering why.

"What is that?" His voice cut through Gisela's moaning.

The last part of Gisela's body that Ylga lathered in the oil was her bare feet. While Ylga coated the oil on certain parts of her body, Gisela convulsed and frothed at the mouth.

Knorren longed for an answer, but Ylga was busy applying the mixture to Gisela. Transfixed by what was happening, he remained quiet and wondered if the girl would pull through her fit.

It was a peculiar thing, worrying over a human, but Knorren recognized it for what it was. But *why*. Did he worry over his hope?

Strangely, Gisela's body grew limp and the moaning subsided. She lay lifeless on the mattress then lurched forward, spewing onto the floor. Ylga grabbed a bowl and held it in front of her as she retched again and again, until there was nothing left in her.

"The oil will continue to work into her body. It is the same tincture as the liquid I sent with you." Ylga spoke to Knorren, but kept her attention on Gisela. Knorren had never seen Ylga display tenderness like she was showing the girl. The way she brushed her curls back, wiped the spittle from the corner of her mouth, and pulled the covers over

Gisela painted her as a motherly figure. An image that tugged at a softer, more vulnerable piece within him.

"You'll need to send for someone who is familiar with this. I cannot and will not come to you every time this happens." Ylga's words held no bite. She told the truth.

Knorren's claws bit into the side of the castle wall as his limbs grew tired from their current position. "It'll happen again like this?"

She turned her gaze toward the window then nodded. "It could."

His gaze dragged to Violet. "You can tend to her, can't you?" Desperation reared its ugly head. He was stuck in a hard place. Knorren wanted the girl alive, but at what cost? Would it not be kind to snuff the life from her now?

"Yes, but I'm not equipped to deal with this. I'm afraid I don't know the signs." She worried on her lower lip.

Knorren paced, tossing his head in annoyance. "And what do you suggest?"

"Send for her handmaid. She knows how to accommodate the princess during these times. It would be nothing but good to have an extra set of hands to help her and to take care of this dreadful castle."

Knorren narrowed his eyes and snapped his teeth in annoyance. "Why don't you grab your brother you were so keen on protecting?"

Violet didn't shrink back. Her spine stiffened and she visibly warred with restraining herself. "I will, and even then we wouldn't be equipped to deal with the princess's ailment, Knorren. I don't know what she has—how to even notice if things are off with her."

"Listen to Violet, Knorren. It's the only way." Ylga

collected her belongings and set them on the vanity. She motioned to them and sighed tiredly. "I'm leaving this here. For when she has another moment like this, you'll need the oil."

Knorren lashed out at the wall. His nails tore through decaying stone and roses then scraped through the stones, emitting an ear-splitting screech. He didn't want to contact King Werner, or anyone at the castle for that matter, but if it meant securing Gisela's well-being, he supposed he had to.

"Very well. When Gisela is well enough, have her pen a letter to her father demanding a staff member to care for her." Even as he said it, he regretted the words and even more so as Violet's eyebrows lifted in surprise. "Your useless brother can deliver it and bring back whoever they send."

Violet glanced at Ylga, then Knorren. She hesitated for a moment. "Fair enough." When she turned around, it was with far too much composure as far as Knorren was concerned. Violet ignored his tantrum, as did Ylga, and both worked to clean up Gisela as if nothing had ever happened.

Knorren pushed away from the wall and curled up on the bridge, waiting until the princess stirred from her room. Unfortunately, she didn't emerge from her room at all, which only added to his foul mood. He hadn't bargained for a dying waif, but despite how she trembled when she was in his presence and the tremor in her voice, Knorren didn't see a cowering maiden.

He saw something far greater. A fighter.

TWENTY

Gisela's eyes popped open the moment a loud, groaning creak cut through her sleep. She bolted upright, hair frizzed from the forced bed rest, and spotted Violet rummaging through a small collection of dresses. She withdrew a deep blue dress and spun to face Gisela, her eyes rounding as she jolted in surprise.

"I didn't mean to wake you." Violet dipped her head and draped the dress over the privacy screen. "I'm sure you need your rest after yesterday."

Exhaustion clouded Gisela's mind, but she was also restless. She didn't want to stay in bed. When she grew tired enough to sleep, she'd rest then, but she wasn't incapable of living—if one could call her current situation *living*. Gisela, in her opinion, had traded one cell for another, but in this case, her warden wouldn't think twice about killing her.

She frowned and rubbed between her eyebrows. Had she been imagining things? "Violet, was Ylga here last night?"

"Yes. Knorren fetched her when you were out of sorts, my lady." Violet stepped around the bed and helped Gisela dress for the day.

Knorren. He was outside of her window too . . . or was that her imagination?

"And Knorren . . . is he here?"

"No, he's gone." Violet paused then. "But he does have a request. You need to write to your father, requesting someone who is . . . more suited to your *fits*, as you call them." Violet guided Gisela to the vanity and took up a brush to comb out Gisela's curls. "My brother, Maxim, is allowed to visit with food from home. He's due to come today, which means he can deliver your letter."

Why would Knorren care enough to send for someone to help *her*? The notion didn't make sense, but she didn't even know what he wanted with her, or what he had in store. If he'd killed Lady Anna for lying, what would he do to Gisela if she didn't fit into his plans—whatever they were?

Gisela nodded. "I'll need something to write with."

Violet left and returned with a well of ink, a quill pen, and paper. Gisela lifted the pen with a trembling hand, flexing her fingers to adjust them. This happened with every episode. Her muscles weakened and it took a few days to recover. Small things that anyone else could do without thinking took Gisela longer to accomplish.

With the tip against the paper, she scratched her words with care.

My Dear Father,

How do I begin this letter? I don't even know what to say. It hasn't even been a week and I miss you so much. I'm alive and well for the moment. Strangely, I haven't

*seen much of Knorren. I suspect that will change in the
coming days.*

*Yesterday, I had a fit, and I know what you're thinking,
so breathe. I'm not here alone. Violet, one of Knorren's
servants, has been caring for me. But, since she isn't
accustomed to my ailment, I'm requesting you send Suli,
as per an agreement with Knorren. A young man by the
name of Maxim will deliver this letter and will wait for
Suli.*

*I miss you terribly, and Jana. Please tell my beloved
Byron I am well and thinking of him.*

Your beloved daughter,
Gisela

When she finished penning the letter, she sighed heavily.
The weight of the situation settled on her shoulders, and her
lip quivered as she fought back the urge to cry. As much as
she'd resigned herself to this months ago, it didn't mean she'd
accepted it and, worst of all, her captor hadn't exactly
revealed his hand to her either.

"Thank you," Violet murmured, taking the letter from
her. "If you'd like to venture outside, you may. Knorren
doesn't really stay around for very long. He does . . . whatever it is Knorren does."

Kill things, Gisela thought miserably. But she wondered,
what did he do? If the truce between him and her father
meant no more deaths, what did he do in the forest?

Musing over this, Gisela turned to look at Violet's
retreating figure. "When he is here, what does he do?"

Violet paused in her tracks, a slow smile tugging at her lips. "He mostly curses, has tantrums, and spews threats, my lady. Aside from that, he sleeps." She laughed softly then left the room, abandoning Gisela to her thoughts.

"Well, that answered everything." She sighed. If he wasn't here, then she supposed she could mill around outside.

Out of her room, Gisela decided to venture down the hallway, opening doors and inspecting the rooms. They were dust filled but intact, unlike the first floor, which bore claw marks in the walls.

The last room on the far side of the hall wouldn't open at first. Gisela frowned, twisting the knob around, and then with a shove of her shoulder, the door grudgingly opened. Unlike the other rooms, this one didn't have standard decorations. Instead, it boasted a giant four-poster king-sized bed. Light wood contrasted with the dark green walls and accents of gold curtains. Tables filled the room.

There were no portraits, no art hanging from the walls. But in the hearth, as Gisela drew closer, she saw fragments of frames and tattered canvas cloth. There was nothing she could piece together to see what it may have been, but it was clear someone purposely destroyed whatever it was.

Golden arrows hung on the wall, crossing one another. Had this been the prince's room? The prince had been a great hunter, so history said, but not even his skills could take down the wicked beast of Todesfall.

With more questions than answers, Gisela left the room, but this time she left it open and then sought out Violet in the kitchen. She needed breakfast first and foremost, then she needed her herbs for the day.

After breakfast, Gisela ventured outside. Sunlight filtered through the thick blankets of foliage above, but it felt good to have the light on her skin, the warmth spreading comfort through her. Even though it was summer, the castle was cold and her thin blanket did little to warm her in the evening.

She drank in the sight of the long stone bridge before her. Old, decomposing leaves, bones, and other matter cluttered the white stones. Gisela bent to brush some leaves away, exposing a tiny green shoot. The green leaves were tipped with red, as if dipped in blood. Curiously, Gisela swept aside more leaves, exposing more tiny rose bushes growing. Where there weren't roses, just like in the woods, there were burdock roots.

How strange, she thought. What would cause them to grow in such an odd place? Especially the burdocks—they couldn't and wouldn't root on the stone properly.

Despite Violet ensuring Gisela Knorren wouldn't come around any time soon, Gisela gazed around the quiet woodland, as if the hulking beast would spring forth at any moment, baring his teeth and hurling threats her way.

"H-hello?" she called out. No answer. Tentatively, she pushed forward, opting to stay close to the castle in fear of growing lost in the thick woodlands.

There were creatures milling around in the woods— chirping, chittering, and even bellowing. An active forest meant there were no predators around, and she took comfort in that.

The farther away from the castle she went, the bigger the rose bushes grew. Vibrant, deep red blooms faced her. Carefully, she reached out and used her thumb nail to remove some thorns, then she twisted the stalk until it snapped. She repeated this several times until she had a small bouquet.

Glancing over her shoulder, she checked to see if Violet called for her, or if Knorren lurked beneath the bridge, but no one was there. However, she noticed the birds suddenly quieted or fluttered away.

Something was off.

Gisela turned on her heel, but her dress caught in the briars. She clutched the flowers in one hand, tugging at the fabric with the other. Thorns pricked her skin as the bouquet jostled in her grasp.

"Oh, come on," she whispered shakily. With a hard yank, the fabric tore free, but it sent her off balance, and her balance wasn't the best as it was. She tried to catch herself, twisting this way and that, but she was tumbling face first into a massive thorny bush. Or at least, she had been.

A furry muzzle caught Gisela, steadying her enough so she could stand upright. Stable, hot breaths washed over her every time the fox breathed, and when he exhaled a rumble sounded. It wasn't the sound of him exhaling, but rather a deep, bone-chilling growl that resonated in her body.

One yellow eye met hers; his other was obstructed by the odd angle he held his head. Half-cocked, trying to avoid the gnarled bushes.

"Kn-Knorren," Gisela stammered. She twisted away from the bush and quickly righted herself in an awkward motion.

He didn't speak, but his eyes narrowed on her and his

growling continued, sounding more akin to a purr at this point.

Did he think she was going to escape, make a run for it like last time? The notion caused a laugh to bubble up. This wasn't the time or place, but it oozed out in quick breaths regardless.

Knorren's lip curled in disdain. "I'm so glad you find your predicament amusing, *Klette*. Perhaps I should've let you fall and blind yourself in the briars." His ears pinned against his head as he moved from the roses, but his eyes focused on the bundle of flowers she held in one hand.

Gisela's eyes widened as his ears fell in warning. She'd seen dogs lower their ears to their skull prior to attacking. Quickly, she attempted to amend the situation. "I don't find it amusing, not in the least. I was merely thinking . . . If you thought I'd try to escape . . . I . . . where would I run to? There is nowhere—" She glanced around, surveying the rows of briars and burdocks. She wasn't the most agile and no doubt, the fox would pin her to the ground in two bounds. In her mind, it was futile.

Gisela froze as Knorren loomed over her, his shrewd eyes narrowing.

"There is nowhere you could run that I wouldn't find you." He stepped around the bush, using his paw to bump Gisela backward. "So I know you couldn't possibly be attempting to flee."

Gisela stumbled, heel catching on the hem of her skirt. Her stomach flipped because she knew she was going to fall on her bottom, but it never happened. Knorren used one of his legs to catch her fall, again. Her fingers grasped at the furry leg supporting her and she shot him a thankful glance from between his legs.

He cocked his head, eyes narrowing on her. "Why do you have those things in your hand? You're making a mess of yourself."

Gisela glanced down, following his gaze to her hand. She hadn't released the flowers when she stumbled twice over, and each time she reflexively clutched harder. Blood trickled down her palm, to her wrist, to the velvet fabric of the dress.

She loosened her hold, but didn't drop them. "They're beautiful."

Knorren loosed a breath, which sounded more like a snort than anything. "No, they're ghastly things. They snag, wound, and annoy."

Gisela watched his expression, too human to truly be that of an animal, but his lips tightened and his brows furrowed, and for a moment she could almost picture him as a man.

"I don't think so. But if you're so sickened by them, why live in a place surrounded by them?" Gisela twisted, moving out from beneath him. Everywhere her eyes searched, there were rose bushes. She'd never seen so many in her life; even her garden at the palace wasn't this extensive when it came to roses.

"And where, pray tell, Klette, do you think I could live? Where would I go so that my hide wouldn't be hunted? Besides, the roses and burdocks are a punishment."

Gisela's brow furrowed in question. "I don't understand. A punishment for what?"

"For killing."

TWENTY-ONE

*K*norren snapped his teeth shut inches from Gisela's face. The scent of death washed over her, making her stomach roil. His breath smelled like a rotten corpse, and it warred with the perfumed fragrance of the roses. A sickeningly sweet blend of crushed petals and congealed blood filled the air, sending Gisela to the nearest tree to spew.

Knorren's laughter bounced off the trees, cruel and hard. "I had my reservations on whether you were another deception in the beginning, because of that wretched king and his lies. But here we are, a little princess reduced to vomiting. How the mighty have fallen."

Her cheeks heated with embarrassment and shame that she'd given the beast exactly what he wanted. A display of weakness. Not that last night wasn't just that.

Knorren wanted to see Gisela's fear, see her unravel, and she'd played into his game. Tears stung her eyes, but she stood up, using the tree to steady herself. "Don't you dare speak of my father."

"Or what?" Knorren's eyes narrowed. "You'll do what exactly, Klette?"

How could he drag Ylga back to the castle to tend to her,

allow her to write to her father, then act as though she were insignificant? Gisela couldn't and wouldn't dissect Knorren's actions, for she could only assume it would drive her mad.

In the end, what could she do to retaliate? Gisela was no match for him physically and the only move she could think to pull was . . . "You are cruel and if it's a game to see who is cruelest, fine. I won't pluck the burrs from your eye or pull a bone splinter from your paw. Your wounds can fester for all I care." She drew in a ragged breath, her heart hammering in her chest and ears.

It was childish, but there was no other weapon she held against him. Knorren could strike her down, devour her wholly where she stood, or draw out her death.

Knorren's ears pricked forward. A foreign expression passed over his gaze—intrigue? Surprise? Gisela couldn't begin to know or even understand what went through his mind.

"Such fiery words coming from a coward's daughter. This apple has tumbled far from its tree." He paused for a moment and then lowered himself a fraction. "Climb on, lest you *do* fall face first into the thorns."

Irritation blazed through Gisela. Did he think for one moment she'd forgiven him or—in the very least—brushed off his comments? She bristled, spine straightening as she glared up at him. "No. I'll walk."

Knorren's eyebrows furrowed, but he walked off. "Very well. I won't offer again."

"That is just fine," she spat.

Except, it wasn't. Gisela tripped, stumbled, and nearly fell face first into several thorny bushes. True to his word, Knorren didn't offer again. He didn't even glance back at her as she lagged behind. His pace remained the same, until she was certain she'd have to run to catch up.

Eventually, the burdocks lessened, as did the rose bushes, until they were in a clearing and Gisela hadn't a clue where they were. The castle spires weren't in sight, there was no hint of the kitchen's smoke in the air, and Gisela was thoroughly lost.

Out of breath, tired, and frustrated, she sank to the ground in a heap. "I can't take another step." She rubbed her throat, which was raw from gasping too much. She hadn't endured this much physical activity in far too long. Even when her fits were at bay, no one really allowed her to run or ride a horse.

"But you will." Knorren sat, curling his tail around himself. "You may have become used to servants tending to your every whim, but you'll not get the same treatment here. You'll have Violet, her useless brother, and even your hand-maid from the castle, but they can only do so much. What are you willing to do in order to survive?" His yellow gaze dragged along her figure, delving past the surface—or at least it felt like it.

Gisela's scabbed-over palm slapped at the ground. "What do you want from me?"

He bared his teeth in response. "What are you willing to do to survive?" he inquired again, the patience stripped from his tone.

Why did it always come down to fighting to live? "What are you asking of me?"

Knorren snarled in frustration. "If I must spell it out for you . . . From here on, you will hunt for yourself. I don't want to hear your excuses. If it wasn't for you, there would be no humans in my castle, which means you'll be hunting for your dinner."

Gisela bolted to her feet. "What? Are you mad?" She recoiled as he launched at her, lips curled to reveal his teeth.

"If you don't, you'll go hungry, and so will the inhabitants. Does that settle well with you, *Princess?*"

It didn't. Gisela didn't have to say it, because Knorren wouldn't have mentioned it otherwise. She looked away from him, frowning.

Knorren stood, shaking off the forest debris from his pelt. "I'm not relying on the nuisance of a dwarf to bestow food on the castle. And Violet nor her brother know how to hunt. That leaves you."

The hatred he felt toward whoever the dwarf was wasn't lost on her. Gisela wanted to know more, but now wasn't the time and she also didn't want to speak to the fox, let alone ask him questions.

She stared down at her hands. One scabbed over from the thorns that pricked it, and the other pristine. No callouses hardened her skin, no dirt caked beneath her nails. This fox expected her to hunt for food? She'd starve. They all would.

"Fine." Gisela turned her back on him, hopelessly surveying the labyrinthine forest. If she ventured down a path, there was no telling where she'd end up. Lost, stuck in quicksand, or eaten by a wolf. Somehow those odds didn't seem nearly as daunting as staying in Knorren's company.

Todesfall Forest consisted of hundreds, if not thousands, of acres of wooded land. Streams, swamps, forgotten structures, and stone caves hid along the way. Gisela knew this from the stories all the maids used to murmur as they tended to her. It wasn't all evil that came from the forest; there once had been good, long ago.

But Knorren made it impossible to remember. The Golden Times, as they were often called. When the Golden Prince had ruled the land and loved his people dearly, there had been no threat of death from the forest.

"Fine?" Knorren echoed her word.

Without speaking, Gisela stubbornly pushed through the woods, deciding there were far worse things than death. Besides, Knorren had already stated there was nowhere she could go that he wouldn't find her. If that was true, he'd seek her out if she became lost and either spare her life or put an end to it.

Brush rustled behind Gisela, startling her enough to spin around. If Knorren were to strike her there, she wanted to see him do it. But no, when she looked up, he was gone. Half expecting it to be a trick, Gisela braced for the worst, but moments ticked by without an assault.

When no threat came, Gisela hiked up the skirt of her dress and ran as fast as she could down a beaten path. One of them was bound to lead back to the castle—at least, she hoped so.

Hours passed by the time she sank to her knees in defeat. The sun weakened in the sky, dimming the forest around her, disorienting her to the point of breaking. What did she think would happen? Gisela cupped her face and smothered a sob lodged in her throat. She wouldn't cry, she *wouldn't*. To cry was to give into this.

Wild curls sprung loose from their braids and tears streaked through the dirt on her face. Her stomach ached from gulping air, as did her throat, and every single muscle burned from exertion.

The castle's spires weren't in view, nor was the beaten dirt path she'd seen on her arrival. Over the course of the day, she'd grown wise and used long blades of dry grass to braid and tie around trees so she knew if she'd been in the area before. None of her markings hung from trees, which meant she was on a different path, likely more lost than before.

Gisela lowered her hands and slapped the ground in frustration, growling at it. She wouldn't be as useless as everyone thought her to be. Amid her frustration, she glanced down at her ruined dress. The hem had torn away after the third time she tripped on it. Holes from thorns peppered the remaining fabric and dried tracks of blood covered her arms. In short, she looked as terrible as she felt.

A twig snapped from behind her, pulling her from the misery tugging her under. A twisted form of relief flooded her as she beheld the figure sitting ever so still: Knorren.

The proud fox sat with his tail curled around his front legs. His cold eyes lingered on Gisela for a moment before he spoke. "You are alive."

"Of course I am." The words tumbled from her lips in a harsh whisper. Gisela felt anything but alive, if she was honest. She tried to push herself to stand, but quaking muscles kept her from achieving her goal.

With an ease Gisela envied, Knorren crept forward and laid down by her side. "Save your arguments and stubbornness for another day. Climb on to my back." He paused, glancing around. Even in the span of a few moments, it'd grown darker. "Unless you'd prefer to stay out after dark, in which case, I don't recommend it. Todesfall wolves are rather . . . aggressive."

More so than he? Gisela didn't want her pride to cloud her judgment further. If she refused Knorren and he left, those wolves wouldn't show her any mercy. Frowning, she pushed herself to her feet, which were covered in painful blisters, and tentatively touched Knorren's shoulder. He didn't bat a lash at her as she clutched his fur, then pulled herself onto his withers.

She groaned involuntarily, each muscle protesting as it stretched and pulled taut. Hopefully, when she returned to the castle, Gisela could slip into a hot bath. As hungry as she was, bathing and sleeping seemed more important to her.

Carefully, Knorren stood and started their trek to the castle.

Surprisingly, no cutting remark slid from him. Gisela took the reprieve without a snide comment and sank into the warm fur beneath her for the duration of the walk home.

Eventually, Knorren wound his way to the castle and lowered himself to the ground so Gisela could dismount. Smoke billowed from the castle's chimney, smelling faintly of spices. The fragrance alone awakened Gisela's stomach with a loud, painful rumble.

The castle at this time of day appeared as horrifying as any tale ever told by the chattering maids. Since the sun's rays didn't possess enough strength to penetrate the canopy of trees, especially just before darkness settled in, the structure was shadowed. The vines growing alongside the stone structure looked like black veins, threatening to devour it.

Gisela slid to the ground, hissing as her muscles rebelled against her. It wasn't a graceful dismount by any means, but Knorren stayed silent. Too silent.

"Go clean yourself up. Tomorrow you have work to do." In the dark, Gisela could see his head tilt to the side and the flash of white teeth in the moonlight that managed to trickle through the canopy of trees.

There he is, she mused. Too exhausted to do anything more than agree, Gisela limped away from her keeper and into a dimly lit castle. Bath first, then food if she had the energy.

"Dear heavens," Violet gasped, placing a hand to her chest. "What happened to . . . did Knorren do this?" Her eyes narrowed as she stepped forward, lowering her voice as if Knorren were about to burst inside at any moment.

As much as Gisela wanted to blame anyone else, it was her own doing. "No," she offered tiredly. "It was me. I ran away from Knorren, thinking I could make it back on my own."

Violet nodded with her lips pursed. "Are you okay?" She paused, holding a finger up. "Let me get a bath ready for you." She disappeared up the stairwell, leaving Gisela to mill around by herself.

Since arriving, she hadn't explored as much as she would have wanted. Between her fits and refusing to leave her room, she hadn't had much time to poke around in the week she'd been there.

Against the stairs, Gisela noticed there was a hidden door. A small knob jutted out and as she approached it, she pulled it open, revealing a long pathway instead of a closet like she'd assumed it was. With no lantern to offer her light, it wouldn't do much good to search.

Just as she was readying to turn, a hand touched Gisela's shoulder, startling her enough that she nearly tripped over her own feet.

"You scared the life out of me!" Gisela rasped, covering her mouth.

Violet bit her bottom lip and had the grace to look sheepish. "I'm sorry." Her eyebrows knit together and her mouth fell open as she stared into the darkness. "Maybe you've had enough adventure for one day, my lady." Violet looked hopeful as she assessed Gisela's figure. "You're covered in blood."

"I know." She sighed. "I need to soak for a while. Knorren said I have a busy day tomorrow."

Violet pulled her head back, squinting as she glanced over Gisela. "Oh? Has he written down an itinerary for you?" Violet teased, but there was a hint of worry or doubt in her voice.

Gisela laughed despite the tension that held her in a tight grip. Her shoulders eased down from her ears, then she rolled her head back. "No, he wants me to learn to hunt." It sounded as foolish as Gisela suspected it to. When she tilted her head forward, she saw Violet's expression, which mirrored how Gisela felt about the idea: horrified.

TWENTY-TWO

Knorren flicked his tail at a cluster of black flies. They yearned to land on his muzzle, hoping to lap up the residue of blood, or perhaps they only longed to sample some of the fox's to annoy him further.

Yesterday, Knorren had watched the princess stumble through briars, pricking her flesh and inevitably bleeding on the cursed ground. Despite the discomfort, she didn't pause amid the rose bushes and only seemed more resolute in finding her perfect blossom.

Foolish girl, he thought miserably. Of course, the roses had long lost their appeal and beauty to him. They were no more than a reminder and a prison of thorns. A reminder that with every time blood was shed, by his doing, another bush would grow from the droplets and the bones would turn to burdocks. Out of the two, Knorren preferred the roses, for the burdocks matted his fur and created knots that tugged at his skin.

For all of the girl's silliness, she was certainly made of steel. Very few outside of Ylga could look him in the eye. Violet was different. That woman was part devil herself, of this Knorren was certain. Once that woman's initial fear shed, the blasted human hurled a pitchfork at him, nearly impaling his tail.

But Gisela didn't spew hatred toward Knorren and he knew he deserved every ounce of it. After the terror he rained upon the kingdom of Tursch, and the individuals he'd slain. Most days, he felt as though he were forgetting himself. Not that he'd ever known who he was, but at least he'd remembered a youthful Ylga summoning him. That day seemed so distant now. It was a foggy memory, and one day it'd vanish. Then what? What would hold him to his small conscience?

Branches snapped as a loud, muttering individual huffed and puffed through the underbrush. A yelp rang out, then another rustling of leaves.

Knorren's eyes narrowed as he watched half-rotten brown leaves fly into the air every once in a while, then eventually a pale, wrinkled face stared up at him. Discontent plastered itself on Egon's face, his little arms flailing in quiet rage.

"You could have helped me, you know!" Egon's face reddened. The black boots he wore were covered in muck from the decomposing leaves and perhaps rotting flesh on the forest floor.

"I could have, but I didn't see much point in it." Knorren lifted a paw to groom. His tongue lapped at the white fur along his toes and he did his best to ignore the pudgy-faced man.

"What?" Egon huffed, bristling all the more. "Why not?"

Knorren's ears flattened against his skull and he hunkered down as he spun to face the little man. Baring his teeth, the fox spoke lowly. "I don't like you."

Egon's bulbous eyes widened, but he didn't flinch. His hand planted on his hip as he tipped forward, then laughter spilled from his lips. "It's mutual, trust me." He wiped a dirt-covered hand on his pant leg. "You're a vile creature, Knorren. If anyone found your company worthwhile, I'd recommend they seek a medicine man or woman, quickly." Twisting around, Egon surveyed the clearing they were in.

They were in the heart of the woods, far from the castle, which brought a question to Knorren's mind: Why was Egon here? He assumed Ylga wished to taunt him further by sending the strange little man. If Knorren had to choose between the pesky flies and Egon, he'd take a swarm of the bloodsucking creatures any day.

Swatting his paw at a cluster of flies near his eyes, he grumbled his question. "Why are you here? Surely you have better things to do than bedevil me with your presence?"

Egon shuffled toward a half-rotten log and sat on it. He fussed over his ruined boots, which he only realized in that moment had the slimy remains of whatever corpses were decomposing on the path he'd taken. He visibly warred with not spewing on the ground, but anger replaced his body's discontent.

"This entire place is disgusting!" Egon blurted in fury.

"You haven't answered my question." Knorren rolled his eyes, then peered down at the sullied boots.

Egon grabbed a handful of fresh leaves and used them to clean off the refuse clinging to his boots. "It is beyond me why Ylga even bothers with you."

"Well, it seems as though it's a mystery for us all," Knorren offered dryly. Egon had no choice but to deal with him, considering the dwarf was in Ylga's service, and if she told him to seek Knorren out whether to annoy or relay a message, then he had no option. In nearly five hundred years, Knorren couldn't remember a time when Egon wasn't with Ylga—or in the very least—doing her bidding. Knorren had asked once, where he came from, why he was forced to do the crone's bidding. In reply, he only said, *"we all have burdens to shoulder, and some have curses to carry out."*

After the vague reply, the dwarf grew distant and eventually sauntered away. Knorren never asked Egon again what or if he was cursed, he only assumed that perhaps he was one of Ylga's toys as well.

In the back of Knorren's mind, he considered the notion Ylga's presence as well as Egon's was meant to infuriate him all the more. What did Ylga care if Knorren's patience turned to ash?

Egon ran one of his knobby fingers along his pockmarked jowl. "Ylga says there is unrest in Tursch and in Hurletz." The small man eyed Knorren cautiously. "There are rumors saying the townsfolk are readying to take the forest back." He spread his hands, shrugging. "And the king gathers an army. Who would have ever thought you'd be the lesser problem?"

Little by little, the muscles in Knorren's face tightened. Knorren should've known better than to let the little human escape the forest. That gesture would likely be his undoing. Yet, what did Ylga care? Why send Egon with such a message? His thoughts turned to suspicion. If troops were marching into Todesfall already, had Gisela sent for an army to take her back instead of simply asking for her handmaid?

Knorren snarled at the dwarf. He crouched down to his level and narrowed his eyes. "You lie."

Egon's face wrinkled as he fell backward with a yelp.

"What are you on about? Why would I lie? I'm simply relaying what Ylga has seen." He recoiled farther as Knorren loomed above him.

Knorren contemplated devouring the annoyance, but as his muscles tensed, the sound of panting caught his attention. He stood, ears swiveling to locate where it came from, then a stumbling figure emerged from the overgrowth.

The delicate young woman curled in on herself as she gulped down air. Sweat glistened on her sandalwood skin and she batted at a swarm of flies.

"The least you could have done was tell me where to find you or how." Gisela swept back the curls from her face and pinned him with a look he assumed was meant to be threatening. It was as threatening as a mouse glaring at a cat.

Knorren's lip curled over his canines. "I could have, but I didn't, and you are no worse for wear." His eyes scanned over her quickly, finding nothing amiss, minus the sullied skirt of her dress and the fact that she was breathless and perspiring. He was pleased to find she wore a quiver on her back and a bow slung over her shoulder.

Knorren stepped away from Egon, the dwarf all but forgotten. His eyes narrowed as his shadow fell over Gisela, who shrank back. *Does she think better of her attitude?* Amusement unfurled within him, though the pinched expression remained on his face as he scowled at her.

Beside him, Egon laughed. It was a small, raspy noise that raked against Knorren's ears. "What are you planning with the girl?"

"She must learn how to hunt." As Knorren spoke, Egon seemed to notice the bow.

"What?" Egon leaped in between Knorren and Gisela.

"Are you mad?" His eyes darted toward the side, then back up to the fox. "Is this one of your tests?" Egon's voice lowered so only Knorren could hear him.

"Quite mad." Knorren offered dryly. "And if it was, what then?"

Egon said nothing in return.

Gisela took a step forward. The bow slid from her arm and nearly knocked her in the head. She huffed in indignation. "I said the same thing." A frown tugged at her lips as she ran a finger along the oak grip of the bow.

"Anyone can learn how to hunt," Egon offered. "And, at the very least, you have a skilled teacher."

Gisela's brows furrowed in frustration. "Knorren is a fox. Perhaps if he were a man, I'd have an easier time learning."

Egon cleared his throat, fidgeting with his pudgy fingers. "I just don't see why you need to learn the skill."

Gisela's frustration clearly mounted. She scowled. "I don't know."

Knorren squeezed his eyes shut. As the two rattled off back and forth, he grew more irritable. "Starvation is your other option. If you're not keen on eating, far be it from me to force you." He opened his eyes and fixed his gaze on Gisela. "If you enjoy meals of venison or boar, you will learn how to hunt."

She made her frustrations quite clear, but Knorren wasn't empathetic to her reasoning. If he were a human, he could hunt for her more effectively, certainly, but it wasn't the point. Gisela had to learn to provide for herself, because Knorren spent most of his days away from the castle. Without him there, there would be no meat. So, it was

Gisela's responsibility going forward to tend to a garden and hunt for her food.

"Away with you, Egon. I've got to tutor Klette." Knorren lowered his head and shoved the dwarf with his nose.

Egon pinned him with a look. "Very well, but remember what I said earlier." Snorting, he hobbled off.

It didn't take long for Gisela to fill the silence. "Knorren, I cannot hunt." She pulled the bow from her body and glanced down at it dubiously.

Although he couldn't smile, his lips pulled back from his teeth in a disturbing mockery of one. "Not yet, but you will." He stood, jerking his head toward a path. "First things first. You must know how to hold the bow and how to stand. Then, you'll need to know how to nock an arrow."

Confusion twisted Gisela's full lips. She looked as if she were a moment from hurling the weapon at him. "Knorren, how do you know how to hold a bow?"

Of course she'd ask. He laughed, a low rumbling noise in his chest. "When you've had as many arrows pointed at you as what I've had, you pick things up through the centuries." Her curiosity amused him, but the way her brow wrinkled and her lips formed a frown gnawed at him.

She sucked in a breath and her eyes widened. "Honestly . . ."

"It's the truth." Knorren chuckled. "All right. I'll cease teasing you, but it is how I know." The tip of his nose poked her in the middle of the back. "Keep your back straight. Square off your stance. Now raise the bow and keep your arms perpendicular to your target."

Gisela followed through with every step, but her arms

shook as she held the bow up. She mumbled in frustration, clenching her fingers tighter around the wood.

He shook his head, then allowed a breath of hot air to wash down her neck in hopes of distracting her. "Don't do that. You'll create more tension."

An array of emotions passed over Gisela's face. Frustration, sadness, disappointment. "It'll never be steady."

Tilting his head to the side, he studied her. "*Never* is a definite word. Are you so certain of your fate?"

She faltered, lowering the bow as she turned to face him. "Are you?"

Knorren snorted. "I asked you first, but no. I'm not." He wished she wouldn't look at him as she was. Her turquoise eyes peered into his very soul, as if she could pick apart his essence. "I didn't say lower the bow. Set up again."

Gisela ran through the motions of nocking an arrow, but her shaking arms and fumbling fingers made it difficult for her to accurately line up her target.

"It's no use. I shake no matter what. Look." A look of defeat washed over her features as she held her hands out and they quaked. Then, as if embarrassed, she clenched her fingers into a fist. The brightness in her gaze had disappeared. Fatigue weighed her down and Knorren wondered if she was about to cry.

He bared his teeth at her. "You are not done yet. Continue."

"How? I can't. You've seen for yourself I lack the coordination. I can scarcely maneuver my way through the woods, let alone use a bow."

Gisela doubted her abilities, which didn't surprise him. As far as hunting abilities, she had none. And she was right:

she was awkward and unbalanced walking, much less trying to take aim with an arrow. However, the girl possessed an iron will that he'd seen firsthand.

"But you will" was all he said in reply.

He wasn't certain how long they spent practicing, but she managed to nock an arrow and let one fly successfully without maiming either one of them.

By the time they were done, she was red in the face from the exertion and frustration. The forest had also grown considerably darker, which meant supper would be waiting for Gisela.

"That was dreadful," Gisela murmured.

Knorren laid down on the ground so she could climb up on his back rather than fumble her way through the woods. "Don't be silly. You didn't shoot my eye out. I'd call it a successful lesson." As Gisela climbed up, she groaned and stiff laughter spilled from her.

"If that's all it takes to be successful, I suppose you're right."

"It's a start."

Knorren wound his way through the tangled mess of briars and bushes. And when the trees grew sparser, they hit the familiar road that returned them to the castle.

Much to Knorren's dismay, they arrived at the same time two riders dismounted in the courtyard. One was Maxim, Violet's brother, and Knorren wasn't certain who the other was. But as she turned her gaze on Knorren, he assumed she was Gisela's handmaid.

She gasped, eyes widening. Immediately, the woman's hand covered her heart as if it'd thump its way from her chest. "Dear Wurdiz, protect us."

"He will not protect you here." His voice rumbled from him like thunder. Knorren didn't bother to soothe the woman's fear. She was a guest in his home and no matter how much she prayed to Wurdiz or held up her fingers to ward Knorren off, he'd still be there and he'd not tolerate her asinine behavior.

Gisela's fingers clutched Knorren's fur as he lowered, then she climbed down and raced toward the other girl. She smiled. "Suli!" She grabbed her hands and tugged the other woman toward her. "You made it."

"Are you all right, my lady?" Suli ran her gaze over Gisela, then turned Gisela's hands over. Raw fingers stared up at her. Lips parting, she sucked in a breath. "What were you doing? Did he hurt you?"

Knorren snorted. He curled his tail around his legs as he sat. "She does that well enough on her own." Still, it rankled him on some level that she'd think he would maim her in such a way.

Gisela cast a glance over her shoulder at him, then looked back to her handmaid. "No. I'm tired and he offered to give me a ride."

Suli looked uncertain. "If you're sure . . ."

Gisela twisted her hands over and caught Suli's. "I am. Knorren has yet to hurt me. In fact, he was teaching me how to hunt."

Yet. He shook his head, but her words hadn't implied he would, nor was her tone chilly.

"Let's get you inside and cleaned up. I've brought more of your belongings with me too." Suli turned to look at the vine-covered castle. Blooms of red hid the stone walls beneath, and the perfume of them hung heavily in the air.

As the girls parted, Maxim took care of the horses and Knorren was left alone to deal with his thoughts. Gisela could have lied and said Knorren had abused her, or could have blown things out of proportion, but she hadn't. In truth, he didn't know what to think of that. Nor did he want to acknowledge the part of himself that wasn't wicked seemed to glow beneath the revelation.

Turning away from the castle, Knorren disappeared into the woods once again. Annoyance rippled through him, because as much as he wanted to evade thoughts of Gisela, she kept creeping into his mind.

Her resilience.

Her honesty.

Amid his musings, he heard the rustling of brush. Knorren swung his head to peer over his hind end and he spotted Ylga. He wasn't in the mood for her, but he hadn't the energy to run away either. He felt nearly as drained as Gisela had looked.

Ylga smiled. "I didn't come to pester you." She waved her hand, sitting on a nearby stump. "I thought you'd find my recent vision interesting."

Knorren sat then let his legs slip out from under him as he laid down. "Hm? Why would I find your vision interesting, witch?" He yawned, watching her with lazy interest. But he was far more interested than he let on. It was odd, in his mind, that she'd arrive on the same day her little helper had. What news did she bring and did it have anything to do with sending him back?

Ylga fiddled with the crystal on top of her cane, running her thumb along the ridges. She sighed. "What I saw was a change, and if your heart is in the right place, you may return to your prior life." She shook her head and strands of silver swept into her gaze. "But mark my words, if you should revert to your cruelties, you'll face dire consequences."

Knorren growled. "That is no different from what I already know. What did you *see*?"

"I saw you restored to your life. Free of your prison. But it didn't come without a sacrifice . . ."

"What do I need to sacrifice to end this life?"

Ylga clucked her tongue. "You'll know when it's time. I cannot say more than that. You know that Wurdiz has their ways."

If that was true, could Knorren return to where he came from? If he made the right choice, could Ylga return him to the depths? With those thoughts racing through his head, there was no way sleep would come to him. Instead, he patrolled the forest, leery that any of the villagers from Burlitz would intrude.

Twenty-Three

*S*uli brought Gisela her herbal tea in the morning. She frowned as Gisela trembled as she took a sip. The bottom of the cup clinked and chattered against the saucer she held. All of the muscles in Gisela's shoulders, arms, and chest protested. She'd experienced soreness from her fits, but this was different and spread from her back down to her forearms and even hands.

"Are you all right?" Suli inched forward, her eyebrows furrowing with worry as if she were readying to catch the cup and saucer at any moment.

"I'm fine. I'm just sore from yesterday." She finished her tea and set the cup down. The warmth of the tea spread through Gisela, soothing her nerves as much as her aching muscles.

Suli didn't look convinced.

"Aside from aches, I feel fine."

She glanced down at her palms, squinting. The skin on her fingers bubbled and throbbed, a reminder of yesterday's archery lesson. Never once in her life had she ever thought a bow would be in her grasp, let alone that she would learn how to hunt. Gisela had been cross with Knorren to start with, and as the day carried on, she grew more frustrated with herself—but after? Afterward, there was something exhilarating about learning how to use a bow.

Even though every muscle in her body ached, Gisela felt empowered. Knorren didn't treat her as though she were a fragile petal on the verge of wilting. It was infinitely refreshing to have him glance at her with a look as if to say, *And so?* The demon of the forest likely didn't realize that, in doing so, he was telling Gisela she was capable of more, and she was beginning to believe it.

What would her father think if he could see her? Gisela doubted he'd stand for it. He would always choose to keep her in a down-padded room so she'd remain safe her whole life.

Suli shook her head, then walked to the armoire. When she opened it, she ran her hands over a select few garments. Sliding some to the side, she plucked a few out only to shove them back into another spot.

The handmaid had been in Gisela's company for years and yet she thought it was possible to hide her discontent? A frown tugged at Gisela's lips. "Out with it, Suli."

Throwing her hands down by her side, Suli spun on her heel. "Why would that beast have you learning to hunt, my lady? It isn't right." Her eyes darted to the floor and she twisted her hands in her apron.

Gisela's eyes narrowed. The truth was, her sisters had been on hunts before. They'd learned archery, had ridden across the fields in search of pheasants and foxes. Gisela had to remain behind in the castle, or waiting on the field to congratulate them, and all the while she felt jealousy brewing within, ugly and angry. *It isn't fair*, she always repeated to herself.

So, what was so alarming about her learning the same skills?

"I don't quite get your point, Suli." She ran her fingers along the blisters, the pain distracting her from the annoyance blossoming in her chest. "You know all of my sisters have learned the same thing." Besides, she knew Knorren was a beast, and he'd been crass with her from the beginning, but he hadn't yet tried to hurt her. She recalled him catching her from the briar patch, saving her from a painful fall.

Suli's eyes widened as if she'd realized her misstep. "No, it's only that . . . I didn't mean . . ." She huffed, looking to the ceiling like it'd give her guidance. "I'm sorry" was all that she said, giving no clarification, and Gisela was fine with that. Somehow, she knew the woman would only dig herself further into her hole.

"He isn't so terrible," Gisela added.

Suli spun around, gawking at her. "My lady—"

She held up a hand, imploring the maid to listen. "I cannot explain. He has moments where . . . he's nothing like the demon everyone paints him to be."

Knorren could have lost his patience amid his tutoring, but he hadn't. He'd stayed with her for the day and not only instructed, but encouraged her in his coarse manner. He was so certain she'd become capable of hunting, even with the unsteadiness of her hands. How could he be so certain? Even those closest to her would shake their heads. If an obstacle presented itself to her, they'd simply remove it or make a work-around so Gisela never had to face it.

Suli's face reddened. Whether it was from her prior embarrassment or withholding a remark, Gisela couldn't say. "Still, to think of putting you in such a position—"

"It was refreshing." Even if in the moment Gisela hadn't felt that way, Knorren found some part of her capable of performing. That, in and of itself, was reflective.

"The king wouldn't be pleased," Suli murmured, closing the armoire. She took a moment to peer out the window, then crossed the room to Gisela. "It's a good thing His Majesty is devising a plan."

Gisela's fingers curled into her palms. She darted to her feet, crossing the floor until she stood in front of Suli. She didn't care what her father thought about her learning archery, but she did care about this plan. "What?" Her heart galloped wildly. That was the last thing she wanted to hear. Why was her father attempting to break the peace between Knorren and everyone else? Whether or not she was his daughter, the greater good depended on her remaining in Todesfall.

Suli pressed her lips together, wincing. "I shouldn't have . . ."

When she tried to pull away, Gisela caught Suli by the wrist. Her grip, although weak, rooted Suli where she stood. "Tell me what is going on." If her narrowed eyes didn't demand it, her tone certainly did.

Suli nodded. Her eyes found a spot on the floor. "The king plans to infiltrate the forest. He's restless and beyond heartsick about you, my lady."

"He cannot!" she shouted, her heart pounding furiously. Gisela released Suli and it was she who took a step back. She pressed her fingers into her eyes and shook her head. "The killings will only continue. Soldiers will die, doesn't he see this? The villagers will continue to die!"

Suli's lips pinched together and her eyes filled with tears

as she went to comfort Gisela. "Your father is amassing an army that isn't just Tursch, it's Drenburg's army as well." She stroked her hand along Gisela's shoulder. "It's a good thing, my lady. Trust your father."

"No!" She pulled away, feeling as though someone struck a blow to her gut. Gisela rushed to her writing desk and withdrew a piece of parchment and a quill. Quickly, she penned a letter, asking her father what his course of action was, if it was true that he was pressing on, and if so, if he could hold. If Gisela could buy enough time to postpone his attack on Knorren, perhaps Gisela could buy time to come up with a peaceful solution for all.

Would her father listen to her this time? She doubted it. But all she could do was hope he'd listen to her this once and truly hear her.

Gisela pulled away from the desk, folding the letter as she crossed the room. "This will never end if someone doesn't stop the cycle. Whether you agree or not, I didn't ask." She ran down the hall then the stairs and searched for Maxim.

When she made it to the servant quarters, she pushed open the door leading outside and found him kneeling in the garden. He turned toward her with a puzzled expression. Maxim shared the same features as his sister. Small nose, ashen hair, and soft brown eyes.

"My lady?" Radishes dangled from Maxim's fist and his brows raised in alarm at the sudden intrusion. "Are you all right?"

"I'm fine." In truth, no, she wasn't, but if this letter could be delivered, maybe then. Gisela lifted her hand and waved the letter. "Can you deliver this letter to my father, as soon as possible?"

Maxim tossed the radishes into a basket and cleaned his dirt-covered hands on his breeches, then stepped forward. The morning sun caught in his hair, lending the top of it a golden halo, and the longer tufts danced in the breeze.

"It's urgent, Maxim." Gisela pressed, then closed the distance between them and pushed the letter into his open hand. "Can you ride as quickly as you can and deliver it? Please?"

He nodded but seemed perplexed by the urgency. "I'll leave as soon as I can mount up."

Relief flooded Gisela. If she could get the letter into her father's hands, then there was hope. "I'll take over the garden."

Maxim's internal struggle reflected itself on his face. His teeth caught his lower lip and he shook his head. "You don't have to tend the gardens. I can do this for you."

Still, she'd finish what he started, whether he expected her to or not. "And Maxim . . ."

His eyebrows lifted in question. "Yes?"

"Ride as fast as you can."

Maxim slid the letter into his pocket and offered a crooked smile. "You have my word."

When he left, Gisela was alone in the garden. Even though she was surrounded by blooming flowers and bountiful beds of vegetables, she hadn't tended to any since leaving her home. Perhaps this was what she needed.

Kneeling in the garden, she began to pluck the weeds free from the new sprouts of vegetables. It wasn't long before Violet knelt beside her and placed a hand on top of hers.

"You don't have to do this. You are a princess of Tursch, and as such, I cannot allow it." Violet frowned, her fingers gently squeezing Gisela's, reminding her of the sores on them.

Violet meant well, surely, but this was one thing Gisela would gladly help with. "Please, I enjoy this."

The woman glanced at her, then pulled a pair of leather gloves from her pocket. "At the very least, wear these. The state your fingers are in . . . they don't need dirt in them."

Relief flooded Gisela. If one more person told her she couldn't do something, she'd scream. Gladly, she tugged the gloves on and ignored the stinging of the blisters. "I miss my gardens at home and if it's meant to nourish all of us, I'd like to help too."

Violet nodded, then grabbed a fistful of weeds to pull from the earth. "What was it like in the castle?"

What could Gisela say to that? It was home, but it was also confining, too. Here, amid the woods, even unable to leave, she almost had more freedom. "It was my home, but it didn't come without its issues." Her voice trailed as memories flittered back to her. Mostly of her sisters' cruelties, and of how worried her father would become. There were also good times too. Like when she and Jana would escape to the market, or to the fields to ride. Sometimes, they didn't have to leave the castle at all, and instead would simply absorb one another's company.

"The castle was chaotic. Todesfall is far more quiet." She laughed, plucking up another handful of weeds.

"And a lot less is expected of you, I suppose." Violet carefully navigated the statement, but still winced as she looked over to Gisela.

"No," Gisela paused, her hands stilling as she considered the statement. Sadly, more was expected of her in Todesfall because whether Knorren voiced it or not, he believed her capable of performing what he demanded of her. Unlike those in Tursch. "More is expected of me here and I'm glad for it."

Violet pressed her lips together and shook the dirt from a clump of weeds. She shifted, seemingly uncomfortable with the tone of the conversation. "Suli seems . . ."

"Suli has a good heart. She witnessed Knorren tearing through a crowd of people, and watched as he took me away from my family. I don't fault her for any of her opinions, especially since she's been with me for so long." Gisela plucked the last bit of weeds from the raised bed and moved to the next.

Violet remained quiet for a moment, then added, "I'm not a fan of that beast, but since you've been here, he hasn't slaughtered anyone and for what it's worth, he is far kinder to you than he was . . ."

"Please don't say her name." Gisela closed her eyes and choked on a sob as Anna's face surfaced in her mind. But her hands stilled in the dirt. If that was what her presence in Todesfall achieved, then she would have done it again if the chance presented itself to her.

And that was exactly why her father must listen. No matter what.

TWENTY-FOUR

*M*uch to Knorren's dismay, villagers had begun entering the forest. He could do nothing as they traversed what he'd claimed years before. As furious as he may have been with them, he still hadn't seen proof of troops entering the forest. It was disappointing. Part of him wished that Werner broke his word, that he'd send soldiers into the woods so that Knorren could once again hunt the humans.

Now that Gisela had sent a correspondence to the king, Knorren wondered how bold the little human was. Would she deliberately send a message to her father, divulging information to him about how and where to strike the beast of Todesfall? He didn't know. And that infuriated him further. Her illness wasn't a farce, that much he knew, but that didn't mean her meekness was no more than a mask.

Although, as he reflected on their tutoring session, how could it be? She had been on the verge of tears from frustration and fatigue.

Knorren snarled as he sniffed at the ground. Vexed by his warring thoughts, he lifted his head, distracted by the intrusion of yet another image of the girl he didn't quite know.

Why did he want to trust her? Why was the idea of her betraying him so unpleasant?

He swung his head toward the side as the sound of a horse whinnying echoed in the woods. The scent of them carried on the same wind that ruffled his fur. Whether or not Gisela sent for them didn't matter; they were dead just the same.

Knorren leaped onto the trodden path and followed the scent of the troop. When the crimson-and-gold banners flew ahead, he knew at once Gisela had betrayed him. With fury fueling his movements, he raced toward them and released a shrill bark.

"He's here!" a man cried.

Horses scrambled as Knorren pounced forward and blocked their path. He loomed over them with bared teeth. "Your foolish king has broken his treaty of peace so easily?" Saliva dripped from his jowls as he stared down the humans and yearned to sink his teeth into their flesh. Their blood would taint the ground, as would their bones, but it would satisfy the thirst for death that grew in him.

One of the men closest to Knorren struggled to control his rearing horse. "N-no," he stammered. "We are on our way to Grunstadt. I swear it on my life. We were sent by the king, but not for what you think. There is talk of a rebellion growing . . ."

Knorren edged closer, which sent the horses skittering backward. "A rebellion against the king?" Ylga had mentioned the unrest, but surely a rebellion against the king wasn't brewing. Or maybe it was. If Werner appeared as weak, what then?

"Y-yes. Against the king and crown. Haven't you s-seen

anything?" The leader of the soldiers pressed his quaking horse forward, carefully navigating the small space between himself and Knorren.

"No." He pulled away from the human and stood to his feet, scenting the air. Aside from few dregs of humans passing through, there was no heavy presence in the area. "They haven't dared to pass yet." He didn't lower his guard, not trusting the men not to turn on him in an instant, but their weapons weren't raised. If they were here to attack him, wouldn't they have drawn them already? "How long has this been going on?"

The man shifted uncomfortably in his saddle then wiped his brow, which dripped with sweat. "For months . . . The unrest has been building. Have you not heard?"

The same man as before spoke, and Knorren assumed he was the captain, especially since he wore a cluster of golden leaf pins on his doublet. "Whispers here and there, but I don't trust any of them." His head cocked, studying the man whose composure grew steadier the longer he was in his presence. "I certainly don't trust you." Knorren's lip curled as he paced back and forth. His plumed tail caught on thorns and several burrs.

The man's gaze shifted as he looked to his comrades. "Your games have led to discontent among the citizens of Tursch, and some militias have formed. There have been attacks in the capital, and elsewhere, pushing for a revolution."

Knorren paused to the side of their path. Guilt didn't nip at his conscience—it was the king's fault for antagonizing him. Every ill deed had a consequence and that was something he knew far too well. Werner's consequence for playing a game he couldn't hope to win would be the end of the king.

With bared teeth, Knorren growled at them. "Go, and don't stray from the path or I may not be so generous next time we cross paths."

He bounded away into the green foliage of the forest, and when he was far enough, he swiped at the dirt in irritation. Ylga had tricked him, or maybe she hadn't. He wasn't certain any longer of what the witch's end game was. Was she destined to torment him for the rest of his days? Confusion aside, something akin to relief flooded him to know that Gisela hadn't written to her father asking for a rescue attempt.

A strange new feeling rushed through his veins and he wasn't keen on it. It flooded him with something other than hatred, and it felt . . . oddly pleasant. A warmth grew within his chest, pulsing, and it unsettled him. What was happening?

A few days later, Knorren lounged in the midday sun, basking in its warm rays. The sound of an approaching horse caught his attention, but the scent was one he was familiar with: Maxim. He barely roused as the boy walked into the yard, but when the rustling of movements became awkward, Knorren forced his eyes open.

Maxim eyed the entrance toward the castle, as if wondering how to get past the fox. When he took notice of Knorren staring at him, he almost collapsed to his knees.

Knorren squinted as Maxim's foot landed on the tip of his tail. It didn't hurt; it wasn't pleasant though, and it made Knorren's voice harsher than he intended. "Well? What is it?"

Maxim's face paled. "I'm sorry . . . I have a letter for Gisela." He waved the sheet of paper in his hand.

From who? Had her father written her again? An involuntarily growl thundered in his chest. Maxim, who had visibly just gained his confidence back, looked as though he wished the bridge would give way and devour him on the spot. With little patience left, Knorren yanked his tail from underneath Maxim's foot, which made the boy stumble backward. "Klette!" he bellowed for Gisela. She was inside after having successfully hunted a deer earlier and, per her words, she wanted to know how to prep one after it was slain.

The princess's curiosity and willingness to learn was commendable, to say the least. Never did he think she'd take to death as well as she had. Although she'd initially feared the castle and the death that permeated the woods, she'd seemed to settle in little by little.

Moments later, Gisela emerged from the castle, dressed in a forest-green gown that clung to her slender figure. Despite living amid a forest, far from the civilization she grew up in, Gisela seemed to flourish. Instead of drawn and pale, she seemed stronger in Todesfall. Color filled her cheeks, and her figure had filled out too.

A familiar animal scent filled the air. Metallic and mouth-watering. *Blood.* Knorren's eyes roamed over Gisela's figure again and noted the blood stains on her apron and on her hands. Tufts of fur also peppered her dress.

So she'd been addressing the deer's carcass herself? *Impressive*, he mused.

"What is it?" she asked, breathless as if she'd been running through the halls. Her pink cheeks puffed as she drew in a quick breath. At once, Gisela's full lips pressed together as she eyed Knorren, then Maxim. Confusion wrote itself across her expression, wrinkling her brow.

"You have a letter." He stood and stretched, only to sit and curl his tail around his legs.

"My lady," Maxim called from behind Knorren, stepping forward with the fluttering piece of parchment.

Gisela's pert nose scrunched up as she took the letter from Maxim and broke the seal. She scanned the words quickly. "There was an attack on the castle," she whispered, eyes widening. "How could they? That is their sovereign."

"And a degenerate," Knorren offered.

Gisela's posture stiffened. Her eyes found his and a challenge swirled within them. "Don't speak of my father like that. You don't know him."

"I know him well enough from his actions, Klette. Haven't you heard the saying 'actions speak louder than words'? His actions beg for someone to rise against him." His tufted brows slanted downward, waiting for her to hurl a verbal barb at him, but it never came.

"Even so, he is still king." Gisela spoke rigidly, her fingers clamping onto the letter. She looked torn, as if she wanted to ride off to Tursch Castle to ensure everyone was all right. Knorren surmised she'd do just that if he allowed it.

"He won't be king for long if he continues on his cowardly path," Knorren drawled as he padded toward the bridge at the opening of the courtyard. Maxim, reading the growing tension in the air, slipped inside the castle, leaving Gisela and Knorren alone.

"And you would know?" She pressed forward, looking up at him.

He did, in fact, know, only because of the soldiers he'd seen in the forest. Knorren lowered his head, his snout close enough so that as he exhaled, his breath tussled Gisela's curls. "I know, because Grunstadt is prepared to move against him. His capital has moved against him, too, so what happens when they all unite and attack the castle, Klette? What then?" Knorren hissed.

Gisela's eyes widened. Horror crept into her face and she turned to her handmaid, who hurriedly walked to her side.

"It's true," the maid agreed, looping her arm through Gisela's. She tried to pull her away from Knorren, but she didn't budge. "What the beast says is true. The attacks are growing bolder and more frequent . . . but I never suspected they'd attempt one on the castle."

"Dear Wurdiz . . ." Gisela's eyes trained on the ground and her shoulders sagged. She looked as if she'd collapse at any moment.

The handmaid lurched backward then turned to run back inside the castle, but not before she pinned him with a gaze that conveyed the hatred she possessed for him. Knorren's nose bumped into Gisela. It was light enough so that she didn't rock backward. "Wurdiz will not help you or Tursch."

"I thought . . . I thought that if I came here, all of this would stop." Gisela's voice broke. She crumpled the letter in her grasp, but even as Knorren pressed his nose more firmly against her, she didn't pull away.

Her voice sounded hollow to him. Oddly enough, guilt nipped at the edges of his conscience, threatening to spread within. *Don't. Don't let it.* Nothing good would come from letting her wheedle her way into his conscience entirely. Gisela would no doubt take root in Knorren like one of the blasted burdocks or roses.

A soft sob shook her shoulders, then she leaned against Knorren's muzzle. Her fingers played with his whiskers, and it shifted a piece within him. Another lock shifted open and rather than snap, or push her away, Knorren endured the gentleness she offered and in turn gave her what comfort he could.

No words tumbling from him would do it, so he remained quiet.

"I must stop this," Gisela finally said, fingers still coming through the fur beneath his chin.

Half drowsing from her soothing scratches, he growled in protest at her words then again as her fingers stilled. "No. You will not." Knorren's voice rushed out, sounding far harsher than he intended. "Gisela . . ."

Her back stiffened the moment the words left him. "Then what is the point of me being here?" Gisela's tear-streaked face turned up, her glistening green eyes staring up at him accusingly.

The point of her being in Todesfall was . . . His mind blanked. Originally, it had been to cease the killings, but now . . . he wasn't certain.

Knorren's eyes narrowed as Gisela rallied. She looked as if she wanted to say something. Those plump lips of hers parted and her cheeks puffed with every breath she took, likely warring with what to say—or not say. She turned on her heel and stormed into the castle instead, leaving him confused and blinking.

Gisela was not some hero from tales of old. Yet, here she was, wanting to dash into the proverbial battlefield with nothing more than her voice. The notion angered him, but as Knorren considered why, he grew uncomfortable with an unfamiliar feeling: worry.

Trouble was coming to Tursch whether the king was ready or not.

TWENTY-FIVE

*W*ith each passing day, Gisela grew more restless. The not knowing kept her up at night and during the day she penned letters to her father, hoping for a response. But nothing came.

When a week had passed, she could take no more and decided perhaps she could face Knorren's wrath with the promise of a return. If it had been her first week with him, there was no way that she would've considered such a careless decision, but in a week's time, they'd formed somewhat of an understanding of one another.

Knorren was by no means a gentle spirit. Nor did he perform acts of kindness in the typical sense, but after her initial fear dissipated, Gisela realized he pushed her to her limits and expected more from her than she'd ever had demanded of her before.

He believed in her.

In turn, she participated in his little games and when she fussed, Knorren found his amusement.

Today, however, Gisela was done with games. She stormed outside, pausing in the courtyard to glance around. Knorren wasn't anywhere to be seen, but as she continued onto the bridge, she saw his face appear in the treeline.

Instead of his laughing smile that usually pulled his lips back, his facial muscles were tense, which gave Gisela pause. She took a step closer to him, quickly glancing over his legs, paws, and chest for any indication of injury. His sides rose and fell, like he'd been running.

"What is it?" Dread snaked its way through her, twining around her pounding heart.

Knorren's yellow eyes flicked toward the side. "Villagers are growing bolder in Todesfall," he began, his voice a low, menacing growl. "Some with weapons, and others purely out of curiosity."

He didn't have to say it. Gisela knew what it meant. Soon, they'd see how far they could push Knorren before he snapped and gave them cause to attack in self-defense, never considering how Knorren would also be defending himself.

She shook her head and closed the distance between them. Lifting her hands, she waited for his snout to meet her fingers. "I need to go to my father."

"No," he growled, finality in his tone.

Gisela withdrew her hands, bunching them into fists. Then what could she do? If he didn't trust her to leave, what other options did she have? She heaved a sigh, pacing in front of him. If not the castle, then perhaps the village?

"If you will not allow me to leave, can you at least show me?" She did her best to keep the hope from her tone, but when she turned and peered up at Knorren, he was scarcely paying attention to her. His head lifted as he sniffed the air.

With a rumble, Knorren lowered himself to the ground. His head moved to the side as Gisela approached him. "I cannot bring you close to Hurletz. But I'll bring you as close as I can."

And that was good enough for Gisela. It had to be.

She clutched his fur, pulling herself up and onto his shoulders. Scooting forward, she twined her fingers into his pelt and prepared for the butterfly-inducing movement. No matter how many times she crawled on his back, when he rose to his full height and moved, her stomach flipped.

But Knorren had given up an easy pace and ignored Gisela's tightening grasp on his coat as he fell into a lope. It wasn't as jarring as a horse's gallop, since he was so large his fur pillowed her body. The motion felt like a massive rocking horse, but this high up it still made her stomach lurch.

Sunlight trickled through the canopy, casting flickering shadows on the ground. Although it meant the pathway had less obstructions, the lighting made Gisela's stomach knot all the more. This time it had little to do with how high she was.

By the time the forest gave way to the village's road, the scent of smoke tickled Gisela's nose. *That's odd*, she thought, *there are no homes so close to the forest . . .*

Knorren swore as they emerged from the woods.

Before them, the once-bountiful fields of wildflowers blazed, catching the nearby trees on fire. Black smoke billowed into the sky, reaching for the hot morning sun. Gisela watched in horror as the fire lapped greedily at the dried grasses, devouring whatever was in its path.

"Who would do this?" Accusation dripped from her tone.

"Humans," Knorren bit. Leaping off to the side, he circled around the fire to see if there was a way closer to Hurletz not blocked by the flames. "Their cruelties surpass mine. And I'll never understand how they can think of me as the villain when they'd do this to their brethren."

Gisela wanted to dispute the fact, but wasn't it the truth? Her heart ached for those that would be affected. Frantically, she glanced around in hopes of finding a source of water or something . . . No, someone. Knorren.

"Knorren, you must run toward the other side of the fire. I have an idea." She hunkered down, coughing as the smoke grew thicker.

"Are you mad?" Incredulity crept into his tone as he stood rooted to his spot. Safe.

Desperation crept inside of her, oozing into every fiber of her being. "Please, Knorren. People and their livelihoods depend on it."

"What do I owe to people?" he quipped. "As I see it, they don't even owe anything to their brethren."

Time was of the essence and if all the fox wanted to do was bicker, then she'd figure out a way without him. She shifted from her seated position, rising, but she stopped as Knorren craned his head around to look at her.

His eyes narrowed on her and his snout halted her. "What are you doing?"

"I'm going to help."

"How?" His eyes rolled, then a deep, resonating growl emitted from him. "The devil take you, Gisela. Sit down, I see a way closer." He bounded around the wall of flames, coughing violently. "Now what?" Knorren wheezed as he looked side to side. His ears fell flat, giving him a pathetic look even from where Gisela sat.

Now what? The question echoed in her mind. "If we don't have water . . . we need . . ." She looked down at the charred earth. The grass had long since burned away, but left behind was ash—dirt. Gisela couldn't hope to dig fast or deep enough to make a difference, but Knorren could. "I need to get down."

"No." Knorren shoved his nose against her, righting her in place once again. "You'll stay where you—"

"Luka!" a woman's voice cried out. "Luka! Where are you?" Wind, created by the fire, shifted the smoke so that Gisela could see a portly woman frantically searching for her son.

"The boy?" Knorren blurted. "Get down," he ordered, tone hardening as tension stiffened his muscles.

Gisela could feel every sinew tighten, and she wondered what was happening. "Are you all right?" The woman's gaze settled on Knorren as Gisela climbed down his shoulder and slipped to the ground. The air was better on the ground, but not by much as the smoke wafted up from the dirt.

"No!" the woman bellowed, as if she realized what she saw was in fact real and not an apparition from the smoke. "You devil," she sobbed. "Not my boy!"

Knorren shook his head and rather than stay put, he leaped over the wall of flames, disappearing behind the curtain of fire and smoke.

Gisela gasped, running forward, but then halted as the heat nearly scorched her from afar. Instead of standing and gawking at the fire, wishing Knorren would return, she ran toward the woman.

"Miss!" she called to her, "Miss! Get away from the fire." Reaching the woman, Gisela pulled her away just as Knorren leaped in front of them. A small bundle hung from his mouth and the mother shrieked in horror.

Lurching forward, the mother grabbed a rock with the intent to hurl it at Knorren, but he carefully lowered the boy onto the ground. Gisela hadn't the time to thank Wurdiz or soothe the woman.

With wide eyes, she tilted her head back to look up at Knorren. "Dig as fast as you can. Create a barrier that the fire can't cross!"

Knorren cocked his head. With narrowed eyes, he glanced down at her as if she'd lost her mind. But dirt was their best option and he was large enough that his paws could unearth more dirt than any shovel.

Gisela watched as he turned and jumped toward the advancing flames. Then, she rushed to the boy's side. Ash covered his figure from head to toe. Small burns littered his bare arms, cheeks, and legs. But he was alive.

Coughing, the boy turned onto his side and vomited. "I-I told you . . . Knorren wasn't bad." His eyes connected with his mother's and then he collapsed to the ground, eyes rolling into the back of his head.

"He needs help. I don't know what the smoke or heat has done to him." Gisela glanced at the mother. "Did you come here on foot?" Her brows raised as her voice rose an octave. If she did . . . How was this boy going to get back home to the aid he needed?

"Luka, my baby," the woman crooned over her son, pulling his head into her lap. She brushed the hair from his brow and rocked.

Helplessness burned in Gisela's chest. But as she searched the area for Knorren, he was nowhere to be seen. The smoke had grown thicker, but the fire seemed to die out, which meant the dirt was working.

Torn between staying put and finding Knorren, she opted for the latter and ran alongside the new dirt path. On the other side of it was a trench—another barricade for the fire. Freshly churned earth melded with smoke. The sun had long since disappeared behind a veil of smoke too.

With no sight of Knorren, worry settled in. Her eyes darted along the ground in search of the fallen fox, but nothing. She couldn't see his shadow looming either. Where was he? She ran as fast as she could, crying his name.

"Knorren?! Where are you?" *Please be all right, please be all right.* She rounded the corner of flames, then saw a panicked Knorren running toward her.

"Run!" he bellowed, then dipped his head, grabbing Gisela up in his mouth. The sound of groaning wood reverberated in the clearing, then the telltale snapping as a tree fell. It shook the ground as it collided with the earth.

Gisela tumbled down as Knorren unceremoniously deposited her in a dirt pile.

The woman crept backward, shielding her son. But Knorren scarcely paid her any mind; his eyes were latched onto Gisela and he was panting hard.

"Who did this?" he finally breathed. "Who set fire to the field?"

Panic filled the woman's eyes, but she stroked her son's back to soothe herself. "The rebels. This is my family's field, and we want no part of politics. They razed our barley fields for it." She nodded in the direction of where the flames were petering out. "Luka tried to extinguish the fire."

"The rebels?" Gisela echoed, then glanced up at Knorren. He was right. Humans *were* awful. As evil as Knorren was painted to be, he didn't turn on his kin—his neighbors. And, despite what everyone thought of him, he was here, helping in some manner. "We need to get him back home, Knorren." Gisela motioned to the boy.

"Luka," he supplied. "The boy's name is Luka."

Knorren had met him before? The mother's expression softened, but it puzzled Gisela.

"Climb on." Knorren lowered himself and because Luka's mother was still unsure, Gisela went first, then motioned for Luka's mother to pass him up.

He was older than Byron, but not much bigger than him. She wiped her fingers along his ash-covered cheek and frowned. Luka shouldn't have had to suffer because of the rebellion. Gisela tugged the boy against herself and he wheezed.

When his mother settled in behind Gisela, Knorren slowly made his way toward the town. But even Gisela could tell he was hesitant. His movements were slow, uneven—was it because he was known as a demon in these parts? Knorren was surely tempting Wurdiz's good graces by venturing into the village.

Maybe, just maybe, Wurdiz would smile upon Knorren for this good deed.

Turning to glance behind them, Gisela was glad to see the fire dying down. Thankfully, there was little wind now so the flames weren't capable of leaping wildly. And, as luck would have it, it started to rain.

Twenty-Six

*E*very pad on Knorren's paws throbbed. Between the digging and treading on the hot grass, and even embers, they had burned. The gravel beneath him did nothing to soothe the pain either, but the little boy needed help and Gisela needed to return to the castle.

After witnessing how empathetic she was to Luka, Knorren felt compelled to help as well. He knew the boy and Luka had trusted him on some level. But why had he felt compelled to help? It gnawed at his mind. Was it simply because Gisela had urged him to?

When he'd found the boy surrounded by the flames, Luka was curled up in a ball, sobbing. But when he'd seen Knorren, he didn't tremble; instead, he'd reached his hands out and his eyes had filled with hope. Not fear. Hope that Knorren was there to save him.

And he did.

Knorren gulped down a breath of fresh air, but it felt like razor blades along his throat and in his lungs. "What house?" he grumbled as he meandered down the road. A farmhouse came into view. It was nothing worthy of poetry. The house boasted a roof in dire need of rethatching. Moss covered it so heavily, it looked as though it were intentionally green. The muddy-colored bricks reminded Knorren of a pig's pen, but he wasn't about to criticize someone's dwelling. Not when he lived in a castle full of skeletons.

"This one here," the woman offered.

The mud-brown house with a green roof. Of course. Knorren lowered himself, grimacing as pain lapped at his paws like invisible flames.

Shakily, the woman slid from his back and took her son. "Thank you." She tentatively stepped to face Knorren, even daring to connect her gaze with his. "For helping us, for saving Luka, and for being exactly how he described you."

Curiosity nipped at him. He'd only ever been called names and told that he was a demon who crawled from the depths. "What did he say of me?"

"That you were kind and helped him before with his friends." She looked down, biting her lip. "I didn't believe him, but now I see . . . Thank you." The woman's gaze shifted over his head. "And you . . . I can't ever repay you—"

"You don't need to." Gisela's voice was hoarse, likely from the smoke she'd sucked in as she ran. "See to Luka and be well." Droplets of water cascaded down her cheeks, dripped from her hair, and saturated her dress.

She was soaked through.

Knorren took that as his sign to stand. His muscles protested, pulling and aching from the exertion of digging. Instead of retreating onto the path they came on, he veered off and pushed into the cover of the woodlands. The ground was slightly more forgiving than the dirt road, but even treading over sticks sent shockwaves of pain through him.

"Knorren," Gisela's voice came, concern straining her tone. "What is wrong?" Her weight shifted as she leaned forward, and he felt her fingers as she combed them through his fur.

"I'll be fine," he ground out, and even though Gisela didn't press any further, he could feel tension rippling from her. She didn't believe him, and why should she? He was traveling far slower than usual and he couldn't disguise the limp as much as he wanted to.

By the time he arrived at the castle's stone bridge, Knorren couldn't stand the searing pain any longer. He stumbled over the bridge, collapsing to the ground. Dust kicked up, as did dried rose leaves and petals.

"Knorren!" Gisela clambered down his shoulder and ran toward his face. Her fingers stroked at his whiskers. "What is it? Tell me, you stubborn fox." When he didn't reply quickly enough, she pulled away, searching for an obvious affliction.

The concern tugging at her lips, furrowing her brow, both amused and touched him. He chuckled amid a growl of pain, then nudged her with his nose. "I'm not dying just yet, Klette." His gaze homed in on her features, watching as the worry shifted into confusion. "My paws are burned and from the smell of it, bloodied."

"You fool," Gisela snapped and rushed to one of his paws, inspecting it. She knelt and gently pushed the tufts of fur between his pads away. Judging by the gasp, they were, in fact, burned and bloodied. "Why didn't you tell me?" she asked shakily and looked over one of his other paws, which was just as burned as the other.

"Listening to you fuss over my well-being doesn't tickle me." Knorren kicked out his legs behind him, his lips tightening against his teeth. Waves of pain tempted him to lash out at her, but he reeled himself in. "Go inside, you're soaked to the bone." He glanced at her and surprisingly, Gisela didn't say a word as she stormed off into the castle.

He watched until her form disappeared through the door and found, for the first time, he wished she'd remain by him instead.

Droplets of rain pelted him, but he lowered his head onto his legs, enduring the shower as it came down. It both stung and soothed the raw pads.

Unwillingly, he whimpered in pain. Licking them wouldn't soothe them.

But the sound of shoes slapping against the wet cobblestone interrupted his misery and when Knorren turned to look at the advancing figure, he was surprised to see Gisela with an armful of . . . what?

"You'll get an infection if . . ." She ducked her head and knelt by one paw.

Knorren barred her way with his muzzle. "What are you doing?"

"Helping you, even if you don't want it." Gisela uncovered a jar and scooped out a gelatinous mixture that smelled of mint. When she rubbed it on his pad he growled, but he was relieved when it numbed and cooled his burn.

One by one, she applied the remedy to his wounds. For as cruel as he had been to her, as much as he'd pushed her, she still showed him nothing but kindness. This puzzled him and that foreign ache within him throbbed again.

Knorren closed his eyes and rubbed his cheek against her. "Silly girl."

"I am not the one who is being silly." Gisela lifted her

hand and scratched near his whiskers. She smiled up at him, her long curling lashes fluttering in the misty rain. Errant curls sprung loose from her plaited hair, kissing her temples.

He grunted at her words but allowed her to run her fingers along his ears and his cheek. But it was the soft kiss she pressed to his snout that startled Knorren. His ears swiveled as he stared down at her smiling face.

"Do you enjoy sitting in the rain?" Gisela lifted a brow, glancing around the bridge before she looked to him again.

"It doesn't bother me, and after the fire, it feels rather nice."

She nodded, then bent to pick up the mess she'd made. "Then I'll leave you to rest. Allow the cream to set before you run off."

As if he'd be running anywhere any time soon. "Have you taken to being a healer rather than a princess now?"

Gisela's lips tilted at the corner's and her eyes shot to him. If he wasn't mistaken, she was smirking. How dare . . .

He laughed as he rolled to the side, focusing on her slender figure. She didn't cower before him, didn't avoid his eyes . . . The brazen princess had somehow flourished in a forest of death and pain.

"There is nothing wrong with being both. Otherwise, you'd have necrotic paws." When he didn't respond, she turned away from him and toward the castle. "Come inside when you have the strength. I don't like seeing you in the rain." Without another word, she left him on the bridge as she went inside.

How he felt about her words he didn't quite know. She continued to show him kindness when he deserved nothing.

Knorren closed his eyes, grimacing as a throbbing pain thudded within his chest.

A faded memory tumbled through his mind, but every time he went to grab it, it vanished. Just a laugh, just a smile . . . from when?

TWENTY-SEVEN

*D*ays turned into weeks. The heat of summer was winding down, and if the subtle cooling of the air wasn't enough to hint to that, a few leaves on the birch trees were turning gold.

Gisela snatched a leaf from a low-hanging limb and ran her finger along the ridges. It was strange to her—in the past few weeks, she'd grown stronger. She felt *good*. Through Knorren's tutoring, she'd learned to hunt successfully and with it came muscles she didn't even know she possessed. Her body may have ached before, but now it felt capable.

Stranger still, it had been because of Knorren that she felt this way. In her time since arriving in Todesfall, his barbs had lessened and she discovered she had grown to care for him. The fox still muttered things he ought not to, threatening to consume her, or implying he'd storm Tursch to ravage the kingdom. Knorren still grew irritated, but it was less and less than before.

Gisela climbed down a hill, using the protruding rocks as a natural staircase as she descended into the gully. It was uncomfortably warm out, and she'd discovered this place while she hunted with Knorren, but without him she was free to strip off her clothing.

She shed the simple layers and walked into the body of water. A fresh pond presented itself to her. Cool enough to cause her to gasp, but it soothed her overheated figure.

"Do you think it's wise to be by yourself?" a voice cut through the silence.

Gisela gasped. She twisted to face the speaker and found a pair of clever yellow eyes staring at her.

"K-Knorren, you shouldn't be here." Gisela folded her arms over her chest in an attempt to hide her curves from him. But his gaze remained unreadable. Why did she care if he saw her bare? He was a fox or a demon.

"Neither should you. Not alone anyway."

He had a point.

"There is no one for miles," Gisela argued, flicking her hand across the top of the water.

"That's not what I meant. There are other tragedies that could unfold."

The initial edge to his voice faded and Gisela knew what he meant by that. She frowned. Even without incident, her ailment was still like a dark cloud hanging in the distance, waiting to drench her at any moment. It reminded her of her father, and how he never allowed her to venture out on the water or anywhere too far from the castle.

"You sound like my papa." She slanted a look in his direction, noticing the way disgust tugged his lips upward— as if he were about to retch. "I cannot simply cease to live because of what *may* happen."

"I am nothing like—like that spineless excuse of a king!"

She propelled herself in the water until emptiness pulled beneath her legs. Gisela hadn't been victim to a fit since the last time she'd run out of the herbs, and it was an exhilarating feeling. The anxiety surrounding when the next one would occur lessened and she felt free to simply live.

How strange in a place that was meant to be her death.

"Are you worried about me?" She cocked her head to the side, eyebrows lifting.

Knorren dipped his head toward the water and lapped at the coolness. "Don't be foolish." But like before, there was no bite to his words. "And how do I sound anything like your father?"

Gisela mused for a moment, considering whether or not to tell him. "When my sisters go on family hunts, I am not allowed for fear of falling and causing a fit. Nor am I allowed to join them on the ship for the same reason. If we're stranded for any period of time and cannot get herbs . . ." She flicked her hand in the water again.

Knorren stared at her and remained as still as a statue, making his expression unreadable. "Hurry. The sun will be down soon enough and we must head back to the castle."

Whatever response she'd expected from him, that wasn't it. A part of her wish he'd shown, just a little, that it bothered him too. Gisela dipped below the surface, then popped back up. The chilly temperature of the water sank into her bones, lowering her core temperature. That was all she wanted. Even if worrying the fox delighted her on some level, because it meant he had come to care about her well-being.

"Close your eyes when I get out."

Knorren eyed her. "Why?"

Gisela gawked at him. Was he serious? "I'm not wearing clothes . . ."

"And neither am I."

"You're a fox!"

Knorren flopped onto the ground. His dark brown paws covered his eyes as they closed. It wasn't necessary for him to take the extra step, but it did amuse Gisela.

She raced to where she left her clothes and pulled them on in haste. "You can open your eyes now." Her fingers tugged on the stays of her bodice, then she quickly tied them.

"Hop on. I don't need you reduced to a pile of skirts and sweat before we even get to the castle."

Gisela snorted. "You have so little faith in me?" She walked up to him, her fingers scratching behind his soft ear. In return, he groaned and leaned against her hand.

"It is but the truth."

She took a fist full of his fur and tugged roughly, then climbed up his shoulder and nestled onto his back. Whether Knorren said it or not, he had more faith in her than she even did.

He'd proven that with the way he pushed her into hunting and every time he pressed her to traipse through the forest. By him forcing her into the scenarios, he'd inadvertently made her stronger.

Knorren treated her as if she were perfectly capable and she *was*. She had always been. It was only that she struggled to show this to her family and over time she'd begun to believe that she was no more than her illness. But Knorren saw beyond that and treated her no differently than he treated Violet, Maxim, or Suli.

"Hold on tightly."

She buried her fingers in his fur as he stood and leaped into the brush to bound off toward the castle. More than a few times, Gisela flattened herself against his neck as he raced beneath lower limbs that would have struck her otherwise. Riding Knorren beat walking miles through the woods for hours, and it was liberating, too.

When they were on an open path, Gisela sat upright and relished the feeling of the wind whipping through her curls, and the way it brushed over her skin.

In no time, they arrived at the castle, and Gisela promptly slid from Knorren's back to the ground. Knorren stretched much like a cat and yawned before settling in a sunny spot.

Gisela smiled before entering the castle. She wasn't the only one who'd changed in the passing weeks. The castle had too. Gone were the cobwebs, scattered leaves, and bones. Much to Suli's dismay, they'd all spent hours cleaning room by room until it felt less like a prison and more like a home to Gisela. In doing so, she'd stumbled on relics of the Golden Prince. Mostly ruined letters that she couldn't make out. Knorren didn't share her excitement.

"Your Grace, you received a letter while you were gone." Violet pulled the paper from her pocket and handed it over. "Maxim didn't seem very . . ."

Gisela took the letter and unfolded it. "Very what?"

Violet fiddled with the hem of her apron. "There were soldiers assembling at the edge of the woods. My lady, I—"

"No!" Gisela's gaze focused on the parchment in her grasp and she pored over every word. The villagers had grown bolder in the past weeks, setting fire to Todesfall as they had the field weeks prior, but none had ventured too deeply, at least not as far as the castle, likely fearing Knorren would destroy them.

As Gisela came to the end of the letter, the sound of her heart pounding in her ears was overwhelming. Her father was coming into the forest? He couldn't come to Todesfall. He couldn't! If her father came, it would ruin the peace between Knorren and Tursch. As it was, the kingdom didn't need Knorren terrorizing it again. More than that, Gisela didn't know if she wanted to return to a life where she was treated as if she were made of glass.

A cry of frustration erupted from her and she ran through the castle doors and to the slumbering Knorren. He roused instantly and blinked his golden eyes at her.

Gisela stared into his eyes for a moment. "If I asked you to go away for a time, would you?"

"What is this about? Another letter?" His ears swiveled then flattened against his head. Knorren touched his nose against Gisela's torso and rumbled. "What has the dolt said now?"

"Please. Answer me." She remained firm.

Knorren appeared to consider her words. "It depends on the reasoning."

Gisela stretched her arms out, wide enough to spread across his muzzle in an awkward embrace. "My papa intends to come for me. I have tried for weeks to soothe him and let him know that I am well, truly well. But he doesn't believe me." Which was true. She'd pleaded with him to let it go, and told him that she was thriving in the woods. He didn't believe her. "And with the rise of the threats from Hurletz and Burlitz . . ." Although, a thought struck her as she lay against the fox's muzzle. What if she allowed her father to see her? Would it calm him?

"Then he is even more foolish than I suspected," Knorren growled. "I will not run with my tail between my legs!" A tension formed beneath Gisela's fingers as he snarled.

Stroking her hand along the underside of his muzzle, she tried to soothe him. "I'm not asking you to run. I'm asking you to trust that I won't flee, and I'm asking you to remain safe." Gisela's fingers brushed along his coarse whiskers. "Please. If anything happened to you . . ."

Knorren remained quiet for too long. Gisela stepped back to look up at him and discovered he was watching her closely.

He sighed. "If I do as you ask, you must do something for me in return." There was no bite to his words, but why did he sound so fatigued?

"What? What do you wish?" If it meant him remaining safe, then chances were she would agree to it. Unless it was something she couldn't promise him.

"What I ask of you, Gisela," he began, and the use of her name sent shivers down her spine, "is that when you come to a crossroads and you're faced with two choices, choose with your heart." Knorren didn't elaborate. His words confused her and the tone of defeat felt like a blade to her heart. Did he believe she'd betray him?

The wind ruffled his fur. "It is nearly autumn, and before we know it, snow will coat the land. I will return when the last leaf falls, but no sooner." Knorren stood and pointed his nose toward the golden sky. The sun still had enough strength to pierce through the thick canopy of pine trees. "You have my word on that. But know that if you trick me, the treaty will have come to an end." He stared down at her, unblinking, and then added, "It would be a shame if I had to devour you now."

Gisela didn't know whether he was jesting or not, but she nodded, knowing that even if he didn't trust her entirely, she knew herself and her heart.

She didn't want to leave Todesfall.

But Gisela did want to ease the unrest.

PART III

"In his deepest heart there surge tremendous
shame and madness mixed with sorrow
and love whipped on by frenzy and a
courage aware of its own worth."

— *VIRGIL, THE AENEID*

TWENTY-EIGHT

A yellow leaf tumbled from the canopy of trees and fell on Knorren's nose. With a breath, he disposed of it and watched as it zig-zagged down to the ground. The leaves were changing earlier than usual. No doubt it would be a cold winter and a brutal season for the surrounding humans to endure.

Normally, Knorren wouldn't take them or their worries into consideration, but with a field of wheat destroyed, and the possibility of other affected crops, it was at the forefront of his mind.

Tap, shhhck, tap, schhhck.

The repetitive noise cut through his musings. Knorren glanced around and found no one, but the sound continued. He stuck his nose into the air, drawing in a deep breath. The smell of salt air and bread wafted toward him. Knorren realized then who it was and growled.

"Egon." The annoying little man leaned into view. He remained seated on the ground, whittling knife in hand, and wore a smug grin. "Aye. Do you need my services?"

"When have I *ever?*" That wasn't entirely true. There were a few occasions when the strange little being came in handy, none of which Knorren would ever admit to.

Egon huffed, then slipped behind the tree again. "I didn't seek you out. You're the one here, aren't you?"

Knorren supposed Egon was right, but he hadn't been looking for him. At least, as he thought about it, he didn't *think* he was.

As he mused over this, his tufted brows shifted. But it was Egon who broke the silence. "I think you ought to visit Ylga. Even I can sense something is troubling you, fox." Egon rose from the ground and dusted his dirtied knees off. He held a half-carved wooden figurine of a horse in one hand along with his whittling knife. With one finger, he flicked a bead of sweat from his wrinkled brow. "Did you eat the princess?" he asked slowly, horror etching itself on his features.

Knorren barely twitched as the question tumbled from the dwarf's lips, and while he should've been insulted, he found the inquiry amusing. At first, his lips puffed with restrained laughter, then they shifted into a wicked barking fit.

"And if I did, what would it mean for you?" Knorren crept forward, looming over the small man. The notion Knorren would even feel insulted struck him as foreign. Why did he care? Knorren shifted his gaze to the side. The phantom touches of Gisela's fingers combing through his fur, teasing his whiskers, and murmuring into his neck distracted him.

I care because of her.

Egon's face paled considerably. "You didn't." His fingers tensed around his tools. "Then hell's gates will welcome you soon."

Knorren's ears flattened against his head as he launched

forward, striking a paw at the dwarf. It was enough force to send him crashing backward. "If only that were true, but your endless need to insult me grows tiresome. And if anyone is on the verge of being eaten, it's *you*." As much as Knorren may have wanted to snap Egon up in his jaws, he turned on his haunches and leaped toward the path that would lead him toward Ylga.

Still, as he trotted down the beaten road, Egon's question and the look of horror and disgust on his face grated on Knorren. *Why, why does it offend so?*

By the time he reached the beach, the tide was high and the foamy waves rolled up the shore, greedily lapping at the sand. The air was still and far too humid for Knorren's liking. Even the seagulls didn't seem too ambitious as they bobbed along the rolling waves.

"Well, look what the tide brought in." Ylga stood in the doorway to her hut, wiping a towel around a bowl. "To what do I owe the pleasure?" Her milky eyes followed him as he sidestepped into the tall grass and off the blazing sand.

Aside from Egon suggesting that he seek Ylga, why was he at the witch's hut? When he thought of it, his mind kept dragging him back to the one who could end his days on this cursed earth.

Ylga's hand paused mid-wipe as her eyes locked with his. "Ah, I see." The way she focused on him was unnerving, but what crept beneath his skin more was what she may have gathered without his consent.

"Do you now?" he ground out.

She placed the cloth into the bowl, then leaned it against her hip while she waved her free hand in the air. "It has begun, has it?" Her words, though vague, made sense to Knorren.

The shift inside of him. The bargaining. The truce. All of it pointed toward a monumental change, which meant, hopefully, his time in this world was nearing the end. But why did the notion strike him like an arrow in the chest?

"I don't know," he replied earnestly. "The king refuses to listen to his daughter and with the rebellion growing steadily, it's only a matter of time before the castle is overthrown." And what then? When Knorren was no longer the biggest threat in the kingdom, what would become of Gisela? *Not him.* Would they infiltrate the forest to capture Gisela and use her to make Werner bend? He couldn't stomach the idea.

Ylga must've seen his uneasiness, because she hummed loud enough to catch his attention. "She is the one who can help you in the end, Knorren. Listen to that tug in your chest. What does it tell you?"

Knorren let loose a breath of frustration. "To listen and wait." Gisela had told him to leave and so he did, because that piercing throb in his chest nudged him. And the genuine worry in her beautiful eyes moved him to believe she truly cared for his well-being. Him. A demon.

Ylga nodded. "Tell me what happened, all of it."

So he did, and Knorren spared no detail. When he finished, the witch's lips twitched. "How about that? Despite your wickedness, someone has grown fond of you. Some would say that the princess knows no better, but I'd wager this is the most freedom she has ever had in her life."

It was. Gisela had divulged that much to him. How she could never hunt with her sisters, or venture out on the ship in fear that she would succumb to her fits while at sea.

Perhaps it was why he pushed Gisela so hard—because she never had been before—or maybe it was his cruel ways, finding pleasure in how it might break her. But Gisela thrived in her lessons, and she grew strong as the weeks passed.

Knorren snarled at the intrusive thoughts.

"You should know, the wind has carried a lot of chatter lately." Ylga smiled, following an invisible *something* with her eyes.

There was certainly no wind here.

Knorren struck a paw in the sand then lowered himself abruptly, his head resting on his forelegs. He was done with her cryptic speeches.

"The whispers say the king plans to march into the forest, but it isn't for you." Ylga leaned against her hut, her eyes growing distant as she stared past him. "The rebellion marches for the castle, and Werner wants to put an end to the threats."

"But not take his daughter back?" Knorren scoffed. "No. I know the truth. He sent word to Gisela already, which is why I'm here." Werner would never step foot into the forest and leave without Gisela, and Knorren wasn't about to let that happen. She belonged to *him*.

"So what I hear is lies, then?"

Did she know something he didn't—that Gisela didn't?

Ylga drummed her fingers on the bottom of the bowl and laughed. It was a wet, hacking sound that inspired Knorren to shudder. "She's wound herself around your black heart, has she?"

He growled lowly, not wanting to admit how fond he *had* grown of Gisela. If he did, then there was a chance something or someone would rip her away from him. And that wouldn't do. "It doesn't matter."

The witch set down the bowl on an outside table, then slowly made her way up to Knorren. She placed her hand on his nose and didn't move. "What are you willing to do to protect the one you care for, and she for you?" Her voice came softly, without a taunt, without bitterness.

"I would do anything I had to." His words came too quickly. He couldn't stop them, but when he glanced up at Ylga, she nodded with a warm smile. His words had pleased her? How? Why? "I would kill *for her*."

"And what, do you think, Gisela would want from you? Do you think she'd be keen on you killing in her name?"

A simple question, but one that clouded his mind with visions of Gisela screaming at him, begging him to stop killing. Exactly as she had at the festival. "No." His voice sounded hollow, even to himself. "But if it meant saving her, then it is what I'd do."

Ylga pressed her lips together, nodding. "Let's hope it doesn't. But remember, each action you take will have an outcome. Choose wisely, Knorren, and you may find your way home." She tucked her hands into the sleeves of her oversized shawl. "Stay here for as long as you like."

Until the last leaf fell, he would abide by his word and remain hidden, as much as he could, and far away from Gisela. But Knorren would be lying if he said it didn't unsettle him. Gisela could take care of herself, of that he had no doubt, but it was others he didn't trust.

Would Werner storm into the woodlands, snatch his daughter away, and lose her to the rebellion? Knorren growled as he stewed over the possibilities.

"Only until the last leaf falls. Then, I suppose we'll see who gets to kill the king first: me, or the rebellion."

Ylga clucked her tongue as she shoved his muzzle. "Then you haven't learned your lesson."

A wicked smile tugged at his lips. "Time will tell, won't it, witch?"

TWENTY-NINE

*N*o matter how many times Gisela told herself that Knorren leaving was for the best, it didn't seem to soothe her. She lifted her hand and brushed a fresh trail of tears from her cheek. It was strange to miss him. Her captor. Gisela knew that. But he'd grown to be so much more. A tutor, a protector, and a friend.

Whether or not Knorren would see it, he'd changed, too. He *saved* Luka and carried the boy and his mother to safety.

"Did His Majesty indicate when he'd arrive?" Suli pressed carefully. Judging by the way her eyes remained trained on the floor, she knew how deeply upset Gisela was. "I will pack your things for you—"

"No!" Gisela shoved the drapes in the castle's front hall open, then turned on her heel so quickly that Suli took a step back. "I'm not going back to the castle. Do I make myself clear?" She clenched a fist at her side, frowning. "How many times must I say it? My father made a deal with Knorren and I won't aid him in breaking it. And I certainly won't have any part in the destruction of Tursch." She strode away from the windowsill and clenched her jaw.

The sound of Gisela's quick footsteps echoed in the empty hall, reflecting the anger boiling within.

"My lady! I'm sorry, I just thought—"

"That's just it, isn't it?" Gisela halted and stiffly turned to face Suli, who was red-faced and on the verge of tears herself. "Everyone is so used to thinking and doing for me, when I'm capable of it." She stretched her hand out, motioning to the castle. "How is it, I wonder, that I've survived here? No, *thrived* here, when I'm so weak, Suli?" Gisela shook her head as she continued down the hallway. The sound of Suli's shuffling told her she followed along. "Within the week, my father will arrive. And for the last time, I'm telling him no."

Suli drew in a sharp breath. "You will spend the rest of your days in this castle of rot and death?" Her voice came out in a shocked whisper. Perhaps she meant no harm, but Gisela narrowed her eyes and spun around.

Gisela stood taller as a rush of confidence filled her. "I will spend the rest of my days living the life that I choose." She briskly turned her back to Suli and walked away.

Perhaps a few hours in the gardens would soothe Gisela, and she could devise a semblance of a plan for when her father arrived. What would she say? How could she evade him if he tried to capture her?

Despite how Gisela's feelings toward Knorren had changed, she wasn't sure how *he* felt. If he still viewed her as an annoyance or a pawn. But his threat before he departed still echoed in her mind. Would he make good on his promise? He'd threatened to devour her if she ran.

She didn't *want* to run.

Gisela placed her hands against the wooden door that led to the gardens, and she glanced over her shoulder to see if Suli lurked behind. She didn't. Sighing heavily, Gisela dropped her head and frowned. "I am done living the life others want for me," she said to herself as if it were a vow.

Turning down the hallway, she pushed the door open to the backyard and stepped into the garden. Immediately, she saw the surprised faces of Maxim and Violet. Instead of dwelling on the upcoming turmoil, she knelt beside Violet, who didn't say a word, and plucked up weeds.

Although Violet had only known her for a few months, the woman knew when to press her to speak and when not to. Unlike Suli, who often overstepped her bounds. Perhaps it wasn't Suli's fault, but everyone in Tursch mirrored the same idea of how Gisela's life should be: quiet, uncomplicated, and controlled.

"Thank you," Gisela murmured.

"Whatever for, my lady?" Violet lifted her eyes, a curious glint within them.

She smiled, leaning back onto her heels. "For simply being you."

In the evening, a strong sense of curiosity struck Gisela. The past few weeks she'd been at the castle in Todesfall, she'd only explored the hidden passage once. That night it felt as though it were beckoning to her, so when the sun had set and cast darkness over the forest, she decided to venture downstairs.

Gisela carried a lamp in one hand and lifted the skirt of her nightdress as she approached the hidden door beneath the stairwell. A cool rush of air swept along her curls, rustling them against her temple and forehead as she opened the door.

It smelled damp inside, musty, like before. This time, she wouldn't allow her nerves to spook her out of the tunnel. Cobwebs as thick as pulled cotton hung above her head and she grimaced, hoping the ones who wove them were long gone.

Water dripped somewhere in the tunnel, but Gisela couldn't make out where it came from. She slid on a wet patch of stones, gasping and gripping the wall to steady herself.

She approached the alcove she visited last but noticed there was a deeper passage, one that led down two steps. Gisela descended then glanced around the room with wide eyes as she took in a wall of shelving. Dusty, web-covered books lined the walls, and on the far side sat a small desk. Or, at least, she assumed it was a desk. It was covered in grime. *What is a hidden study doing here?*

As she looked around, she found a lamp full of oil and used her own flame to ignite it. The wick crackled as it burned away the dirt, but it remained lit.

Gisela yelped as a face loomed above her, but when she squinted, she realized it was only a portrait. Lifting the lamp, she studied the face. The red hair, smattering of freckles, and confident tilt of the lips. It was the Golden Prince. With her heart hammering in her chest, Gisela slid around the desk, both intrigued and driven to find out more about the prince that Knorren devoured.

What had he been like outside of what history dictated?

She blew a fraction of the dust away from the desk before she pulled open a drawer. Nothing. She sighed, then pulled on another one. This time, the drawer contained yellowed pieces of paper. Pulling them out, Gisela laid them on the desk, and her brows furrowed at the first line on each one.

My darling prince.

My dearest one.

My heart.

Love letters hidden in the prince's desk? *But why?* Gisela drew up one letter and took her time reading it.

My darling prince,

How I've missed you! Mother says it's pointless pining away for a life that isn't attainable, but I know the strength of our love. I count the days until we can meet in secret again. When you return from the hunt, please tell me all about it. I can nearly imagine you sitting on top of your horse with a bow in hand.

I miss you.

Always yours,

Lenora

The prince had a secret lover! Gisela's heart fluttered. From the sounds of it, she wasn't a noble. No history lesson spoke of this, or mentioned the prince's love life at all. They only knew him for the abrupt end of his reign.

"What sort of secrets did you possess, Prince Jannik?" Gisela flipped through more letters, stilling as she scanned another. The ink had been smudged in some spots, as if water had dripped onto the words. The letter wasn't addressed to anyone, but the words leaped out at Gisela.

Jannik, please rethink your decision. I love you. Mother says your greed drives you, but I know you're only thinking of what is best for the kingdom. I stand by you no matter what. Please, meet me on the edge of Todesfall.
Lenora

What had changed from the first letter to this one? Gisela twisted in the chair and glanced up at the portrait. The prince's yellow gaze stared out at the room and his eyes held a wealth of secrets. She didn't miss the sparkle deliberately painted in them, and there was also something almost familiar about them.

Instead of continuing to read, Gisela rummaged through the open drawer. Her fingers grazed something metal that gave her pause, then she pulled it out and realized it was a locket. As she opened it, a miniature portrait of a woman stared at her. Hair the color of autumn tumbled down the woman's cherubic face, and her dark brown eyes brimmed with life. On the other side of the locket the words "Keep me close to your heart. Always" were inscribed.

"You truly loved him, Lenora. But what happened between the two of you? Was it Knorren?" Gisela wound the chain of the locket around her hand, then grabbed the lamp. How long had she been in the passage? She stood from the chair and gave one good look at the prince's portrait. "Whatever you did, I hope it was for the best." She blew out the extra lamp, then left the secret study.

Gisela yawned. Her discovery weighed down on her, even as she left the tunnel. If only she hadn't sent Knorren away, if she could ask him a question about the prince . . .

There would be a time, but for now, she needed sleep.

But a restful sleep would not come once she settled into her bed. No, instead she dreamed of a flock of crows with beady red eyes. All but two flew away, and they stared at her with their beaks gaping. Concern flooded her as she approached them, but they scattered, settling on the road once again. This time, they sat on opposite roads.

Before Gisela could focus on the signs, a familiar shriek cut through the air.

"Choose with your heart," Knorren's voice rumbled through the woods.

THIRTY

O f all days to be exhausted, to feel the worst she'd felt since arriving, today was not the day.

Gisela ground her teeth together as she slung her bow over her head and tightened the quiver strap on the other. It took a moment to balance herself; the waves of dizziness passing over her made it difficult. A sour taste formed on her tongue, making her feel nauseous, but it was all a part of the prelude. All hints that a fit was lurking around the corner surged within her. *Not today, you will not do this today.*

Suli followed her into the stable, remaining as quiet as she had been since Gisela had snapped at her. It wasn't within Gisela to be mean, but she was through listening to others attempt to control every piece of her life and tell her what she was or wasn't capable of.

The little mouse was no more, and in her stead was a lioness.

At the end of the barn, Maxim's horse stuck its black head over the door. He bobbed his head in excitement and nickered softly to Gisela.

"Good boy, Orin," she murmured as she approached. Reaching into the pocket of her dress, she produced an apple and held it so the horse could bite into it. "I hope you take care of me today." She'd been riding him when Knorren wasn't around. It'd been so long since she'd ridden on a horse, and she had needed the practice.

Suli fidgeted at the opening of the barn and, judging by her pinched lips, there was something she longed to say.

Gisela arched a brow in question, but then thought better of pressing her handmaid. She could swallow her concern along with whatever chastisement likely rested at the tip of her tongue.

Gisela ignored Suli and tacked up Orin, then led him outside. She mounted him and stared down at her hand-maid's pale face. "Someone must break the cycle, Suli."

The other woman rubbed her eyes tiredly. "I know. Believe me, I know." She sighed heavily. "And I've seen how you communicate with that . . . with Knorren. You speak to him as if he's not a monster. If I hadn't I don't think I ever would've believed how he is with you, but—"

"But this still isn't a place for me to live?" Gisela supplied, refusing to let her shoulders slump as much as they may have wanted to.

Suli nodded.

"But it is my choice." With that said, Gisela urged Orin on and, rather than wait for her father to approach, she opted to seek him out. The bow was for precaution because although she had seen no rebels walking about, she also hadn't dared to venture too far from the castle since Knorren had left.

The late morning sun peeked through the canopy above, casting a warm golden glow throughout the woodlands. Autumn touched the flora with her crisp fingertips, painting the tips of the birch trees yellow and the maple leaves a brilliant red.

Orin's hooves churned up the softened earth from the previous nights' rain shower. It lent the forest a heavenly aroma. Pine mixed with the smell of ozone and dirt. A fragrance Gisela loved. And on particularly humid days, she could detect a hint of salty air.

She pushed the horse on faster through the woods, leaping over fallen logs and darting through various paths she'd come to know. Then she heard it: the sound of men shouting in the distance. She slowed Orin's pace and halted him so she could listen more closely.

"I've not seen a thing, Your Majesty! No sight of the beast!" a man cried.

"He won't be far off. Keep looking!" It was her father. Gisela hadn't realized how much she'd missed the timbre of his voice and it pained her to hear it.

"Papa," she whispered. Doubt slithered into her mind, hissing and whispering how weak she was. But then, Gisela focused on all she'd accomplished so far and urged Orin forward. *No mouse*, she told herself, *no mouse any longer*.

The horse propelled them over a fallen log and into the clearing where her father's men waited. In the middle of them sat her father on his puffing mount.

His eyes widened as realization dawned on him. "Gisela!" Werner urged his horse forward and looked her up and down, then focused on the bow. "My Mousy, is he here? We will surround him." His voice trailed off as he surveyed the immediate area.

Already his attention was elsewhere, and Gisela grimaced. "Papa. Knorren isn't here. I sent him away."

"You?" He sounded surprised and his expression said as much. "How?"

"I asked him."

Her father laughed as he leaned forward. "Come home while the beast is out hunting." A shadow passed over his gaze, unsettling Gisela. There was something he wasn't saying.

"Why?" Her tone was quiet, meeker sounding, even though she felt anything but that. "Why now? What's going on?"

For a moment, it looked as though her father would simply brush it over, but he sighed and, with an exhale, his composure fled. Her father looked exhausted, as if a strong breeze would unseat him at any moment, and when she truly glanced him over, she saw the bags beneath his eyes and the worry furrowing his brow.

"The rebellion grows each day. We received word that they're setting fire to the forest to flush Knorren out, and they'll be coming to Tursch Castle next." He sounded defeated already, but how could that be? They'd not even fought yet.

"No," Gisela breathed. "They can't do that." Wherever Knorren was, she hoped he was safe. She hoped he'd taken her words seriously and hid.

Werner nodded, frowning. "I'm afraid it has come to this. We must vanquish them before they grow anymore. They've already amassed quite the following."

"When?" Gisela pressed, taking advantage of the fact her father was divulging the most he'd ever in her presence. He wasn't brushing her off, nor was he chastising her for asking. As long as he was willing to speak, Gisela would question him.

"Within the month, I'd wager." He rubbed his fingers along his brow, smoothing out the wrinkles. "Gisela, please come home. We've all missed you."

In the past weeks, Gisela had thought less and less of home. She'd wondered how her sisters were, had even asked Suli, but they hadn't cared. None except for Jana.

"You and Jana are worried. The others are no doubt relieved to be rid of me." She shot him a look, frowning as her father stammered in an attempt to protest. "Don't bother denying it. I know them, and they know little of me. But I will not leave this forest and break the treaty between you and Knorren."

Aside from the horses snorting or pawing at the ground, quiet filled the clearing. Her father broke the silence by coughing. "You will come with me." It was an order.

Gisela's eyes narrowed. "I said no." She pulled back on Orin's reins and the gelding backed up. It was enough signal for her father to attempt blocking her from escaping, but Gisela had spent hours riding and maneuvering through tighter spots than the pathetic attempt at a blockade he'd created.

Orin reared up and Gisela shifted her hands up his neck, clinging to his mane. He pirouetted with ease, then bolted forward as she jammed her heels into his sides. Her father cried out to her, and with one last glance at him, she shouted, "Return home! Don't come for me again!" The words struck her heart like an arrow, but it wasn't safe for either of them. Knorren would return and if she wasn't there, the kingdom would fall, but if the rebellion truly grew and they were going to burn the forest down . . .

When Knorren returned to find ash where his home once was, what would he do? Who would he attack then? And more importantly, how could she even stop him if he were truly enraged?

A flash in the corner of her eye distracted her. She saw one of her father's men riding along on another path. Panic crept up her throat, clenching it tightly. He was going to make this difficult. Gisela understood it came from a place of love, but he was foolish and oblivious, too.

"Come on, Orin, don't let me down!" she shouted as the horse leaped over a fallen tree, following her every subtle movement as to where to run. Gisela opted for a narrow path with lower hanging branches. Typically, she avoided them, but she refused to be caught.

A loud and wet *thud* sounded behind her, but she didn't take a moment to look over her shoulder. She sent up a prayer to Wurdiz, hoping the rider would recover.

Orin didn't cease galloping until they were at Todesfall Castle once again. Gisela's chest ached as she gulped down air and the horse's sides puffed quickly. Even though there was a chill in the air, perspiration dripped down her neck. That was close. Too close.

"Gisela?" Maxim rushed to her side. "Are you all right?" His eyes scanned her from head to toe. Worry wrinkled his brow and tugged at his lips.

"Yes," she managed, swallowing another mouthful of air. "But the forest won't be for much longer." Gisela lifted her eyes to the trees above and shook her head. They needed to prepare for the worst, and if they could find any allies, they needed them now.

"What do you mean?" Maxim held Orin's reins as Gisela dismounted, but his eyes never left Gisela.

A well of frustration bubbled within her. All of this could have been avoided if it hadn't been for her need of herbs. No, she wouldn't allow herself to dwell on what had been. They needed a solution for the problem at hand.

She stepped forward, bracing her hands against Maxim's shoulders. "Listen. Tomorrow, I must ride into the village to find allies."

Maxim's face reddened. "Absolutely not." His dark eyes searched hers, attempting to find an answer that wasn't there. "What is going on?"

Gisela told him. She told him what had transpired between herself and her father. Maxim cursed as he pulled away.

"I'll come with you. I don't want you to go alone . . . especially if this is what the rebellion is planning." His eyes softened as he caught her gaze. "Let me help you. Please?" His voice was quiet, on the verge of an intimate whisper, and something in it sent a chill up Gisela's spine. It wasn't unpleasant, but it forced her to take a step back and keep a respectful distance from him.

When had an underlying tension formed between them? Gisela swept curls away from her eyes and chanced looking at him again. Maxim was still studying her closely, and it made her cheeks warm.

"I'd appreciate the company."

Maxim nodded, smiling tightly, before he led Orin toward the stable.

When he disappeared around the corner of the castle, Gisela released a breath. A companion on the journey would comfort her, and Maxim was from the village. He'd know who to trust, who to ask for help, and who to avoid.

Which meant Gisela needed to solidify a plan of where they'd go and what they aimed to accomplish once they were there.

The library was Gisela's favorite spot in the castle. One wall consisted of all windows, which showed the sloping hills. She could see the tops of the trees, the changing colors, the evergreens, and even a small lake. The other wall was all empty shelving. She supposed once there were books, but even when she'd arrived, nothing had been there. Just torn pages, decomposing leaves, and bones.

As she sat near the window at the desk, she lifted a quill and scratched down her ideas.

Gisela was never taught diplomacy, but some things people were born with, and that was one of her strong suits. The villagers would need someone to trust and look to for strength and support. She could be that person for them.

The sound of approaching footsteps gave Gisela pause. She looked up to see Maxim striding into the room. As he walked up to her she could smell hay, and the scent of Orin's sweat clung to him.

"Writing a letter that will change the course of history?" he teased, grinning roguishly.

It wasn't out of the ordinary for Maxim to grin at her, but

there was something else hiding in the crinkle of his eyes that formed butterflies in Gisela's belly. It confused Gisela at times, but he never purposely made her feel uncomfortable. He was too sweet and far more soft-spoken than his sister.

"If only." Gisela shook her head and stood from the desk, motioning to the couch in the middle of the room. "Come, sit with me. I'd prefer to not have someone looming over me." She plopped down on the couch, adjusting the skirt of her maroon dress.

Heat crept up Gisela's neck and into her cheeks. But to Maxim's credit, he said nothing on the subject. "Let's devise a plan to create our own militia." He leaned into his corner of the couch and arched a thick brow.

"A militia to stop a militia?" She laughed.

"Well, if that's what it takes. Maybe instead of weapons we can lob ears of corn at them." He winked and twisted a lock of hair around his finger. "It's an idea."

While it was nonsense, Gisela laughed and it was a welcomed break as the weight of the situation settled on her.

THIRTY-ONE

*I*n the morning, Violet found Gisela in the courtyard, staring out across the changing leaves. A light fog spread through the trees, making it almost impossible to see between them. It was eerie and beautiful all at once. An apt description of the forest.

"Good morning, my lady," Violet murmured, then cast a look toward the stable. "Are you and Maxim ready?" There was a lilt in her tone that caused Gisela to glance at her. Violet smiled, a glint in her eyes. "Maxim will ensure you're safe, I promise." She hesitated before continuing. "He's fond of you, you know."

Gisela's cheeks warmed at Violet's words. Unsure of how to reply, she murmured, "Is he?" She didn't know how to feel about it. Part of her felt as if she were betraying herself, but that was a silly notion. Maxim was kind, handsome, and treated her as every bit of a capable being as she was. However, Gisela never took a moment to process how she felt beyond a friendship with him.

Violet bit her bottom lip and glanced over her shoulder. Horse's hooves clapping against the cobblestone courtyard announced Maxim leading Orin and his other horse, Tula, out of the stable.

For a moment, it looked as though Violet may tease her in front of him, and Gisela was readying to grab a hold of her wrist if that were the case, but when Violet smiled at her brother, Gisela relaxed.

"Protect her with your life, Maxim, because it'll be your life if anything happens to her." Violet's tone was hard, but love shone within her eyes as she closed the distance between them and embraced him. "If Knorren returns and anything has happened to her—"

"I know," Maxim murmured.

If? No. *When* Knorren returned. Gisela had told none of them he'd left because she had pleaded with him, nor had she mentioned when he'd return. Everyone knew the beast of the forest enjoyed coming and going as he pleased. This time, Knorren would be gone longer, and Gisela hoped it would keep him safe.

Violet squeezed Maxim tightly, then gave him a kiss on the cheek. "Don't be stupid, either."

Gisela's lips twitched, then she gave in to a laugh. "I promise I won't let that happen. No idiocy allowed."

Violet locked eyes with her and said, "I will hold you to it."

Gisela nodded, then slung her bow over her shoulder and took Tula's reins before mounting. "I expect nothing less." She smiled and looked at Maxim. "Let's ride." When he mounted, they were off and rode carefully through the forest.

The fog didn't let up even as they left the woods. The charred earth was so bleak, particularly on the crisp, sunless day. A shadow hung over Hurletz, as if the village knew what lay ahead. It unsettled Gisela.

"It's all right, I promise." Maxim attempted to soothe her. His dark eyes locked onto hers. "We will do exactly as planned. We'll seek Luka's mother out and go from there."

Maxim sounded so sure of himself, but doubt gnawed at Gisela. She could see things from their perspective. What had her father done to protect them from Knorren? If they couldn't exact their vengeance on the beast, what was the point of siding with Gisela?

Orin moved closer as Maxim guided him toward Tula. His hand reached out and grabbed Gisela's, squeezing it. "Trust in yourself." When he pulled his hand away, he motioned to the dirt road in front of them. "Besides, it's too late to turn back now."

Gisela groaned, but urged Tula forward into the village proper. It was quiet even though it was late morning. The few individuals who milled around outside barely glanced her way. There was nothing that currently screamed royalty about her. She wore men's breeches instead of a dress for ease of traveling. With no banner, no entourage, Gisela looked like any other traveler.

Soon, Gisela halted in front of Luka's modest home. She could smell something baking in the oven. The warmth of bread or some baked dessert.

A little boy hung halfway out of the window, his eyes rounding as he saw Gisela. "It's you!" He finished climbing out of the window, and was followed by a scolding.

She laughed, waving to him as he beamed at her, then she glanced at the mother. A frown tugged at Gisela's lips. She never got the woman's name.

"Oh, Your Highness," Luka's mother lowered her eyes and bobbed a curtsy before scooping her son up in her arms.

Her brow furrowed in question as she looked at Maxim, then Gisela again. "Is there—why don't you come in?"

"Of course, but please, what is your name?" Maxim slid from his horse and then moved to grab Tula's reins as Gisela slid down. She stretched her legs, withholding a groan as the blood flowed into them again.

The woman blinked and placed her hand over her heart. "Adeli." She bowed her head. "Come. I've just baked some fresh apple strudel."

Gisela's stomach growled in protest. She'd eaten a light breakfast, but knew since she'd be on a journey, that a heavy meal would sit like lead in her belly. Now she was famished.

Adeli set Luka down and corralled him into the cottage. She took up a broom and fussed over the dirty floor. "I'm sorry it's a mess." Color rushed to her cheeks and she refused to glance at Gisela again.

The home was cozy and far cleaner than where Gisela currently lived. "Don't apologize for what you have. Your home is lovely." She smiled, waiting for Adeli to motion toward the small table near the window Luka had crawled out.

Adeli was quick to grab a plate and cutlery as she brought the fresh streusel over to the table. "I made fresh cream too." In a blink, the woman grabbed a bowl of freshly whipped cream and Gisela fought the temptation Luka did not. For he swept a finger in the bowl and promptly licked his finger.

"Yum!" Luka grinned.

"Now, let's hear why you're visiting us so soon." Adeli scooped a portion of the streusel for herself and settled down at the table, looking from her to Maxim.

Gisela and Maxim took turns explaining why they were there and what the rebellion was planning. Adeli didn't seem surprised, but she appeared worried.

"I don't-I don't know what you think I can do..." Adeli shifted in her seat, fiddling with her fork as she stared down at her empty plate. "I'm nobody."

Those words tumbled around in Gisela's head. "No," she said, reaching across to still Adeli's hand. "You're not a nobody. I think you're capable of more than you know. But what you can do for us, you can be our ears, and you know the villagers. See who you think will rise against the rebellion and fight for the kingdom."

"The king, you know, he's angered so many people." Adeli spoke carefully, but Gisela wasn't blind to her father's faults. She knew. "I don't know how many will rise for him, when he's done little for them."

Gisela relinquished her grip on the woman's hand and turned to look at Maxim. He nodded encouragingly to her. "Believe me, I know. But this is for the kingdom, not for the king. If the rebels take the castle, they will plunge the kingdom into chaos, which will solve nothing. They will destroy the forest, burn Tursch to the ground, and leave what to Hurletz?"

Adeli nodded. "I will help and do what I can."

"You won't be doing it alone," Maxim added. "I'll be helping you too."

Adeli chewed at the inside of her cheek. "There is one thing, though. Do you know His Majesty is coming to Hurletz in three days' time?" When neither Maxim nor Gisela said a word, Adeli continued. "His efforts to soothe hurt feelings in Hurletz, I suppose. I guess we will see what transpires then."

As soon as Adeli's words tumbled from her lips, Gisela froze. She stared at the woman, seeing, but not entirely hearing. "He's coming to Hurletz?" Why hadn't her father said anything to her? He had spoken openly about everything else except this. Anger rose up within, forcing her heart into a steady gallop. Gisela cupped her face, inhaling a sharp breath. "To a village full of people who want to kill him?" Her voice trembled as a wave of fear melded with the anger. Surely he had to see it was a trap, that by coming here he was playing right into the hands of the rebellion.

By killing the king, it would make overthrowing Tursch all the easier. But was this a trap for him—or was it a ploy set by her father's men to vanquish the rebellion?

The sound of thundering hooves on the road made everyone forget the current topic and lean toward the window. Outside, a gathering of riders approached the houses on the road. Riders slid from their mounts and went to doors, knocking. They weren't soldiers, that much was clear. They bore no uniform, no crest, which meant they were likely the rebels.

Adeli pushed away from the window. "They've been desperately looking for recruits. Mostly the younger men with something to prove." Her eyes darted to Maxim, and she jerked her chin at him. "Like him." She hurriedly walked toward the back of her cottage. "Follow me. I have a small shed outback. Hide in that until they're gone."

Gisela's face paled. "Hide?"

"I doubt most know what you look like, but on the off chance they do, it wouldn't be a bad idea." Maxim led the way outside and opened the shed door. It smelled of moldy dirt and was barely big enough for the two of them to fit inside. His arms wrapped around her protectively, forcing her bottom to nestle against his hips. A wave of heat washed over her and she couldn't discern whether it was from embarrassment, or that a tiny piece of herself enjoyed the feeling.

Gisela couldn't hear whether the men had entered the cottage, because the sound of her heart beating thundered away in her ears.

Maxim didn't move. He barely breathed, and she'd know because his nose was inches from her ear.

"It's clear," Luka whispered moments later.

Gisela pushed the door open. Maxim's hand swept along her hip, sending goosebumps along her flesh. "We should stay here tonight, since we don't know when my father arrives."

"Here?" Maxim's voice cracked.

Gisela blinked, then laughed. "Not here, but somewhere close by. If my father is due to arrive in a few days, it makes no sense to leave and arrive after he's in the village." She looked from Maxim to Adeli. "Do you know of anyone who would let us stay? While we're here, we can see if anyone will house us." Gisela walked to the window and glanced outside. No one milled around, not even a villager. She frowned, wondering if Knorren was safe. Gisela hoped he would remain hidden, and that word would not reach him. Could she be that lucky?

"My family farm," Maxim offered. "I know my mother wouldn't mind. I believe she'd be honored to have you house there."

Gisela nodded, then turned to Adeli. She stepped

forward, closing the space between them, and took up the woman's hands. "Thank you. I will see you soon, and in the meantime, be safe." She glanced down at Luka's chubby face. "Especially you."

Luka hurled himself at Gisela's leg and squeezed tightly. "Tell Knorren to stay safe too."

She smiled at him, smoothing his hair away from his face. It was strange how things could change so quickly. Even stranger that the beast of the forest had captured a boy's affection.

THIRTY-TWO

The ride to Maxim's home was a quiet one, full of tension from the rising threat. Even the village remained quiet, too quiet for an early afternoon. Very few villagers bustled in the streets or toiled in their side gardens. Gisela's stomach knotted with apprehension, similar to how she felt before a fit, but thankfully she had the foresight to pack herbs in the saddlebag. They weren't a cure-all, but they would soothe her enough and hopefully chase away any impending episode.

Maxim led the way down a secluded dirt road. Spindly trees lined the path, but behind them were open fields full of corn and wheat, which were ready for harvest.

A small breeze danced in between the cornstalks, brushing them together to create a melody. With it, the smell of a fire wafted toward them. Panic crept inside Gisela, but Maxim shook his head, smiling.

"It's only the masonry oven. My mother bakes bread and sells it at the market." Maxim nodded to the field of wheat.

"Oh." Gisela glanced at the field again, then urged Tula to walk faster as Maxim pulled ahead in a steady trot.

The road gave way to a larger farmhouse. It was bigger than Adeli's cottage. This home was two floors and although the roof was thatched, it wasn't moldy and looked as though it had recently been done.

Outside of the home, an older woman with graying mousy hair carried an arm full of wood around the house, but she paused as they approached.

"Maxim! Good, you're here and you brought—"

"Mama, let me introduce you to Her Highness, Princess Gisela." He bowed his head, lips twitching as he spoke.

There was a playfulness to his words that Gisela appreciated, but it brought doubt into his mother's gaze. She focused on Gisela, scrutinizing her.

Gisela dismounted and approached Maxim's mother. "I'm pleased to meet you. Maxim has told me a lot about you." While she didn't know what Maxim's father looked like, both Violet and Maxim looked so much like their mother. Rounded cheeks; dark, expressive brown eyes; and ash-brown hair.

"Princess?" the woman echoed, looking between Maxim and Gisela, as if a joke was being played on her. "Wurdiz . . ." she breathed, then clumsily curtsied with the wood in her arms. "I'm sorry, had I known, I would've prepared something."

"This isn't a joke, Mama. We have much to fill you in on." Maxim's words sobered his mother. She hurried to the outdoor oven, leaving them to deal with the horses.

Once everyone settled, Maxim and Gisela took turns relaying everything. His mother, Erna, paled at the mention of Knorren. "That ghastly beast . . . so it is true, all the reports of him abducting the princess. It's you." She placed her hand against her chest and shook her head. "Wurdiz be with you.

How have you managed?" Her eyes softened as she drew up Gisela's hands.

I am alive, aren't I? she mused. But it was more than that. Knorren had been cruel in the beginning and there were days when Gisela thought he'd surely end her life, but in the end, he'd taught her more than she'd ever learned in Tursch Castle.

"Well enough. Knorren took care of me." Doubt filled the other woman's eyes, but Gisela wasn't here to discuss Knorren or his flaws. She was here for help if it came down to needing to protect her father. And she wanted to be ready when push came to shove.

Erna nodded and bit her bottom lip. "Adeli mentioned a run-in with Knorren, but I didn't believe it." She focused on the cloth she held in her hands, running it through her fingers nervously. "Do you think the deaths have stopped for good then?"

Gisela didn't know how much Knorren had changed. But she'd seen him grow less coarse and more amiable in her presence. He gave her freedom and with it, she became stronger.

"I will do what I can to make certain of it."

Over the course of three days, Maxim, his mother, and Adeli gained a militia. They were villagers who didn't agree with the rebellion. Individuals who were furious over the loss of crops and the senseless violence.

No one wanted war or a battle, nor did they wish for

their people to be slaughtered by a demon. There was a treaty in place with Knorren, and there hadn't been a death since Anna. The mere thought formed a pit in Gisela's stomach. In the forest, burrs and roses grew for every drop of blood shed and every bone shattered, but what would grow for all the deaths Gisela caused? Perhaps it was contempt among the kingdom's people.

And that was a thought that didn't settle well with her.

In Maxim's barn, Gisela fidgeted with the strap on her saddle bag, aware of him lurking behind her. He'd gone above and beyond the past few days, but today he acted as though there was something he wished to say.

"Gisela," he called softly. Still, his voice sent a chill up her spine. She enjoyed their friendship, but that was it. "Can we talk before we ride out?"

For a moment, she allowed herself to see a life with Maxim. Her father would no doubt fight it, but eventually would relent. Maxim would live a life of luxury instead of toiling in the fields or feeding his animals. Would he be happy?

"What is it?" Gisela half turned to face him, eyebrows lifting as she forced a smile. Her fingers stilled on the strap, but they curled around it tightly as tension flooded her body. Maxim didn't notice. He stepped closer and tucked one of her curls into place.

Before he even got a word out, his mother rushed into the stable, her eyes wide and face flushed. "King Werner's party was spotted just outside of Todesfall."

Whatever calm she'd felt a moment ago was gone. Gisela's adrenaline kicked up because she knew what lay ahead of them. If it was possible, Gisela would try to stop a battle, but sometimes battles were inevitable. But death—she wanted no part of death.

Maxim pulled away from Gisela and snatched the reins to Orin. "We need to move now then." He motioned to Tula with his hand. "Whatever you do, don't ride ahead without me."

Gisela scrunched her nose. "I wouldn't, because I'm not daft."

He chuckled. "I know." Maxim's eyes lifted to take in his mother's reddened face. "Don't worry so much." He opened one arm and hugged her as she stepped in against him.

"Just come back," she murmured.

Gisela turned away, feeling as though she were intruding on an intimate moment. She thought of her own mother. What would she have thought? Certainly her father would shout at her loud enough for the kingdom to hear.

When Maxim pulled away from his mother, Gisela slipped out of the barn with her horse in tow. She swung up into the saddle, thankful for the breeches she wore instead of a dress, which would only get in the way.

Maxim mounted his horse, settling into the saddle. It creaked as he shifted his weight. Sighing, he inclined his head toward Gisela. "Are you ready?"

She exhaled, looking at the gray sky. "Not really."

"Neither am I." He urged Orin forward, and the horse obliged. "My father was the soldier. Not me, but here I am . . ." Maxim shrugged, then whistled a low tune that echoed in the streets.

The sound of shutters opening caught Gisela off guard. Not just one house, but several of them as they rode by.

They didn't exchange a single word, just opened the windows and moved away.

Maxim led them through the village, continuing the strange tune. And when Gisela turned to look over her shoulder, she noticed people emerging from their homes. But it was only those who opened the windows. Maxim's whistling. Was it a code?

At the end of the village road, where it branched off to the king's highway, Gisela halted Tula. "That was—"

"Yes." Maxim nodded, spinning around to face the direction they'd come from. "Now, we ride directly to the king." His eyes slanted as he homed in on her bow. "I hope you've been practicing. We may need that."

She glanced him over, looking for something that stuck out as a weapon, but he didn't have one. Not unless she counted the thick wooden walking stick strapped to his saddle. That hardly counted.

"You didn't bring a weapon?" Her question came out shrill. Gisela would hardly call herself a proven archer, especially under stress.

"I may find one along the way." He grinned sheepishly.

This was hardly the time for humor. "You better." She clucked to her horse, spurring her on in a steady trot. It was difficult not sending Tula off into a gallop, but Gisela couldn't risk drawing attention to them. But Wurdiz, she wanted to run as fast as her horse would go until she was near her father.

The road seemed treacherously long on the way back, but as soon as the field near Adeli's home came into view, so did the royal banners, which flew high. They flapped in the breeze, signaling the king. As if that wasn't announcement enough, the horses in the party thundered their way down the king's highway.

The display was elaborate and instilled pride within Gisela, but also horror, for they were announcing to *everyone* that they'd arrived. The rebellion hadn't thought out their attack well, for if they did, they would've left Adeli's fields intact to hide in. But now, with no wheat, and nowhere to hide, her father's party couldn't dodge any attacks either.

So where were they?

Gisela glanced to the woodline on her left, her eyes scrutinizing every minute detail. Just as she went to turn her head, the glint of something caught her attention. She focused better and saw a face.

"Maxim, to my left, archer," she whispered softly, continuing to march Tula on as though she hadn't noticed at all. But her hands clenched the reins so tightly that she thought the braided leather would leave an imprint.

He nodded. "Just smile and ride along. Our help will make their way into the woods too, if they haven't already."

The royal party surrounded the king, blocking him from view except for the flash of his armor. He sat proudly on top of his horse, wearing a stoic expression. Gisela knew what lay behind his helm: a crippling worry for his kingdom. The need to gain control.

"Halt. Do not come any closer," the captain shouted, barring the path from them.

Gisela arched a fine brow at the man. While he was only doing his job, didn't he recognize her? "I will come closer." And she did. Her horse plodded forward, setting the soldiers on edge. "Would you keep a daughter from her father?" Gisela jerked her chin toward the king, smiling despite the nerves threatening to snuff the air from her lungs.

"What?" the captain cried. "Nonsense. You are not—"

Maxim snorted at the soldier.

"Move aside!" her father grumbled, pushing his horse through the throng of other mounts. "Gisela?" Disbelief filtered into his gaze, rumpling his brow. "Why . . . how are you here?" He urged his horse forward until he was beside Gisela. Twisting, he leaned over to hug her with one arm.

The cold metal of his helm pressed into her cheek as she embraced him and as he withdrew from her, bewilderment wrinkled Gisela's nose. "What do you mean, how? I rode here."

"But Knorren . . ." When he pulled away, he shot a look to Maxim as if asking, *Did you have a part in this?*

"That's neither here nor there. You must go back into the forest." Gisela grabbed a hold of her father's chainmailed arm. "I know why you're here, but the rebellion awaits you in the treeline. They have arrows on you as we speak."

Werner didn't look surprised. Gisela surmised it was the reason he wore his battle armor, and she was grateful for it. "You need to get out of here, now." His words came out rushed, panicked.

Whatever argument Gisela may have had at the tip of her tongue died off as an arrow plunged into the neck of a soldier's horse. Squeals erupted as the horse bucked, ramming into his surrounding comrades. With the chaos erupting, the other men rallied around her father.

"Gisela! Come to me!" Maxim cried out over the shouting, but it was no use. The soldiers barricaded her father and in the mad dash, Maxim's gelding and her mare panicked.

"Nevermind me! Cover Gisela," Werner barked.

Amid the madness, Gisela's mare reared, twisting in a clumsy pirouette. Not ready for it, Gisela lost her balance at the same time the mare did. It happened so fast—too fast—that Gisela didn't have time to propel herself away from the falling horse. Instead, both rider and mount collapsed to the ground with a hard thud.

She screamed in surprise and pain. Fire erupted in Gisela's hip, then spread down her back and down her leg. Unsure if anything was broken, she scarcely moved, but as her mare scrambled to right herself, Gisela found the moment to slip out from under her.

Her ears rang loudly, and the sound of shouting seemed distant even though she was amid it all.

"Gisela!" her father called from a distance, but where was he?

Dazed, she spun around, then a shriek tore its way from her as a rider brandishing a sword came straight for her. This was it, this was how she'd die. This time, when she screamed, her body lifted from the ground. She was floating, staring down at the assailant, but as her body jostled, she realized she was being carried.

Gathering her wits, Gisela craned her neck to take in Knorren's narrowed eye. He was glaring at the gathering rebellion. Carefully, he placed her down on the ground and growled at her.

"You fool." His words lacked bite and in them she heard worry.

She hissed the moment she sat up. Gisela lifted her hand to brush against his muzzle as he nuzzled her. "Says the one who is here."

"And if I weren't, you'd be dead. Thanks to that fool of a boy." Knorren twisted around, assessing the melee. "Stay put."

It wasn't Maxim's fault. Surely he must've known that. Frowning, she nodded. Gisela could hardly move without it feeling as though a knife were burying itself into her hip.

Knorren dug his claws into the dirt. His eyes kept darting back to the chaos, and it was clear he was torn on whether to scoop her up and run away, or stay and help. A moment passed, then he pressed his snout against her. "Stay," he breathed.

"Knorren, you cannot kill them. They're angry, hurt . . ." The words seemed feeble even to her ears. His lips tightened against his teeth. He looked positively feral, as if he'd launch at her.

"Are they? I suppose that gave them the right to attack you?" Knorren lifted his head and sniffed the air. "There is no way to come out of this without death, Gisela." With that, he leaped into the fray.

In a blink, Knorren lifted a rider from his horse and tossed him aside. To his credit, he spared them impalement by teeth and claws. Still, his sheer size and presence inspired men to retreat.

Where was Maxim? Gisela searched the faces frantically. She finally spotted him close by her father. Relief flooded her, but it was short-lived as an arrow embedded itself in his neck. Blood sprayed even as he toppled from his horse.

"Maxim!" she shrieked as she hobbled toward him. Not Maxim . . . not another death. Tears burned her eyes from pain, horror, and shock.

This time, Knorren used his teeth to snap the assailant in half. Whether it forced the rebels to rally or it was their plan all along, they focused their attention on the king, and an archer was aiming directly at him.

"Papa!" Gisela shrieked, grabbing her bow and rummaging for an arrow in her quiver. It wasn't full like it had been. Most must have fallen out during her fall. Her fingers found purchase on one and as she notched the arrow, readying to let it fly toward the archer, Knorren leaped into her line of sight and the arrow meant for her father disappeared into his fur.

Knorren hit the ground hard. An ear-piercing bark erupted from him as he slowly stood back up and his yellow eyes, filled with such hatred, focused on the men who remained.

"No!" With pure adrenaline fueling her movements, she limped across the field. With every step she sucked in a breath, grimacing as bursts of pain followed suit. "Knorren!"

With a whoop, the militia she and Maxim had gained converged on the field, weapons drawn. It wasn't as if they *wanted* to fight their neighbors, but the need for protecting the king was stronger.

Most surrendered. They kneeled with their hands behind their necks, unwilling to cut down their brethren.

Gisela fell next to Maxim. She crawled to him, pulled the collar of his shirt down, and withheld a gasp. Blood. So much blood. The strong metallic scent washed over her, making Gisela dizzy. He gurgled as he tried to speak, choking as he clawed at the arrow. "No, Maxim, no. Don't try that." Maxim rasped as he found her hand, then squeezed it. She held on until his grip loosened. "I'm sorry. I'm so sorry."

Scooping his head onto her lap, she rocked him as the surrounding chaos continued. Violet, Adeli . . . Gisela had promised to watch over him, to keep him safe. She squeezed her eyes shut, sobbing.

Something pushed at her shoulder lightly, then harder. A humid warmth washed over her, and as she focused, she could hear her name over and over. "Gisela!" Knorren wheezed, before scooping her up into his mouth and running as fast as his injury would allow.

THIRTY-THREE

*I*n hindsight, Knorren should've remained on the beach outside of Ylga's hut. But the moment Egon shuffled into view and mentioned the king passing through to Hurletz, every muscle in his body stiffened. There was no way Gisela didn't know of this, which meant she'd foolishly attempt something.

Ylga only clucked her tongue and shrugged. Ever the helpful witch, she refused to give him any insight. How was he supposed to make the right choices when Ylga didn't shine as much as a candlelight on the proper path?

Egon's panic was tangible, which oddly set him on edge. *Damn it all.*

Which was why he leaped into the forest full of rage, readying to shred the rebels into ribbons if they'd harmed a hair on Gisela's head.

When he saw her toppling over, it sparked a fire beneath his paws and he bolted for her. How had his anger transformed into fear so quickly? He'd snapped at her, but it came from a place of worry, not anger.

If he'd stayed on the beach, Gisela more than likely would have joined Maxim in the afterlife. And as much as he was loath to admit it, it meant he cared *deeply*. The notion of a life without her seemed bleak. She was the sun to his moon.

A deep, gnawing pain blossomed with every breath he took. The arrowhead had met its mark, and if Knorren was right, it'd punctured his lung, which meant it was filling with blood. Knorren had no choice but to rise to his paws, if only to take Gisela away from the madness. She was injured already and the longer she remained on the field, the likelier a secondary wound was.

Knorren swept his gaze toward the king's men, who were converging on the remaining rebels. He longed to sink his teeth into their wretched bodies, but time wasn't on their side. With a sharp intake of breath, he propelled himself into a slow run.

"Knorren, please bring me back," Gisela sobbed, but she barely moved in his mouth.

Unable to speak, he listened as she wept for the boy. Although Maxim was an annoyance, he didn't deserve to die, and the thought gave him pause. Never once had Knorren considered whether death was deserved or not, and now he was.

Knorren withheld a cough. His body quaked as he fought off the feeling of a thousand fire ants crawling up his throat.

Dying. He was dying.

By the time he reached Ylga's hut, the light in the gray sky was dwindling. Knorren swayed then collapsed to the ground, careful not to let his jaw slam into the sand. As he opened his mouth, Gisela emerged.

"Knorren!" She limped toward his eye. "Knorren, stay with me." She turned her head, fresh tears spilling down her cheeks as she screamed. "Ylga! Someone!" Gisela's fingers stroked his brow, and she leaned her face against his.

Knorren closed his eyes, far too exhausted to talk. At that moment, he was nearly at peace. If this was how he'd die, then so be it. Let him die with Gisela stroking him and knowing she cared enough to shed tears for him.

Hopefully it was enough to send him back to the demon realm.

"I am too old for this, and you're far too heavy." Ylga's raspy voice stirred him.

Ylga?

His eyes popped open, and he nearly leaped to his paws. Her milky blue eyes stared down at him and she wore a satisfied grin.

"You're not dead yet," she offered quietly, lifting a finger to her lips. "Gisela is asleep. Between the injury she sustained and fretting over you and that poor boy, she wound up in a fit. Not a bad one, but enough to drain her further." Ylga turned toward the bed in the corner of her hut but instead of frowning, she smiled. "I couldn't heal you while you were in your other form." Ylga ran her thumb along the silver ring on her middle finger. "I think we've played this game long enough."

His form . . . this game? Knorren shifted, but his body felt wrong. He couldn't feel his paws, his tail . . . He blinked, glancing around the room again. He was *inside* the hut. Not simply sticking his head in it.

Ylga lurched forward, hand held out. "Don't do that . . . stay still."

But he didn't listen as he leaped to his feet. *Feet*. He collapsed to the dirt floor and his skin slapped against the cool surface. Knorren cursed as it sent a shockwave of pain through him, but the floor against his body distracted him from it.

Lifting a hand, he peered down at his pale, freckled fingers, then up at Ylga. "What is this?"

"This is you," she said tiredly. "The true you."

No. This was one of her games. Knorren crawled to the cot he'd been propped on and clumsily crawled onto it.

"If I had more time you'd have remembered upon waking, but now it'll be the hard way."

He could hear every word she spoke, but she sounded so far away and a throbbing pain in his head drove him down into the pillow. He fisted the linen sheet in his hands, gritting his teeth so hard he thought they'd snap.

Knorren thought the arrow in his chest had hurt, but this was like a bolt hammering straight through his temple. Images of a younger Ylga flashed behind his eyes. Silky white hair, smooth skin, and crystalline blue eyes. She wasn't looking at him but at a young lady with warm brown hair and laughing brown eyes. The sight of her caused Knorren's heart to ache.

"No, I don't want to remember," he rasped, clutching his short cropped hair. "Don't do this."

"It's time. You took an arrow for the king, the very man you so loathed. You did it for his daughter, despite how you felt about him, and you further endangered yourself by bringing Gisela here. That, old friend, is how you broke the curse."

Lenora. Her lips on his, her hands clutching his back as he drove them to pleasure. The sound of her laughing, rasping breaths against his chest. He loved her. Worshipped her.

"Time doesn't heal all wounds, does it, Knorren?"

Knorren. The name didn't feel right; it gnawed at him. He frowned as he rocked onto his heels and stared out the window, watching as the sea grass wavered in the moonlight. "I loved her."

"You did, but you loved your power, too." She frowned, settling down in the chair next to his cot. "Your kingdom loved you nearly as much as my daughter did. You were fierce, willing to protect those you loved. But when it came down to it, you chose your power over love. Your carelessness with my daughter's heart killed her." Ylga lifted a hand to smooth back her silver hair.

"You were to meet at the edge of Todesfall, since you were hunting and living in what I believe you affectionately deemed *the castle of thorns.* But while there, you chose to upstage some petty lord during an impromptu hunt. My Lenora waited for you, and do you know who found her, Knorren?"

Not Knorren, his mind hissed. Tears of frustration and pain welled in his eyes, but the memories raked against his mind, throbbing and beating. The memory of Lenora's soft body cold in his arms, battered and bruised, sprung at him. "Highwaymen. If I'd been there, I would have slain them. I would have killed them." He growled, curling his fingers into his palms.

Lenora's mother, Ylga, had been the royal witch, in charge of aiding the kingdom when they needed magical tactics, or a healer. She'd been so devastated by her daughter's death, she'd blamed Prince Jannik. It was his fault, after all.

The day of her burial was the same day Knorren emerged from Todesfall and devoured the Golden Prince. It was him.

Knorren was Jannik.

He swiped at his eyes. "I never meant—"

"I believe you, Jannik, and I've forgiven you." Ylga's gaze slid toward the slumbering Gisela. "Do you care for that girl?"

Jannik glanced down at his bare chest and ran his fingers along a fresh scar. The memories from both lives collided, dizzying him. "Gisela?" he murmured her name and slid from the bedding.

"Yes, *that* girl, Jannik." Ylga huffed as she leaned into her chair. He hadn't noticed how drained she looked. If he was nearly five hundred years old, and she was older than him, it was no wonder she tired easily as of late.

His feet touched the cool floor, and this time, he carefully crossed the room to her side. Kneeling, he watched as she slept peacefully. "She has known me at my worst. Nevertheless, she found a place within her heart to care for me." Jannik's fingers lightly ran along her curls, then up to her temple, where he brushed the pad of his finger. "I care for her beyond measure," he whispered, leaning forward to leave a featherlight kiss on her brow. "That even while I was a demon, this willful girl forced her way into my heart and gave me little choice." He chuckled softly.

Gisela wasn't unlike Lenora. Both listened to their hearts, possessed a strong love for the community and their families. But Gisela had a distinct quality that seemed to keep him in check. She demanded more from him, expected better of him, and challenged him.

Jannik rested his chin against the mattress. "Ylga, get some rest. I'll watch over Gisela."

She nodded, rising to her feet with a less-than-subtle groan. "There is a linen shirt on the bench for you. Even as old as I am, I'd prefer a level of modesty in my home."

He grinned as he rose from the floor and walked toward the bench. Jannik pulled the loose linen shirt over his head, then caught his reflection in a dirty mirror. It'd been so long since he'd seen his face. A pert nose, a smattering of freckles, and wild red hair, so dark that in dim lighting it looked brown. His eyes, even as Knorren, hadn't changed. Light honey-colored irises traced his features, unsettling him. Being human again, possessing memories of both forms, was maddening. The guilt of every single death weighed heavily on him, and Jannik knew no amount of love could erase the blood staining his conscience.

"Jannik, let it be known," Ylga cut through his thoughts. "I am just as much at fault for those deaths." She pulled at the blanket, settling her head on the pillow.

"Even so, you weren't the one who ended their lives. It was me."

THIRTY-FOUR

Seagulls chattered loudly, rousing Gisela from her deep sleep. Every muscle ached and as she stretched her legs, pain flared. She grimaced as she pushed herself upright and opened her eyes only to find a yellow pair staring back at her.

She yelped, sliding as far back as she could. Where was she? Gisela frantically searched the room, slowly recalling that she was at Ylga's. That Maxim . . . she cut herself off from that thought, feeling the rawness of reality wash over her. But Knorren. Wurdiz, where was Knorren and who was this man?

"Gisela," the man's gruff tone was as familiar as his eyes. She'd seen him before, knew that glint in his eye and the tilt of his lips. But that was impossible . . .

"You're . . . I'm dreaming. You're Prince Jannik."

The redheaded man lifted his eyebrows and remained rooted where he sat. "Aren't you a clever one? I suppose you were rummaging around in the castle. Did you find anything interesting while you were snooping in my secret study, Klette?"

That voice. Those eyes. "Knorren?" She squinted and this time really scrutinized his features. She'd seen his pale freckled face in the study, the same confident smirk. Gisela held her hand up, blocking the rest of his face. In response, the man's brow furrowed in question and he cocked his head.

"What are you doing?"

Gisela could almost see the fox sitting primly, his paw half lifted, as he questioned her. "Knorren . . . you're Jannik?" she whispered, then threw her arms around his neck, hugging him tightly. He was alive! Gisela squeezed him harder, willing this to be real and not a dream. Knorren was alive and . . . a human? "How? How is this even possible? I thought you were dead. The arrow, the poison!" She pulled back, searching his eyes, and felt a tug in her chest. Not an ache, but something warm and wonderful spreading from within.

Jannik's arms wrapped around her, his fingers combing through her hair as he leaned his forehead against hers. "There is much to tell you." He pulled back, tucking her curls behind her ear, then tapped beneath her chin with a finger. "I believe it all begins with *once upon a time*." When he withdrew this time, he stood and fetched a steaming cup of tea as well as a scone. "Drink this and eat up as I tell you my story."

Even as Jannik told his story, Gisela stared in disbelief. The fox she'd grown to care about, despite his malicious ways, was the Golden Prince. But as he mentioned Lenora, everything snapped into place. The letters, the disappearance of the prince, and why Knorren felt bound to the castle in Todesfall.

"But that means Ylga is—"

"Older than dirt itself." Jannik grinned.

And so was he. Lifting her hand, Gisela brushed her

fingers against his cheek. The pads of her fingers brushed against the fine stubble there. "It's truly you, isn't it?"

Jannik leaned his head into her palm and kissed the inside of her wrist. "Shall I bark at you to prove it? What more can I say, Klette?" His voice rumbled in a familiar growl.

In this form, his growl sent chills down her spine but for another reason entirely. His eyes focused on her lips, but rather than lean in and claim them, Jannik hesitated. "May I?"

She nodded, unable to speak. He leaned forward and place a chaste kiss against her forehead, although a part of her warmed at the thought of his lips against hers. It brought forth questions, though. Did she care for Jannik as she had for Knorren, or was there more? The scent of him washed over her. That familiar pine, earth, and musk that always seemed to linger on his fur and now, she supposed, his skin.

This, she thought, *this feels right*. Being with him, like this, and the tenderness he displayed, fed the flickering flame within her.

Jannik pulled back and framed her face with his arms. "I believe I said if you left Todesfall I'd have to devour you," he rumbled. "I will make good on that vow." Jannik chuckled, his eyes lightening, and it was clear he was teasing her.

Gisela closed her eyes, knowing that this must be a dream. When she woke, Maxim would be fine, Knorren would be alive, and her father would be safe at the castle.

"For the love of Wurdiz, I told you to have a sense of decorum, you wretched beast." Ylga came up behind Jannik and yanked him off Gisela as if he were a little boy in need of scolding.

Jannik's brows drew together, and he bared his teeth as if he were about to snap at Ylga. So like Knorren, but then he looked away and folded his arms across his chest. "I am—we are—we're both clothed."

Ylga rubbed at her forehead. "I'm not here to argue. Only to say the king is on his way. I soothed his worries since he spent the better part of the night in search of you two."

The dream-like quality of the moment faded and with it came a tightness in Gisela's chest. If this wasn't a dream then . . . "Maxim, he—" She couldn't bring herself to say it. Jannik nodded, then wrapped his fingers around hers. The same deep ache formed in her chest that she'd felt the day before, tempting Gisela to succumb to her grief, to simply lie there and weep over the loss of yet another friend.

A shadow passed over Jannik's face. Could he read her expression? Did guilt weigh on him?

"And all of those lives . . ." It sickened Gisela to think of all the death that had occurred because of Ylga's anger.

Jannik's eyes lifted toward the ceiling, then settled on her once again. Sighing, he nodded. "No amount of good that I may do will ever erase the blood on my hands."

Despite the horror she'd witnessed, despite his cruelties, Gisela had seen the good he could do, too. And although he'd fought against the right path, inevitably, Knorren gave in. All he'd needed was a conscience.

"Gisela, hear me now." His tone broke through her misery. Low and raspy. "You are stronger than you know. Now isn't the time to wallow in grief. There will be time for that. Now is the time to rise and take a stand. There is still much to do."

"He's right." Ylga leaned against the door frame to her

hut. Her pale skin had a sickly green cast to it and something was off about her eyes. They almost appeared sunken in. Had reversing the spell taxed her? "And Egon tells me he saw the rebels lurking in Todesfall."

Jannik stiffened. His jaw muscles leaped furiously as he stared down at the floor.

Gisela slid from the bed, grimacing as the pull of tight, sore muscles reminded her of yesterday's fall. If she closed her eyes, she could see everything happening in slow motion. The rearing of her horse, the cry from her father, and the panicked expression on Maxim's face.

"Jannik, don't—"

"Don't what?" He turned to face her, lifting his dark eyebrows in question. "Run after them? Strip them of their skin, hang their heads on a pike?"

"After everything that has happened, you daft creature!" Ylga rumbled and snagged her cane from a nook by the door. She looked as though she intended to use it on Jannik.

However, this was his twisted sense of humor at play. Gisela had grown used to it, but she didn't find him amusing in the least. She frowned at him, shaking her head.

When he garnered no laughter, Jannik flicked his fingers beneath his chin, then rolled his eyes. "I won't skin them or hang their heads on a pike. But I am going after them. I created this mess and I aim to fix it."

"This mess isn't entirely yours. If I wasn't ill—"

Jannik's jaw shifted. "If you weren't ill, it would've been another poor fool to cross paths with me and not your father. And if you weren't ill, would you still be Gisela? The courageous woman I've come to know?"

Her eyebrows furrowed as she processed his words. He

thought her courageous? She loosed a breath, which sounded more akin to a halfhearted laugh. It would take a demon of the forest to find Gisela courageous.

She watched the hard planes of his face soften as he crossed the room, but minded his proximity. Occasionally, he glanced at Ylga, who lifted her cane as if she were about to knock Jannik again. He sighed, jamming his fingers through his hair. "None of this is because of you."

Gisela clutched the fabric of her breeches, grounding herself. Guilt unfolded within her, at first trickling, then flooding her. However, Jannik's words relieved a hint of the weight she'd carried with her for fifteen years.

She wanted to believe it was true.

"And I *vow* to make amends for what I've done. For all of it." Jannik pointedly glanced over at Ylga, who nodded.

Bottles on the shelves clinked together and herbs swayed above their heads. Gisela stared at a bundle of dried sage as it swung like a pendulum.

"The king's horses," Ylga murmured.

Gisela's eyes widened, then she slipped out the door, grimacing as her hip throbbed, reminding her that Ylga hadn't entirely healed her. Her father emerged from the woods, a mixture of panic and pain etched itself on his face. His lips were tight, his eyes full of sadness. For perhaps the first time in her life, Gisela could relate to her father.

"Gisela!" He slid from his horse and rushed to her, enfolding her in his arms so tightly she couldn't breathe. "I thought . . . I thought I'd lost you to that beast." Werner glanced around as if half expecting Knorren to saunter out of the tall grasses. However, there would be no fox anymore.

Jannik strolled up beside them. Her bow was slung over his shoulder and the quiver held replacement arrows. He turned his intense gaze to Werner. She saw Knorren there, in the way he refused to balk in the presence of her father and instead challenged him silently. She saw the shrewd mind at work, thinking, planning, and waiting for an opportune moment to pounce.

Werner's gaze shifted from the newcomer to Gisela. "And you are?"

Where did they begin? And was telling the truth in their best interests? Her shoulders inched up to her ears as tension built within. By law, Jannik should be hung for his crimes a thousand times over, but what would her father think of the circumstances?

"It's complicated." Jannik's lips twitched into a confident smirk. "But I think Jannik will suffice for now, until we've cleared the air." He peered down at Gisela then back to Werner. "I know we haven't much time because the remainder of the rebellion is lurking in Todesfall. But if you lend me a horse, I'll do what I can to hunt them down so they may be tried for their crimes."

Werner's eyes widened at the name and Gisela wondered if he saw flashes of the prince whose portraits once hung in Tursch Castle, and whose story had been passed on through generation to generation, creating the lore that was Knorren.

With a nod, he motioned for one of his men to dismount. Jannik walked to the horse and jerked his head toward another. "Give Gisela a horse too." It was an order.

For a moment, she didn't think her father would argue, but then his dark eyebrows furrowed and his lip curled in anger. "My daughter will not be joining us. After yesterday—"

He still viewed her as a timid mouse. No doubt the fall, the ambush, and not knowing whether or not she was alive rocked him to his core, but Gisela's voice wouldn't be silenced any longer.

"I didn't ask and it isn't up for discussion. Your daughter —Gisela—can speak for herself." Jannik's eyes hardened as he stared down at him. "Is it your wish to join, Gisela?" He held a hand out to silence her father's argument.

Lifting her head, Gisela walked to the horse Jannik sat on. One look at her father and she could feel his upset, but to his credit, he only pursed his lips. Hopefully he would see she was not an invalid. That when she fell, she'd rise again. "It is precisely what I wish." She would go to be his conscience, to ensure no more death occurred in the forest.

THIRTY-FIVE

"**I**'ll be right behind you," Werner promised Gisela. Although the sound of his quaking voice only served to annoy Jannik.

He watched Werner hover over her as she mounted. She was strong enough to do so on her own, even with the deep bruising on her hip. For weeks, she'd clambered up his thick fur and nestled onto his neck, relying on her grip to keep her steady.

Gisela had arrived full of excuses and no confidence, and discouraged. But the woman he saw today wasn't the same one he brought to the forest of death.

Perhaps it was all for a reason. If Jannik told himself that, maybe it would alleviate the guilt of everything he'd done.

"Ylga, which way did the dwarf say to go?" She'd emerged from her hut, looking half amused and even more drained than moments ago. He frowned as she swayed on her feet. "Are you—"

"Toward the castle of thorns, and never mind about me. Go." She flicked her hand, gripping her cane with the other.

Jannik wasn't keen on leaving Ylga, not when she appeared so feeble and he feared for the worst. But he had little choice. If he stayed, who knew what the rebels would do to the castle, to Violet and Suli.

He grunted, then kicked his horse into a gallop. Werner rode behind them with his entourage following suit, no doubt watching his daughter in horror, but Jannik wished it was in awe. His daughter was far stronger than he knew. "Ride like I know you can, Gisela!" It felt strange to be on a horse again after so long. He was unbalanced at first, then it came back to him when he relied on the horse and not his own movements.

Leaves crunched beneath the horses' hooves as they traversed the land, grinding it into the earth beneath them. Cool air rushed against Jannik's face and he felt the kiss of autumn in every single caress.

"Jannik, do you smell that?" Gisela pulled up beside him on the path, staring ahead in horror. "Smoke."

"Smoke from where?" Werner bellowed.

A string of curses left him. It was possible that a traveler had lit a campfire, but he wasn't willing to chance it being the forest or the castle ablaze.

By some stroke of luck, or Wurdiz's meddling, there was no inferno to greet them. It likely had been a traveler, but as Jannik pulled his horse to a halt, the flash of metal in a tree close to them grabbed his attention.

He held his hand out, then placed it to his lips before pointing upward. To Werner's credit, he didn't argue with Jannik, he remained as silent as his daughter.

Jannik pulled the bow from over his head. It'd been so long since he'd held one in his hands, but the recent tutoring sessions with Gisela proved to him that he at least recalled how to use one.

Notching the arrow, he pulled the bowstring and lined up his shot. He couldn't see anyone, just an occasional flash from a sword or a piece of armor.

"This is your one chance. Come down from your hiding place and we will resolve this peacefully." *Not that I want to.* That dark, twisted part of him still wanted to see them suffer as he tore into them as if they were only a ribbon. For nearly killing Gisela, for killing that boy.

"Jannik," Gisela whispered, but he didn't so much as glance over his shoulder. If he did, no doubt they'd use it to their benefit. "You cannot—"

"If I must, I will, but should they come down without an issue, I will have mercy." He purposely raised his voice. "I offer my mercy once and once only."

When no one budged, Jannik guided his horse forward with his legs, then focused on the limb he saw the glint of metal on. Just one slip, that was all it took. Jannik saw an arm come into view and he took the shot.

He let loose the arrow, and it zipped through the air, hitting its mark. He knew because a scream tore through the air, then the figure dropped from the tree, hunched over and holding the arrow. It wasn't a mortal wound, but it would smart just the same.

Jannik scowled at the young man. "Do not te—" An arrow whizzed by, narrowly missing his shoulder. Relief washed over him, but then panic crept up as he as he frantically searched for Gisela. Had it hit her? A quick once-over eased his worries, but he turned his horse so he could block Gisela from any stray arrows.

"Get him, you fools," Jannik ground out as he jerked his chin toward the whining rebel on the ground.

Rousing from their stupor, two of the guards slid from their horses and bound the fallen man. Jannik smiled grimly as they wrenched his arm behind his back, not heeding his cries from the arrow.

He deserved far more discomfort.

"Gisela, you must get out of here," Werner bit out behind Jannik, and it wore thin on his nerves.

"Now isn't the time," he snapped at him, catching movement in the nearby bushes. "Little bird, it's time to flush you out," Jannik hummed to himself as he notched another arrow. How many were left? And what would it take to squash their efforts?

This time, when an arrow whizzed by his head, it glanced off Werner's armor and fell uselessly to the ground.

Jannik slipped from the saddle and stalked toward the bushes, arrow pointed at the rustling bush. It was too big of a movement to be fauna, but as he approached, chaos erupted behind him. Horses bolted forward, shouting filled the clearing, and as the figure popped up from behind the bush, Jannik stared into the eyes of a middle-aged woman.

He squeezed the fletching of the arrow, stilling as the woman raised her hands in surrender. Inwardly, Jannik screamed at himself to let the arrow loose, but as she begged, he lowered it. "Someone, grab her before—"

"Jannik!" Gisela cried out.

Spinning around, he stiffened as a man came into view, sword held high and poised to strike Jannik down. He braced, readying to leap out of the way, but there was little time. In the next breath, his attacker froze and choked, then collapsed.

Behind the assailant, Gisela stood, shaking like a leaf as

she held the other end of a sword. Her sandalwood complexion paled considerably, lending her a green tone. There was a wild look in her eyes, not that of one who was bloodthirsty, but much like a rabbit, cornered and fearful. She'd acted out of fear, not anger.

"G-Gisela," he breathed, glancing down at the sword she still clung to as the man slid to the ground. "Klette, darling." Jannik moved closer to her and wrapped an arm around her shoulder before pulling the sword away.

"I killed him," she squeaked.

The sound of her voice cracking might as well have been a sword to his heart. She never should've been in this position, and yet here she was. "Yes." He frowned, softening his tone, knowing that no matter what he said, it wouldn't comfort her. Jannik peered around. The discord had died down, but the king, who'd witnessed the death blow given by his daughter, stared at the two of them.

Pressing a kiss to Gisela's temple, Jannik turned her away from the lifeless body. "It's done now," he murmured. Around them, the remaining guards pulled the rest of the rebels from the woods and threw them to the ground, binding them to the horses. It would be a long walk back to Tursch, but they'd suffer for the crimes they'd committed.

Still shaking, Gisela pulled away from the group of men and turned toward the castle. He assumed she wanted to speak to Violet, who still didn't know about her brother's demise. A deep frown creased Jannik's cheeks.

If anyone could comfort Violet amid her grief, it would be Gisela, for he knew she'd adored him much like a brother.

Sighing, Jannik leaned against a tree trunk, reveling in the sound of the birds, only to be disturbed by an unkindness of ravens. He'd never seen so many of the black birds in one spot before, but one with a gaping mouth looked down at him and ruffled its feathers.

"Who are you?" Werner asked as he made his way up to him. "You're familiar and my Gisela acts as if she knows you well." He removed his helm and set it against his hip.

Jannik turned his gaze toward the bridge leading to the courtyard. He frowned as he watched Gisela disappear, but the king had asked a question, and Jannik didn't care if he knew the truth or not. "What I'm about to tell you, you may choose not to believe. But it is the truth." He slung the bow over his shoulder and arched an eyebrow. "I am both the Golden Prince of Tursch, and Knorren—the demon of Todesfall. Long ago, I was cursed for a foolish mistake, and the witch, Ylga, bound me to the fox form. If it weren't for Gisela's courage to care for me despite my cruelty, I'd never have found my way back."

Werner laughed, but when he saw Jannik wasn't smiling, he scrutinized him. If one looked close enough and paid attention, they'd hear the roughness of Knorren's voice, they'd see the cleverness in his eyes, and the sneer, that even in fox form, he'd managed to wear.

"The witch . . ."

"Ylga doesn't just makes herbal remedies for worthless kings who stumble into my forest. She is quite capable of bringing anyone to their knees with a flick of her wrist." He placed a hand to his chest, bowing. "And she did, nearly five hundred years ago, *Your Majesty*." His voice slipped from him, rough and taunting, like it had the first time they'd met. When they'd made a bargain in his forest.

Werner's eyes widened. "It is you . . ." A war of emotions

played across his face, all vulnerable ones in Jannik's opinion. Fear, doubt, anger.

"The rebellion has been squashed—for now. Go back to Tursch, deal with your prisoners, and I'll return Gisela once she has made her peace here." He glanced away from Werner to the castle of thorns. He'd grown accustomed to his life in the forest, and recently the comfort Gisela gave him, despite his cruelty. Jannik cared for her and to be without her—even the thought—gnawed at him.

Werner shifted toward his horse, shaking his head. "We are not done yet, Jannik."

"No, I didn't think we were." He spared one glance to Werner, then walked away from him toward the stone bridge. For if his time was limited with Gisela, he wanted to bask in her presence before she returned home.

THIRTY-SIX

A week had passed since Gisela returned to Tursch. It felt strange being among so many people again, but when she'd returned, Jana had tearfully welcomed her back. Which released the dam Gisela had been fighting.

So much had happened that Gisela had little time to process it, but it had poured out of her the moment Jana's arms wrapped around her.

It was early afternoon when Gisela stepped into the castle's garden and she hesitantly walked toward her roses. After her stay in Todesfall, she wasn't sure she could ever look at them the same. Still, they were beautiful, but she'd always recall the way they sprung up when blood was shed.

"Even as autumn's chill touches the land, they still persevere and grow." Her father's voice startled her, forcing her to turn and face him.

He wore a deep red doublet, with golden buttons trailing from his neck all the way to his waist. Despite the turmoil that continued in the kingdom, the tension had eased from his expression as the week went on.

She smiled, nodding in agreement. "They are some of the most resilient flowers, even if their petals are delicate."

He walked to the bench and patted the spot beside him.

"Come sit. I've had a few things on my mind since Todesfall."

She bit her bottom lip and toyed with one of the silken buds as she carefully assessed her father. While tension didn't ripple from him, something made him uneasy, which made her feel anxious. Was it about Jannik? She hadn't seen him since returning home, but that wasn't before she journeyed to Erna with Violet to return her son's body. It was one of the hardest things she'd ever done.

With a sigh, her father twisted so he could look at her. "I realize my mistake in not allowing you to live your life as you should've. When I held you back, I wanted to keep you safe, but in doing so, I took away life experiences from you." He wiped at his brow, frowning. "For that, I am sorry. But never once think I looked at you as weak, Gisela. You are the strongest person I know and have fought since you were born to find a place in this world."

Until that moment, Gisela hadn't realized how much she needed to hear those words from her father. She reached for his hand and squeezed it. "Oh, Papa."

"You've proven that and then some." He patted her hand with his free one. "You did what no one could do in five hundred years by breaking the Golden Prince's curse." He shook his head, grimacing as if he were still trying to process it. "And for that, the entire kingdom owes you a debt of gratitude."

The people owed her nothing and yet, the words warmed her. After years of being shoved aside as though she were an invalid, Gisela was seen as *capable*. That in and of itself was enough.

Unsure of how to respond, she remained quiet.

"But, Knorren committed crimes against the crown and against the kingdom itself. For that, he deserves an immediate death."

Gisela dropped his hand and bolted from the bench. With wide eyes, she stared down at her father. "You can't prosecute him!"

Her father lifted his brows and schooled his features into that of a king. Unable to read him, she scowled. "I may do as I please, considering I am king."

It dawned on her that perhaps her father hadn't changed. Simply because he was king didn't mean he could do as he pleased.

When he didn't elaborate, Gisela felt her pulse quicken. He couldn't actually hunt Jannik down! "Papa!"

"However, the fox is dead and therefore the price of his transgressions has been paid." His lips pressed together in a thin line as he stared at the stone pathway. "What Knorren did is unforgivable, but he saved you, me, and likely the kingdom—with your help, of course. Which is why I *did* hunt him down."

Confusion wrinkled her nose as she looked to her father and off to the side, but when she did, she saw a flash of red hair and pale skin. Maybe it was her mind playing tricks on her and that she only *hoped* it was him.

The man stepped into view, wearing a forest-green doublet and tan breeches tucked into his knee-high boots. He wore a grin that she'd know anywhere and those eyes that warmed her heart. "Good afternoon, my darling."

Not *Klette*, but *darling*. Did she miss the wretched nickname? No, she rather liked the sound of *darling* from his lips.

Gisela smiled as she looked at him then at her father, who fidgeted uncomfortably.

Werner stood to his feet then cleared his throat. "I will allow you some privacy, but respect my daughter." He inclined his head to Gisela then left the garden.

Unwilling to keep the distance between herself and Jannik, she walked to him and wrapped her arms around his neck. "Why have you stayed away?" She hated how weak her voice sounded as she whispered against his neck.

"Ylga isn't well. I couldn't in good conscience leave her alone, but the damn crone demanded I come to you. It just so happened your father was searching for me too."

It seemed as though there were more to that story, but Jannik didn't elaborate.

Gisela pulled her head back and looked up at him. "I will take a page from Ylga's book and demand you tell me about that later, but for now . . . I missed you." And she did. *Oh, she did.* She'd missed his laugh, how he'd grumble when she was right about something. It'd occurred to her two days after he'd left her that she loved him. Gisela had adored Knorren, but it was the pieces of Jannik that remained in him that she grew to love.

Jannik lifted his hand and stroked her cheek with his knuckles. "A day without you was worse than a sunless sky. But when I thought about it, it made sense. You're my very heart, Gisela, and without you, I'm just Knorren." His words grew soft toward the end, just above a whisper.

She swallowed roughly as what he said sunk in. Gisela slid her hand down his shoulder to rest above his heart. "You're more than that." And she knew for certain it was true, because Knorren would never say such a thing, even if he might have thought it.

Hesitantly, she lifted herself on her toes and pressed her lips to kiss softly at first, then as his fingers raked through her hair, Gisela leaned in to his kiss. He tasted of honey cakes and tea. And as clumsy as her lips may have been, he guided her along at a slow pace. Suddenly, his hips pressed into hers, and she was more aware of her body than ever. Tingles of anticipation raced through her as he melted into her body. Gisela opened her mouth, welcoming the probe of his tongue against hers, and she couldn't help but moan as the kiss grew heated.

She withdrew, feeling lightheaded and something far more wonderful. "I love you, even when you were a coarse fox." Gisela laughed at the last part of her words. She paused, considering how he'd saved her in so many ways. "And for showing me how strong I could truly be."

He smiled down at her then brushed a kiss against her forehead. "I'll need to improve my behavior if I'm ever to live up to the pedestal you put me on." Jannik chuckled.

"Pedestal?" she cried and gave his shoulder a gentle shove. "Next time you're covered in burrs, I shall leave you to them."

Jannik's eyebrows furrowed and he lifted his hands in surrender. "I am at your mercy, my darling."

Gisela laughed. It felt good. There hadn't been much cause to do so as of late. Especially after Maxim's funeral and the guilt she held onto for his death. And the fact that she'd killed a man. Even months after the attack, Gisela still dreamed of that moment, when she'd thrust the sword into the man and watched as he fell lifelessly to the ground. It haunted her. No matter how much her father told her it was to protect Jannik, it didn't make her feel any better.

Sighing, she rested her cheek against his chest, listening to the thrum of his heart. "What now, Jannik?"

His chin rested atop her head and his arms settled around her. "Now we heal. Now we begin a new life—an even better one than we could possibly imagine."

Gisela liked the sound of that. No matter what life threw at them next, she would be ready. With Jannik at her side and with the strength as well as courage she'd gained. She would thrive.

EPILOGUE

*A*utumn's frost turned into winter's bite, which inevitably lost to spring's hopeful blossoms. Fragrant blooms perfumed the air once again, inviting bees to sip at the sweet nectar inside. It was Gisela's favorite time of year because despite the harsh winters, life began again.

In the past few months, Tursch had calmed, but there was still discontent in the kingdom, which Gisela understood would take time to heal. All grievous wounds did.

Inside her father's study, Jannik sat next to her as rigid as a rod. He'd seldom left the castle unless it was to tend to Ylga, who had recovered and sent him away for the last time once she relinquished the recipe for her herbs.

Everyone was in the study. *Everyone.* Tilda, Pia, Mina, and Jana, as well as their father, who was currently pacing the room, adding tension to the already unsettling mood.

Even with Jannik present, Tilda scowled at Gisela when she thought he wasn't looking, and when he caught her—as he did in that moment—he glowered as fiercely as the demon of Todesfall.

None of them knew the truth of who he was. If any of them ever remarked on how keen of a resemblance he bore to the Golden Prince, Jannik simply said he was a descendant.

"I'm sure you're wondering why I've called you all here." Her father broke the silence and folded his arms behind his back. "No matter how hard I've tried to make amends for my admitted cowardice, our citizens still don't possess the confidence in me that they once did. So, with much thought, I've decided to abdicate in favor of my heir."

Gisela's heart thrummed in her chest wildly. If Tilda was crowned, then it didn't matter if Gisela had banished the demon of Todesfall or not. She glanced at Tilda, who stuck her chin up and wore a smug smile. She'd been waiting for this moment for most of her life.

Jannik slid his hand over Gisela's and squeezed, but his eyes never wavered from her father.

"The people deserve someone strong, who will not waver in the face of an adversary, and who will rule with her heart as well as her mind. Which is precisely why I'm—"

"Oh, Papa! I've waited for this moment. I will make you proud, and Mama too. I promise!" Tilda rushed toward him, placing her hand to her chest as she willed tears to her eyes and feigned choking up.

As if she didn't know it would be her.

Except their father didn't so much as look at her. He turned his gaze to Gisela and smiled while he pointedly said each word. "Naming Gisela queen because I have no doubt that you, my heart, will aid this kingdom."

Gisela's eyes widened. For a moment she thought she'd heard wrong, but as she flicked her gaze to Tilda, who was truly crying at this point, and then to Jana, who was beaming at her, it sunk in. "What?" she stammered.

Werner walked to his desk and poured himself a glass of pear brandy, then lifted it to her. "To the future of Tursch.

May you and your kingdom prosper." He took a sip, then bowed at the waist to her.

"Long live my queen," Jannik whispered into her ear, causing her heart to flutter wildly.

Everything in her life added up to this moment, and if someone asked if she'd go through it all again, Gisela knew she would. Jannik was right. While life certainly hadn't been a bed of roses, it led to this moment and created the person she was.

As Tilda stormed out of the room, Pia followed in her wake, but Gisela didn't so much as watch as they disappeared.

"What now, my darling?" Jannik crooned.

"Now, we turn the page and live, my love."

ACKNOWLEDGMENTS

Elle in 1996 with her mom at Children's Hospital in Boston, Massachusetts

First and foremost, I need to thank my 'family' of 9N at Children's Hospital in Boston, Massachusetts. In my younger years I spent more time there than at home due to my severe epilepsy. A huge thank you to my mother who sacrificed so much to be with me at every doctors appointment, every overnight, ambulance ride or medflight. You'll always be my hero. And my father for always providing for us in my darkest time. Also...huge shout out to my sister Aimee-Beth and brother Zachary, thanks for enduring me being an 'attention hog' ;)

I can't forget to thank The Epilepsy Foundation of New England, without you, my struggle and my family's struggles would've been so much worse. I was honored to be the Winning Kid two years in a row, which is a poster child/speaker for Epilepsy, showing that we can do so much more than just be 'ill', that we are strong and capable like anyone else, and sometimes even better.

Tanya, the reason why this story even stayed around is because of you. If you hadn't encouraged me, pushed me, threatened me. I wouldn't have ever finished this. Knorren owes his life to you.

Yentl, you've been with this story since the beginning and I can't thank you enough for your encouragement . . . for finding the failed competition we entered (haha) and inspiring me to write this story. It never would have existed if it wasn't for you.

To my beta readers, Candace, and Christis, without you this story wouldn't be what it is, so thank you from the bottom of my heart. Honestly, you guys lit a fire in me to continue writing this story.

A special thanks to Donna, for encouraging me to write. Your cheerleading means more than you know.

Amber H and Amber D, thank you for proofing this baby of mine!

A massive thank you goes out to my editor, Brenna, for taking this story on and loving it as much as I do. Thank you for molding it into the final product!

And finally, thank you readers for taking the time to pick up Gisela and Knorren's story. I hope you enjoyed it!

THE OFFICIAL PLAYLIST

Want to listen along while you read and immerse yourself into the world? Listen to the playlist below! Or follow Elle Beaumont on Spotify!

1. Lay By Me by Ruben
2. Cure by Barcelona
3. I'll Be Good by Jaymes Young
4. Forgive Me Friend by Smith & Thell
5. No Angel by Birdy
6. Walls by Ruben
7. Devils Backbone by The Civil Wars
8. Somebody To Die For by Hurts
9. Let's Hurt Tonight by OneRepublic
10. Ghost by Chelsea Lankes

ABOUT ELLE BEAUMONT

 Elle Beaumont loves creating vivid fantasy and science fiction worlds. She lives in southeastern Massachusetts with her husband and two children. When not writing or chasing around her children she can enjoys making candles. More than once she has proclaimed that coffee is life blood and it is how she refrains from becoming a zombie.

Stay up to date and receive some free books by signing up for her newsletter! ellebeaumontbooks.com/newsletter

Join Elle's Facebook group and hang out with her
facebook.com/groups/ElleBeaumontStreetTeam

For more information visit
www.ellebeaumontbooks.com
Follow Elle on social media!

facebook.com/ellebeaumontbooks

twitter.com/ellebeaumont

instagram.com/ellebeaumontbooks

MORE FROM ELLE

Standalones

Die From A Broken Heart

The Dragon's Bride

Immortal Realms Trilogy

Seeds of Sorrow (May '22)

Tides of Torment (coming soon)

Wages of War (coming soon)

Demons of Frosteria

Frost Mate (Dec '21)

The Hunter Series

Hunter's Truce

Royal's Vow

Assassin's Gambit

Queen's Edge

Secrets of Galathea

Brotherhood of the Sea

Bindings of the Sea

Voice of the Sea

King of the Sea

Galathea Saga

Changing Tides (July '22)

Anthologies

Of The Deep

Blood From A Stone

Cirque de vol Mystique

Link by Link

Something in the Shadows

Beyond the Cogs

Stories for Nerds Vol. 1

SNEAK PEAK!

Continue reading for the first chapter of The Dragon's Bride by Christis Christie & Elle Beaumont!!

1

IMARA

With a slight press of the blade tied to her belt, the stem of the witch hazel snapped between her fingers, coming away from the body of the plant to be placed in the small pile in her lap. Overhead, the sun shone down upon her shoulders with an almost blistering heat—unobscured by even the smallest of clouds. Imara couldn't remember the last time the noonday sun had been pleasant, rather than a sweltering force to abide, the days trying to hold on to the last dregs of a fading summer as fall approached.

"Oh, this won't do," she murmured to herself, examining the sprig, then the bush as a whole.

"What was that?" came a voice from over her shoulder.

Leaning back on her heels, Imara lifted her hand to brush the back of her wrist across her forehead, ending with a swipe of her fingers through the blond strands of hair at her temple, tucking them behind one delicately pointed ear. The grass-covered roof beneath her had seen better days. Where once thick, luscious green blades had grown, now yellow spiky strands fought to stay alive. What life was left in the soil had been driven toward the herbs and flowers Imara had planted several years ago, her father doing what he could to keep her garden alive.

"This witch hazel is dry as a bone. I don't know that I'll get much more than this harvest out of it," she stated, glancing over at her sister currently struggling to draw water from the soil around the house, sprinkling it over the rooftop garden once it had gathered upon her fingertips in small, perfectly formed spheres.

Words hardly free of Imara's lips, a spray of water splashed over her face and down the front of her. "Asta, the garden, not my face!"

Imara shot an irritated glare at her sister, who released a giggle of surprise before offering an apologetic smile.

"I'm sorry, that wasn't intentional, I promise. I wasn't paying enough attention to where I was pointing," Asta explained, reaching out to brush a few drops of water from Imara's face. Collecting them with a soft tickle of magic upon her skin, she turned to sprinkle them over the bush of witch hazel.

"Fortunately, it was rather refreshing." Imara cast an accusatory glance toward the sun. Whatever relief could be found from its rays was welcomed.

Brushing a trickle of water along her own temples, Asta turned and plopped down at the edge of the roof, her feet braced where the roof became actual ground. "When do you expect Birger today?"

Clipping one last branch from the bush, Imara turned to sit beside Asta, her eyes drifting over their lands. Situated just a stone's throw away from the village of Omdahl, their little farm was immersed in a breathtaking landscape of rolling hills dappled with tall, branchy trees and split below by a winding river that reflected the blue skies above. The seidr had chosen this valley to settle in many moons ago due to the snow-capped mountains that loomed on either side, majestic giants of protection that graciously supplied fresh spring water to the village and its inhabitants. The valley had also been a land of opportunity, its soil rich and fertile—the perfect place for a people known to cherish the earth and all that she supplied to take root themselves.

Their family plot had been the ideal location for raising sheep and growing cotton—the supply for Dagny Hjelmstad's beautiful woven fabrics and tapestries. Erlend had seen in these fields everything he had hoped to give his new wife: the home, the opportunity, the prospering family. It was everything—until the rains stopped coming, the river began to dry up, and the soil turned to dust beneath their feet.

"He usually arrives about midday, once he has passed through Omdahl proper and spoken to anyone who has dealings with him there." Imara glanced down at the small pile of witch hazel in her lap—not nearly the offering she had hoped to have once he arrived but the best that she had to give.

Asta peered up at the sun, gauging the time by its position in the sky. "It's half past two, but is there time for a quick drink before we need to bundle and prepare that?" she asked, eyes flicking quickly to indicate the witch hazel.

Nodding slightly, Imara pulled up the corners of the blue apron-skirt layered over her green shift, containing all of the branches she had cut, and rose to her feet. Having been outdoors for some time now, a break from the sunshine was more than warranted by both.

"Yes, let's fetch ourselves some water and perhaps run some down to Father. He's been working in the fields since early this morning." Keeping the corners of her apron-skirt swept up, Imara walked off the roof and down the small bank to the front of their home, the curved white frame set just inside the hillside as familiar to her as her own self.

Toeing the partially opened door all the way, she stepped into their home. Her mother, Dagny, stood before a loom, a finger tapping idly upon her lips as she contemplated it. Moving easily to her side, Imara pressed a soft kiss to her cheek.

"It looks beautiful, Mother, as all your pieces do. Jorunn will love it," she murmured in passing, slipping by to deposit her collection of branches onto the table.

"Thank you, Mari," was her mother's contemplative response.

Behind her, Asta came into the house with a flourish of cotton skirts and the scent of spring rain, her elemental affinity so strong she wore it like a mantle upon herself. As Imara brushed a few lost yellow petals off her skirt, her sister got busy pouring them glasses of water from the tap in the wall.

"Is Father down in the western field today?" Imara asked, reaching for the clay goblet Asta held out to her. The fresh mountain water was crisp and cold, sending a blessed chill through her body. A grateful sigh escaped her lips, shoulders relaxing as she soaked up the moment of relief.

"No, he took the sheep to the north pastures, so he ventured to the southern field instead to see how it is faring," Dagny murmured in a distant tone, her attention remaining more on the tapestry before her than on the girls.

Her questions answered, Imara finished her goblet of water and placed it on the counter beneath the tap. Freeing a water flask from the cabinet below, she worked on filling it with water, the tap squeaking softly in her grip.

"I'll take Ishka down," she said to Asta, letting her know there would be no need to walk down with her. "Should I take him a bite to eat as well?"

Her sister plucked a ripened apple from the basket on the table and brought it over to her. Once upon a time, Magnhild's apples had been so large one needed almost to hold it up with two hands to take a bite. Now, the crisp fruit nestled easily in her palm as she accepted it and slid it into the pocket looped around her belt.

"If Birger arrives before I've returned, please ask him to wait. I will be but a moment," she asked of Asta, who nodded with understanding.

"Of course."

With a smile of thanks, Imara stepped out the door and back into the bright sunshine, the ground crunching beneath her soles with every step toward the paddock. Sensing her approach, Ishka wandered over, her snowy coat gleaming against the backdrop of hills, mountains, and sky. There was a brief moment of nuzzling as girl and horse greeted one another, and then Imara mounted the mare and they were off, down the lane leading to the cotton fields closest to the river.

Fingers twined lightly in the horse's mane, Imara started her in the right direction, then left the rest to Ishka. This trek down to the lower fields had been made so many times in days past that both horse and rider could have made it in the dead of night without even the glow of the moon to light their way. While communication with animals was not an elemental strength, nor could she have tapped into it if it were, there was an unspeakable bond between them, a way of understanding each other that had been there since Ishka had been a foal and given into Imara's care.

It was a swift, and easy ride down to the southern field. Spotting her father kneeled down with his hands in the soil, Imara slid off the horse's back. Smoothing a soft touch down the side of her neck, she praised Ishka for a job well done.

"Stay here, girl." With her parting words, Imara pulled her skirts up above her ankles to keep them from sticking to the cotton as she went by and headed down the row her father was in.

Down on one knee in the brown soil, his palms on the earth itself, Erlend Hjelmstad was muttering softly beneath his breath. While she could not make out the words, Imara instinctively knew that they were words of summoning, and her father was trying desperately to pull nutrients and life from deep within the ground and up into the topsoil their crop was planted in. Sensing her behind him, Erlend stopped. His head lifted and he gazed back at her over his shoulder, blue eyes a mirror of her own, shining with love as he took her in.

"Imara, haven't you a trader to meet with this afternoon?" he asked, running a soiled hand through short-cropped blond hair.

"It isn't quite time for that, and I thought you could do with some fresh water." Her hands were already upon the flask at her waist. Loosening it from her belt, she uncapped the top and held it out to him.

A look of gratefulness came over his features, and without further prodding, he stood, taking the water flask from her and tipping it back. As her father drank, Imara held a hand to her forehead, shielding her eyes from the sunlight so that she could survey the area around her. While the soil was meant to be brown, the cracked nature of it was worrisome. Both her mother and sister had been down here the day before, pulling what water there was left to the surface. It looked as if nothing had been done at all.

"It's not going so well, is it?" she asked, eyes returning to her father at last.

Erlend swiped a hand across his lips.

"No, it is not. I'm doing what I can, but there is simply nothing left in the ground to pull out of it." His hand motioned to the grounds around the cotton field. Just two months ago, they had borne green grasses and wildflowers; now they were withered, yellow, and barren.

"Is it even worth it anymore?" Imara questioned, taking in the sight of the cotton plants, perhaps only a third of them bearing anything worth gathering.

The decline had started gradually, beginning with hotter-than-typical days and a lack of fresh rain. With two water elementals in the family, fewer rainy days had never been an issue before. But then the grounds dried up faster than what had made sense. The grasses withered, flowers began dying, and everywhere one looked, the world was turning brown.

There had been difficult farming years in the past, but elemental abilities had always been able to combat it.

"To be honest, I'm not so certain. This won't be enough to supply what your mother needs for her fabrics . . . The yield simply isn't there this year." Erlend shook his head, his frustrations melting away into something resembling defeat.

It would have been nice to reach out a comforting hand

and reassure him. However, reassurance wasn't something that Imara had to give. Not when, everywhere they looked, their neighbors were fighting the same effects. Each day seemed to bring new struggles, and with the lack of crops this harvest, people were beginning to question if they would have enough to get them through the winter, let alone hold over until next year for planting.

"Will there be enough wool to compensate?" They had not lost any numbers from the flock, the sheep hardy enough to withstand poorer grazing. Whether their coats had held up would be the next question.

"We'll see when we start sheering in a couple of weeks." The look in his eyes wasn't necessarily hopeful, which was difficult to see.

"What of our offerings for the Dragon Master? Do we need to lessen the amount we give?"

Each Fallfest, the residents of Omdahl welcomed Lord Lajos the Dragon Master to their celebrations. A powerful being who resided in the forests surrounding the mountains, he had centuries ago come to an agreement with the founding Elders of their village. At the commencement of the fall harvest, each household in Omdahl would provide a portion of their yearly produce, cattle, or craftmanship to him, and in return, he would keep the dragons in the woods from raining fire down upon them all.

It was a burden felt heavily by each citizen this year.

Erlend sighed. "We cannot, you know it. Each family offers up the same portion of their goods. We are not the only ones suffering this season. There can be no leniency for us if it is not offered also to them." His features were pinched with concern.

Imara's father had always been a lighthearted man. While he worked long, hard days to care for their crops and the flock, he had always upheld a cheerful countenance. Worry was a weighted cloak that had come only recently to rest on the Hjelmstad family's shoulders.

"Something will work out," Imara assured him, feigning confidence she did not feel. Pressing a soft kiss to his cheek, she left him to his work and returned to Ishka, who awaited her patiently.

As Imara came up the hill to the family house, she was welcomed by the sight of a small horse-drawn cart covered by a canvas tarp that hid several items beneath. It was a sight that brought a smile to her lips, and without thought, she urged Ishka on a little faster. The days of splurging were behind them, but her trade relationship with Birger was the one allowance Imara still afforded herself. It came at no cost to her family, her small rooftop garden supplying the barter items Birger required for their exchanges.

The cart's seat sat empty, his horses standing unattended and unconcerned. Releasing Ishka back into the paddock, Imara was drawn toward the open door of their home, familiar voices sounding out from its depths.

Inside she found her mother and sister seated at the table with Birger, who was in the midst of sipping tea from a clay mug. Her presence did not go unnoticed, and all three turned to look her way, greeting her with three unique smiles.

"Miss Imara!" Birger called. Setting down his tea, he held his hand out to her, which she took as she approached. The rough fingers used to holding leather reins gave hers a fond squeeze. "As always, it is a pleasure to see you. I managed to find not two but three of the volumes you were seeking."

Smiling at the warm greeting, she pulled out the wooden chair beside him and took a seat, noticing that the witch hazel she had picked this morning was neatly bundled in cheesecloth and tied with twine—Asta had been kind in her absence.

As they began to speak, her mother left the table to fill their little teapot with more water from the tap. As she turned back toward the table, her hand rested upon its ceramic side until steam rose from the white spout. A mug with tea leaves nestled in the bottom was placed before Imara, and then her mother poured in the now steaming liquid, leaving the perfect amount of room for a dollop of cream to be added once she was ready. Imara waited for the leaves to settle at the bottom, then added a tiny portion of cream from the small jug on the table. Letting it all steep for the time being, she peered over at their guest.

"That is wonderful to hear, but I don't know that what I have is worth three hard-sought-after books on mage medicines. Try as I might, I couldn't keep the witch hazel from drying out," she explained.

"Nonsense," he replied. "Our arrangement has always been my books for one bunch of witch hazel, and that is what you've offered up."

"Yes, but—"

"Imara." He reached out to rest his hand over the top of hers on the table. "I've seen the state of Omdahl." He shook his head before continuing. "I'm not looking for more than what you are able to give right now."

THE DRAGON'S BRIDE BY CHRISTIS CHRISTIE & ELLE BEAUMONT

**If you loved the first chapter, you can snag it at
midnighttidepublishing.com/thedragonsbride**

Available in ebook and paperback

MORE BOOKS YOU'LL LOVE

If you enjoyed this story, please consider leaving a review!

Then check out more books from Midnight Tide Publishing!

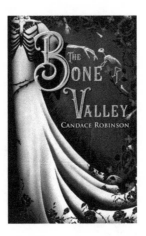

The Bone Valley by Candace Robinson

He's a lover. She's a thief. A magic bond like no other will tie them together.

After the death of his parents, Anton Bereza works hard to provide for his younger siblings. Love has never been in the cards for him, especially after desperation forces Anton to sell himself for coin. And he has no idea that, beneath the city of Kedaf, lies a place called the Bone Valley.

When Anton's jealous client plots against him, he is cursed to spend eternity in a world where all that remains are broken bones. There, Anton meets Nahli Yan—a woman who once tried to steal from him—and his cards begin to change. But as the spark between them ignites, so does their desire to escape. All that stands in their way is the deceitful Queen of the Afterlife, who is determined to wield her deadly magic to break Anton and Nahli apart. Forever.

Available Now

A Cursed Kiss by Jenny Hickman

Living on an island plagued by magic and mythical monsters isn't a fairy tale... it's a nightmare.

After Keelynn witnesses her sister's murder at the hands of the legendary Gancanagh, an immortal creature who seduces women and kills them with a cursed kiss, she realizes there's nothing she wouldn't do to get her back. With the help of a vengeful witch, she's given everything she needs to resurrect the person she loves most.

But first, she must slay the Gancanagh.

Tadhg, a devilishly handsome half-fae who has no patience for high society—or propriety—would rather spend his time in the company of loose women and dark creatures than help a human kill one of his own.

That is until Keelynn makes him an offer he can't refuse.

Together, they embark on a cross-country curse-breaking mission that promises life but ends in death.

Available 11.24.21

The Prince's Wing by Amber R. Duell

A ROYAL GUARD. A FORCED REBEL.

Lord Saer Tufaro was raised to be the prince's Wing—the truest and most loyal personal guard a royal could ask for. He would gladly sacrifice his life to save his best friend—the future king of Eradrist—but that may be exactly what the rebels have planned.

The Red Asters were the ones to place Saer in the palace after the old king was usurped. Close to the throne and above suspicion, he was to be an invaluable tool for the cause. But a spy is only useful if his loyalties aren't torn.

When the prince is manipulated into an arranged marriage to the former king's bastard daughter, tension in the palace grows. The lady is as innocent as she is beautiful and would make the prince a wonderful wife. If only she didn't make Saer's heart race...

Available Now

CPSIA information can be obtained
at www.ICGtesting.com
Printed in the USA
BVHW080834301121
622781BV00005B/105